LETTING GO
A CONTEMPORARY ROMANTIC THRILLER

A. L. AWTREY

Published by H3T, LLC, 2016.

This is a work of fiction. Similarities to real people, places, or events are entirely coincidental.

LETTING GO: A CONTEMPORARY ROMANTIC THRILLER

First edition. November 1, 2016.

Copyright © 2016 Anthony L. Awtrey.

ISBN-10: 0-9894761-1-1

ISBN-13: 978-0-9894761-1-9

Written by Anthony L. Awtrey.

Published by H3T, LLC

   3564 Avalon Park Blvd E Suite 1
   #197
   Orlando, FL 32828
   http://h3tllc.com/

10 9 8 7 6 5 4 3 2 1

To single parents everywhere. You've got a tough job. Here's to hoping you find your own Alex or Molly.

Tony

Chapter 1: Vizcarra

Vizzy watched the cloudy drops disappear into the cup of herbal tea and put the small vial back in his pocket. *Let's see if this does the trick.* His lips thinned into a tight smile, but his steady heart rate never changed. He turned towards the living room and let the smile soften.

"Are you still making my tea or do I need to come show you how to do it again?" Maria called out from the living room in their native Spanish tongue.

"Here you go," Vizcarra said as he handed his twin sister the cup and saucer.

"Thanks." Maria sat the warm saucer on her swollen belly while she took a sip from the cup. "Ugh, I hate this part about being pregnant. It makes everything taste bitter and metallic."

Vizzy gave an involuntary shiver when she smiled down at the twins pushing her stomach out like an alien with a parasite. At almost eight months pregnant his sister looked like a cow. A pregnant woman was the living example of a mistake someone had made. While a beautiful woman might provide a warm place to fulfill his needs, the idea of allowing his seed to grow there was as repugnant as finding weeds choking his coca fields.

"My pleasure." He smiled sweetly at his sister as he sat across from her, his face never betraying his thoughts. "I've missed you."

"I know. I've missed you, too," she said as she took another sip of the tea. "Unfortunately, the doctor made me give up traveling months ago. And I *dread* the next month of bed rest."

"It's preeclampsia, right? Like Auntie Isabel?" he asked with a sympathetic frown. Their family had a history of twins and troubled pregnancies, but he already knew the answer from their mother. The diagnosis had sparked the idea that brought him to visit.

"Yeah." Maria shut her eyes and lay back against the overstuffed chair. "But the medicine is keeping my blood pressure down and the headaches at bay until the twins get a little bigger."

While she relaxed, Vizzy studied his sister. Her swollen bare feet stuck out of the legs of her soft pink pajama pants. He couldn't fathom how she could be happy with her body so bloated. His actions really were a mercy, he thought. A slow, rolling nausea at her appearance made him look away around the elegant living room. "It's hard to see you living so…small…here."

Maria chuckled. "It's not small, it's cozy. It fits us perfectly for now."

"I know you have plenty of money. Why not at least get a house?" Vizzy had never understood why his sister married so far beneath her station or settled for such a plebeian lifestyle in Houston. She could have married a prince or a CEO. Instead she had married the glorified stock broker who worked for their parents.

"This *is* a house—a townhouse," Maria sighed and took another sip. "You know I love you, but if you flew all this way just to criticize my lifestyle again, you can let yourself out."

Her teasing tone irritated him even more. "I am only critical of you calling my nephew *Manny*. Why don't you name him after me? And *Hannah*, what kind of name is that for a de Cervantes?"

"She's not a de Cervantes." Maria frowned and rubbed at her forehead. "She's a Thompson."

"That we can agree on, at least." Vizzy sat back and templed his fingers as he watched his sister's expression change at his words. "Too bad they're getting our grandfather's trust."

"Not that again." Maria's glare shot across the room at Vizzy. "I told you, I'm perfectly willing to split it with you when I get access to it in a few years. You need to get over *Papi* cutting you out of the trust because you were a rebellious teenager. Besides, you've more than proved you can live without the family money."

"It's not about the money," Vizzy muttered. It was that Maria had led a charmed life while he'd suffered for every scrap he got. And his traitorous parents were already planning how they were going to spoil their mongrel grandchildren with his inheritance. "I just hate losing."

After drinking the rest of the tea, Maria blew out a long breath and rubbed her forehead again. "You know I love you, Vizzy, but I also know you better than anyone in the world. You haven't come all this way to fight about Papi's trust."

Instead of responding, Vizzy watched quietly as his sister shifted around in discomfort. She squeezed her eyes shut and pushed her hand against the side of her head, as if to squeeze the pain out. *Good, the drug is working*, he thought to himself.

Her eyes opened, and he noticed her right pupil was widely dilated. "Something's wrong," Maria slurred, her face noticeably drooping on her right side.

"Yes, it is," Vizzy whispered calmly as he got up to collect the cup and saucer from her pregnant belly. Ignoring her obvious discomfort, he went to the kitchen to wash her cup thoroughly. Once it was clean of the evidence of the drug, he refilled it from the teapot with fresh tea.

As he walked back into the living room, he saw Maria in the throes of a violent seizure. With a smirk, Vizzy spilled the warm tea over her belly and dropped the cup and saucer to break on the floor next to her chair.

"I am not letting what should be mine go to a *filthy Thompson*." He spat the last two words out as if they left a bad taste in his mouth. He hoped she could still understand him as her left eye seemed to meet his. "It was hard enough watching you fall so far. I love you so much, but this is about more than just you. It's about our family's legacy."

She appeared to be straining to say something, but nothing more than a gurgled noise came out. The drug Vizzy had put in Maria's tea had caused a spike of blood pressure that might give anybody else a bad headache or nosebleed. But for a woman suffering from preeclampsia, it was a death sentence.

"I'm glad I didn't have to shoot you," Vizzy whispered, more to himself than his sister as her twitching slowed. "But I was willing to, if this didn't work. Now I can leave you for Alex to find while I'm safely on a plane back to Mexico City."

With his mission accomplished, Vizzy had a spring in his step as he walked out of the townhouse. His rental car was a sleek black sedan parked nearby on the quiet neighborhood street. He pulled out his phone as he sat down in the driver's seat. After starting the car and pressing a contact on the screen, the phone rang through the car's stereo system.

"Yes, sir?" a male voice answered.

Vizzy pulled into traffic as he spoke nonchalantly. "It worked. File the petition to claim the trust."

"Right away." The call disconnected with a beep.

He turned left and headed toward Bush International Airport. It should have felt different to kill someone he loved so much, but it didn't seem different from any other execution he had performed. If anything, he thought, it was a relief to get it over with.

Then a wave of sadness washed over him. Maria was gone. His twin. She had been the good one, the lucky one, the happy one. The sadness quickly turned into hope. Maybe with her out of the way, Vizcarra de Cervantes would finally get everything he deserved.

Chapter 2: Alex

Alex taped the last box of books closed and stood to stretch out his back. Moving day had finally arrived, which meant it had taken forever to get his five-year-old twins, Manny and Hannah, to stay in bed. Arching his back with a groan, Alex moved the box of books into the stack near the door of the home office, then made his way into the kitchen.

The townhouse near downtown Houston had been perfect for him and Maria before the kids came. Leaving it was just another way of letting Maria go. The first time had been the hardest; the doctors explained about pregnancy, preeclampsia, and strokes, forcing him to make the decision to let her go and save their children. The second time had been letting go of Maria's family and their mutual friends when his in-laws put him through a wrongful death lawsuit. This time he was finally ready to let go of the rest of his life, their townhouse and investment business included, and give the twins his full attention. Their new house was truly a dream home made real in the hill country of central Texas.

The buzzing cell phone in the pocket of his jeans made his stomach clench. He pulled it out and stared at the *Unknown Caller* on the display for a moment before accepting the call.

"Hello?"

"We're still watching you."

He froze. At first he thought the voice belonged to Maria's twin brother, Vizcarra, but the tone and accent were off somehow. Alex remained silent as the familiar fear gnawed in his gut.

"You think we don't know you're moving?"

"No, I just don't care," Alex lied. The harassing calls always came from stolen or prepaid phones. The voices could be men or women, young or old, and they almost always had a Spanish accent. But no matter who had called over the past three years, Alex knew his wife's wealthy parents, Consuela and Rubin de Cervantes, were the ones making the threats.

"You can't escape justice that easy. You don't deserve to live after what you did to her."

"I only did what she asked me to."

Alex had said those words a thousand times in a thousand different ways, but he could never shake the feeling that he might have done more. That somehow, if he'd loved her enough, he could have found a way to save her and the kids. The downward spiral of his thoughts were interrupted by the caller.

"So do what you know she wants you to do: find a nice high place and jump off so you can join her!"

"Fuck you," Alex growled, his temper overriding his sense. The callers always tried to get a rise out of him before they hung up.

The call dropped, cutting off the deep chuckle on the other end and leaving Alex clutching the phone in his fist. It was time to change numbers again, even though they always found his new number eventually. His security company, Context Security, could never prove how they did it. Even using special secure phones and switching cellular carriers hadn't stopped the calls for longer than a week.

Alex pressed the number at the top of his frequent caller list. "Context Security," a female voice answered.

"It's Alex Thompson. I've had another call."

"Have you forwarded the recording yet?" she asked as he listened to her type up the report through the phone.

"Not yet. I just wanted to make sure Larry's gonna get me a new phone and number before we leave tomorrow."

"Yes sir, I see Mister Hanover is scheduled for a visit in the morning. Would you like me to have him call you tonight?"

"No, it's okay. It's late."

Larry had become more than his liaison in the three years since he'd hired the security firm. Most of his friends had come through Maria's social life, but her family's influence had changed that. His employees were sympathetic, but being the boss meant keeping a certain distance. His colleagues and college friends were too involved in their own lives and careers to keep in touch after their condolences at her funeral. And despite being close to his parents and sister, they had never been a warm family. And Maria's death had tainted their relationship in a way he'd never quite understood.

"I'll be watching for the recording when you get a moment. We'll analyze the call and let you know if we learn anything relevant. Please remember to keep your house alarm armed and your panic button with you at all times."

"Thanks," Alex said and dropped the call. Thumbing through his apps he found the one that automatically recorded his calls and sent in the file with a touch.

The soft knock on the door made his heart thump. Three years of threatening calls had Alex leaping at shadows. He brought up the security camera feed on his phone and saw Larry Hanover standing at his front door with a six-pack of beer in his hand and a file folder under his arm.

Alex smiled and shook his head, walking over to disable the alarm and open the door for his friend. Larry stood there for a moment thumbing through his phone.

"Got another call?" Larry asked when he looked up.

"I told her not to bug you so late," Alex said as he stepped back to let his friend in.

"She didn't. I get alerts when your account gets activity." Larry bumped shoulders with Alex in a brief one-armed hug, refusing to look him in the eye. "I brought beer."

"You know, I'm only moving a few hours from Houston." Alex took the six pack and led the way to the kitchen. "And you know that back patio's gonna kick ass for weekend games and cookouts."

"Yeah, but it ain't the same," Larry said as he twisted off the top of his Shiner Bock. "Cheers."

Alex did the same after putting the remaining beers in the empty fridge. "So, is this a social call?" he asked, nodding at the folder.

"I got you copies of the background checks on your neighbors that you asked about."

"Thanks," Alex said as he opened the folder.

There were pictures and small bios of everyone who lived in the vicinity of his new house. Roger Dunlop was a former Marine drill sergeant who lived on the other side of the creek at the back of his property. Grant Singleton looked like a crusty farmer whose kids had left him alone to go work in Dallas. Alice Mayberry was an ancient widow living her declining years with her grandson, Terry, who still raised cattle as his family had for generations. And his next door neighbor was Geraldine McDill, who sold Alex his thirty-two acres of prime Texas hill country.

"So, what the hell are you gonna do out there in the sticks?" Larry asked.

"I don't know, exactly. I mean, I know the kids and I are gonna put up a fence around the house and plant a little garden this summer, but I'm gonna play it by ear. I make enough money from my investments to live comfortably for now, but I'm sure something'll come up."

Larry laughed, "Hannah told me she wants a horse and Manny made me promise I'd teach him how to shoot a BB gun."

"See? Now you gotta come out to visit," Alex joined him in laughter before polishing off his beer.

Larry smiled as he stared down the neck of his bottle. "It ain't gonna be the same around here, man."

"Any news on that big television network contract?" Alex asked to deflect the topic away from his impending move.

"We're in the top three bids, but we won't know anything until late summer or fall. Ever since the story broke about those reporters being kidnapped overseas, they've had the heat on to do something, so I'm hoping that'll move things along."

"That'll keep you busy if it comes through."

"Yeah," Larry sighed. "Busy's good."

Alex knew that look on Larry's face. He was thinking about the woman who divorced him. Security wasn't a nine-to-five career and she wanted the nine-to-five life.

"So, you been on any good dates lately? As a widowed father of two, I need to live vicariously through someone else's love life."

"Still lookin', but nothin' so far," Larry chuckled and got another couple of beers out of the fridge. "You might wanna check if there're any single moms out there."

Alex smiled sadly as he took the beer from Larry. "Maria's a hard act to follow."

"But you're not the same man you used to be. Maybe there's someone out there for the new you."

"Maybe." Alex sipped the beer and tried not to hope too hard. "Maybe."

Chapter 3: Molly

"I like the chocolate ones best," Will said as he smeared the brown icing on the last cupcake with a butter knife.

Molly used a dish towel to remove the evidence of the sampling he'd done earlier. "I can see that."

She washed and dried her hands as she studied the new neighbors through her kitchen window. The man who built the house next door to Molly's family home had been a mystery for months. When Alex Thompson got out of his SUV that morning with his two kids, Molly immediately recognized him from the tragedy and trial that had been a top story on the local news off and on for years. A quick Google search on her phone confirmed it and provided forgotten details.

Will, Molly's six-year-old son, had been bugging her all day to meet the new neighbors. She held him off with the promise of making cupcakes to welcome them. The neighborhood may only be a long two-lane country road with more cattle than people, but the families who had owned their land for generations kept a close-knit community.

"Do you think they like to ride bikes?" Will asked.

"I saw the movers carrying bikes into the garage earlier," she said. "Help me put these cupcakes in a box and we'll head on over."

Will was impatient as ever and left Molly to finish packing up the treats so he could pull his shoes on without wasting any time.

"Come on, Mom!" Will yelled from the kitchen door as Molly finished up the plastic wrap.

The moving van was pulling out of the neighbor's front yard as Will waved to hurry Molly along. She smiled at his exuberant joy as he ran through the tall grass and ever-present thistles towards their newest neighbors. He skidded to a halt at their driveway to wait for her.

"Manny," a little girl called as she peeked around the edge of the garage. Her unruly hair was flying every direction, but her dusty face was adorable. The suspicious look she was giving Will contrasted sharply with Dora's happy expression on her t-shirt. "Come see!"

Manny showed up wearing a Houston Dynamo soccer jersey and a scowl. "What?" When he saw Will, his eyes lit up. "Hey! I'm Manny! You wanna play?"

Will grinned over his shoulder at Molly who nodded her approval. By the time she arrived in the garage with the box of cupcakes, the kids had disappeared inside the house.

Alex walked out the door to the garage wiping his hands on a towel. He was a tall man with broad shoulders, but he had the soft look of someone who sat at a desk for a living. There was a touch of gray at his temples, but his face was still youthful with an easy smile and expressive blue eyes. Even wearing jean shorts and a dirty gray t-shirt, he gave Molly a little flutter.

"When I suddenly saw *three* kids run through the kitchen, I realized someone must've come by."

She extended her hand, holding the box of cupcakes against her hip with her other arm. "I'm your next-door neighbor, Molly McDill. The extra kid in the house is my son Will."

Molly noted Alex had nice forearms and a strong grip when he took her hand, but was completely unprepared for the warmth he created in her stomach. He seemed just as stunned as their unblinking eyes met.

"Alex Thompson. My two are Manny and Hannah."

She realized she was holding his hand a bit too long and let go to present him with her housewarming gift. "Will and I made y'all chocolate cupcakes. No nuts, just in case."

"That was sweet of you," Alex said as he gestured toward the garage door. "The place is a wreck right now, but you're welcome to come in if you want."

Molly was dying to see the interior. She'd watched the house being built and had even snuck in a few times to see the layout before the windows and doors were installed. It was a one-story ranch style house finished with stacked river stone and topped with a gray slate roof. The front door opened to the west, leaving the large covered patio out back in the shade when the sun set.

Entering the sunny kitchen took her breath away. Alex had made it the center of the house, with golden marble countertops and professional grade appliances. "Wow," she muttered, not having to pretend to be awed by the room.

"I like to cook," Alex said with a shrug. "Hey kids, who wants cupcakes?"

His shout brought the three kids out singing a chorus of "Me!" and "Me, too!"

He pointed to the stools around the island in the center of the kitchen while he pulled wet wipes from a container on the counter. "Clean first, between your fingers and the backs as well. I saw you playing in the dirt out back after I told you not to."

"Sorry," Hannah muttered as she cleaned her fingers, leaving the wipe filthy.

"But Dad, I had to finish the road for my dumptruck!" Manny barely used the wipe before grabbing one of the cupcakes out of the box and licking off the icing. "Can Will stay over tonight?"

"No, we need to finish unpacking," Alex chuckled. "The faster you get your rooms in order, the sooner we can talk about friends coming by."

Will had icing smeared on his lips when he said, "I'll introduce you to my best friends Noah, Jen, and Lisa. They visit their Papa Roger all the time. He lives on the other side of the creek."

Molly had stepped away to look over the living room and through the French doors into the patio and outdoor kitchen. The dark exposed wood beams in the vaulted ceiling were lightened by the pale yellow tile on the floor. The contrast made the room seem balanced somehow. She already liked the basic arrangement of the leather furniture, side tables, and lamps despite the disarray of boxes around them.

"You've done a great job with the house," Molly told Alex as he joined her while munching on a cupcake. "I hope you like the cupcakes."

"They're awful," he said as he took another bite. "Keep them to yourself next time. Blech!"

It took her a second to see the amused twinkle in his eye, but she chuckled when she realized he was teasing. Stealing the last bite from his hand, she popped it in her mouth.

"Hey!"

"I couldn't stand to see you suffer another bite."

"You." Alex grinned at her and nodded once. "I like you." Alex opened the French door to the patio and invited her out to see it with a nod.

"Well that's good because you're stuck with me living next door. Wow, this patio is amazing!"

The screened patio was as wide as the whole back of the house and was covered under the house roof for a dozen feet. On one side, he had a small outdoor kitchen with a fridge, counter mounted propane burners, and an inset propane grill. In the middle was a large wood slab table that could comfortably seat a dozen people on rustic chairs. The rest of the area was filled with padded outdoor furniture near a ceiling mounted flat screen television.

"Thanks. Is that your old two-story up the road?" Alex asked.

"Actually, it's Will's. My grandmother left it in a trust for him, but I'm the trustee and responsible for the upkeep."

"I met her when we closed on this property and thought *she'd* be my neighbor. Is she…" Alex paused with an uncomfortable look on his face.

"Oh, she's fine most days, but there's a family history of dementia. She wanted to move somewhere before she, as she put it, *became a burden on us*." Molly shook her head. "Stubborn old goat. She lives near Dallas in the Rolling Meadows Retirement Villas' thanks to you paying the asking price for this land."

Alex gave her a warm smile. "I love the way you've restored the house."

"I didn't restore it, it's been in my family for generations. That's just how it looks." She sighed at the amount of money it cost to keep it running. From electrical and plumbing problems to leaks and structural issues, the house was a giant money pit. And because she had to do so many of the repairs herself and on a tight budget, she never seemed to get ahead.

"I'd love to have a legacy home like that. Two generations back, my family was mostly rough necks and bootleggers. What do you do?"

Molly wandered around the patio, looking at the various furniture pieces and running her hand over the backs of chairs to feel the cushions. "I do call center work from home. What about you?"

"I used to own an investment firm. I still dabble in the business for some of my original clients, but I moved out here to raise my kids." Alex watched Molly meander through his back patio.

"So, how're you settling in?" she asked, finally pausing her steps to look back up at him. She wasn't sure what she was expecting, but there was a softness in his gaze that caught Molly off guard.

"Not a bad first day. As you can see, the movers got the furniture assembled and placed where we wanted it. The beds are made and ready for later, even if the rest of the bedroom stuff is still in boxes. We've got the kitchen mostly set up, and tonight I'm gonna spend a few hours working in my home office."

His eyes got a faraway look as he scanned the trees at the back of the property. There was something about Alex that stirred her up beyond his looks. Molly had dated nice looking guys before, but Alex had something solid and comforting she could pick up like the scent of honeysuckle on the breeze.

To keep him talking she whispered, "Alex? Where'd you go?"

"Sorry." He came back to himself with a self-conscious smile. "So tell me about yourself."

Molly hesitated, unsure how much she really wanted to share. She had spent a few years in the Army, where she met her ex, but some men were intimidated by a woman with a military background. She didn't see the sense in bringing it up. "Well, there's not too much to tell. I grew up next door, moved away for a while, got married. I had my beautiful baby boy… and got dumped when my ex-husband decided he wasn't finished sowing his wild oats. How about you?"

"I got a business degree, went to work doing investment management, and eventually started my own firm. I married the love of my life, but she died giving me the two best things that have ever happened to me." His jaw clenched a few times and he looked down.

Molly looked down as well. "I have to confess; I Googled you."

Alex let out an uncomfortable chuckle. "Yeah, the media attention was the worst. Going through something like that was bad enough, but it got to a point I couldn't even watch television anymore. The kids saved me."

"Kids can do that. Mine did, too. And Nanny Gerry. So what are you gonna do now that you're out here?"

"Build a fence around the property. Plant a garden." Alex paused as he pondered something that made him frown. "I want to learn to shoot, but I don't know where to begin."

"How did someone grow up in Texas without learning to shoot?" Molly laughed.

Alex rolled his eyes and shrugged. "Liberal parents."

"I know Roger Dunlop has a nice range and berm set up on his property. I'll give him a call to see if he can teach you. He was a Marine drill sergeant and really knows his stuff." She took a deep breath and decided to make the offer she'd been considering. She only did the call center job after Will went to bed in the evenings, so she had her days free when Alex might be busy. "And if you ever need kid-sitting services, I'm always looking for a little extra money."

"I'll keep that in mind," he said cautiously. Molly had thought they were getting along quite well, so his hesitation confused her.

"Mom, can I have another one?" Will called from the patio door, interrupting their conversation.

"Nope, I don't want you spoiling your dinner. Let's say goodbye for today to let Mister Alex get his kids ready for their dinner."

The kids moaned their disappointment, but Molly clapped her hands at Will and pointed to their house.

"It was nice meeting you," Alex said as they moved back towards the outside patio door.

"Nice meeting you, too." Molly looked him in the eyes and saw shadows there. She knew some of what he'd been through and it filled her with a mixture of admiration and pity that magnified the physical attraction she felt towards him. "Let me give you my number. Call me if you need help or want me to watch the kids while you get work done."

"I really appreciate that." Alex pulled out his phone and they swapped numbers. "Thanks again for the cupcakes and for coming by to welcome us."

"It was my pleasure," Molly replied with a smile and took her son's hand. "I'm sure we'll see you around."

Molly took a deep breath and let it out slowly as she walked away from the house. Talking quietly with Alex on his patio had been more interesting than her entire date with that redneck she'd met in the grocery store a month back.

Will raced ahead of her with his arms out, pretending to be an airplane. Following him back to their house suddenly set off her paranoia. Maybe it was Alex's guarded attitude whenever his kids were mentioned. She couldn't put her finger on exactly what it was, but her eyes swept the tree line looking for someone out there watching her.

Chapter 4: Alex

Early the next week, a long flatbed tractor trailer pulled up in front of Alex's house loaded down with wooden fencing materials, bags of concrete, and a gas powered post hole digger strapped to the bed. Alex was dressed in brand new work boots, jeans, and a gray t-shirt that did nothing to hide the small pooch he'd developed over the last few years. The driver and two younger guys got out of the cab and walked toward him waiting on the porch.

"Mister Thompson?" the driver with the clipboard called as he approached. He was older, with thinning hair under a dirty red ball cap advertising fertilizer.

"That's me," Alex said as he strode out to meet them. He had been looking forward to getting his hands dirty for months. His plan was to fence in four square acres around the house to let the kids raise small animals like goats and chickens. Since Hannah had been going on about having a horse for as long as she could talk, Alex hoped that one day he could get her one as well.

"I'm Bubba Caldwell. Where do ya' want this stuff?" he asked with a heavy Texas drawl, gesturing with his thumb to the loaded flatbed.

"Right here in the front yard is fine."

"You gonna install all this fence by yourself?" Bubba moved his cap back to scratch his head while he gave Alex the once over. The two younger guys were smiling at each other like there was an inside joke Alex didn't get. *Just because I've never done something before doesn't make me a chump for trying,* he grumbled to himself.

"Daddy! Daddy!" Manny and Hannah came running out to hug his legs despite being told to stay in the house.

"As you can see I have plenty of help," he said, giving his kids a weary look.

Bubba chuckled to himself. "Yeah, I see that. Lemme get ya to sign here and I'll get the boys started unloading everything."

After a quick double-check of the bill of lading and signature, Alex hustled the kids back into the house. "I need you to stay here until the men finish working then I'll let you come out and help me later. Okay?"

"But we want to help now," Manny pleaded.

"The best way you can help is to stay out of the way for a little while. Okay?" He got them some pretzels to snack on and sat them back down to finish their favorite pirate cartoon.

By the time he got back outside, the young men had made short work of unloading the flatbed. The bundles of morticed fence posts lay in the middle of his yard, their pre-cut holes facing up. They lay next to the split rails, staged next to where the two young men were loading the forklift back onto the trailer.

"Okay, you ever use one of them post hole diggers 'afore?" Bubba asked as he gestured to the large auger on the ground next to the front porch.

"No, but the videos I watched online made it seem easy enough."

Bubba barked a laugh, then checked himself. "Just don't hit the throttle too hard or you'll break your arms. I'm serious. Ease into it slowly, but if it feels like the drill is workin' too hard, you might be hittin' a big rock or clay deposit. Gettin' that thing *into* something is a helluva lot easier than getting it back *out* again. I can't tell you the number a' times I've had t' come back out with a backend loader to yank one out of the ground."

"Thanks, I'll keep that in mind." Alex was getting a little steamed at the condescending attitude the men were giving him.

"Here's your receipt. I put down my cell phone number for when you give up and need a crew to finish it up for you. Joshua and Isaac are good boys and work hard."

"I'm going to do it myself," Alex growled as he snatched the paperwork.

"I sure know you're gonna try, buddy," Bubba said fighting a smile. "Good luck."

After the men left, Alex stood looking at the piles of split-wood rails, mortised posts, and bags of cement with a sinking feeling in his chest. It had seemed like a great summer project to do with the kids, but seeing what over sixteen hundred linear feet of fencing looked like was daunting. He reminded himself he wanted to raise farm animals someday and that required he put up a solid fence before he could do anything else.

Since he'd already staked out the property line with flags and string, he knew where to plant the fence posts. The next step was to dig the starting corner post, so he picked up the digger by the handle and dragged it to the corner where his property and Molly's property met the road.

As soon as he got it positioned and pulled the starter on the motor, he heard the kids charging out of the house like lions. "Stay back," he shouted as he eased the throttle on the digger.

The auger spun slowly and he had to fight the counter-rotation, but the strong motor made short work of the sandy soil that spilled out around the hole. The kids stayed back, but their eyes were glued to the auger sinking slowly into the ground. When he was down about three feet, Alex backed it out and turned the motor off.

"Dad, that was SO cool," Manny exclaimed.

Alex grinned at his enthusiasm, but there was already a growing ache in his back and shoulders. The machine did the hardest work, but holding it upright and keeping it from spinning was harder than he'd thought.

"Dig out the dirt with your hands while I go get the concrete and corner post." Alex left them digging like mad, throwing dirt between their legs to get it out of the hole.

When he got back with a wheelbarrow full of wet cement and balancing a corner post along one side, Molly's son Will had joined his kids as they lay on their stomachs to dig out the loose soil at the bottom of the post hole.

"Hello down there," Will shouted through cupped hands down the face-sized hole. He had mud up to his shoulders and a smear of dirt across his forehead where he'd wiped his face.

"Does your mother know you're here?" Alex asked Will as he glanced around looking for Molly.

"No, sir," he responded. "I can go tell her if you want."

"That's probably for the best. And make sure you're wearing clothes you can get dirty if you wanna help."

It took two more trips to the house to get his hammer, bubble level, the bracing stakes, and sunscreen for himself and the kids before he got busy putting the post in the hole to see how it fit.

Will came running back just as Alex was dropping the post in the hole for the third time with a grunt and muttered curse.

"Did I miss anything?" he asked.

"No, Dad just put this gunk all over us," Manny complained about the sunscreen.

"And he made the hole too deep and then said a potty word, so now he has to fill it back in a little," Hannah added while Alex muttered under his breath again.

It had taken him more than an hour to get to the point of getting the post in the ground. The concrete in the wheelbarrow was setting up too fast and the temptation was growing to call that insufferable bastard who delivered the fencing for help. He grabbed his t-shirt and pulled it up to wipe the sweat from his face and hair.

"How about I keep an eye on the kids while you work for a bit?"

Alex jumped as he lowered his t-shirt to find Molly standing behind the kids holding a big glass covered with condensation. "Would you please?" he begged without any shame.

She brought the glass over and handed it to him with a patient smile. "You look like you could use this."

He drained the entire glass of sweet tea in a few large gulps and gave her back the empty glass. It was just what he needed to cool off his frustration and approach the problem afresh. "Thanks."

"Come on kids, let's go exploring!" Molly led the three kids off toward the stacks of wood.

He lifted the post back out of the hole, kicked in some more rocks, then tamped the post back down to measure its height. After a couple of more attempts he got the height correct then got the mortises oriented down the fence line. The thickening concrete was like stuffing pudding around the post, but he scraped it out of the wheelbarrow with a shovel before it was stuck there permanently. Using the bubble level, he adjusted the post against the stiff concrete until it was true, then braced it with stakes until the concrete cured.

When he stood back with his hands on his hips, Molly brought the kids over to inspect his work.

"One down, one hundred sixty-something to go." Alex stretched his back and looked at the pile of wood that remained. There was no way he could do this and watch the kids at the same time. "Were you serious about kid-sitting during the day?" he asked Molly with weary resignation.

"Of course," she said with a suppressed smile.

He didn't know if the smile was because she really needed the money or was happy she could help him. Either way, he'd take all the help he could get. *God, she's pretty,* Alex thought to himself before he realized she was giving him an expectant look.

"Would you mind watching them over here? It's nothing personal. I just hate my kids being out of sight for too long."

"I wouldn't mind at all."

Her smile distracted Alex again, and after a moment he had to shake his head clear again to get back to work.

Chapter 5: Molly

Molly watched Alex set fence posts for a week with a growing sense of wonder. The first two days he could only set four posts before collapsing on the back porch. His skin turned bright red despite the sunscreen he applied every couple of hours. With one hundred fifty-six posts left to set, he was obviously frustrated. But then he got a determined look on his face as he said goodnight to Molly and Will.

The third day he got up before his kids and worked from dawn to dusk to set eight posts. His system was to drill four holes in a row, stand posts in each of the holes, mix enough concrete for them all, and then bolt the rails to support each post. When he finished working that day he was utterly wiped out, but he had a happy smile on his face when Molly went home.

By the end of the first week, he had set forty-eight posts and in the process he also developed a ruddy complexion, calloused hands, and lost some of the softness around his middle. Watching him working hard warmed something deep inside Molly. Alex was already good looking, but seeing his determination and generosity toward her made him magnetic.

While Alex was busy outside, Molly spent her time doing what she normally did. The difference was that his huge kitchen was an absolute dream to cook in. Their laundry that seemed to take her forever at home only took one afternoon with his huge front loading washer and dryer. And with the kids keeping each other company, she almost felt guilty taking his money for watching them.

When Alex had suggested an amount for Molly to watch the kids, she had thought Alex meant per day and agreed. But he had insisted on paying her that much per *hour*. Between her low-income job and the reality of living in a poorly maintained, seventy-five year old house, the accumulating debt had nearly broken her heart along with her checkbook.

With Will's two playmates and new toys keeping him busy, Molly actually had time to catch up on her own, long-overdue tasks. At the quiet kitchen table, she worked out a new budget that used the temporary income Alex was paying her to pay down some of her debt. Then using the tricks she'd learned from her call center job, Molly had been able to spend the necessary time to renegotiate her credit card rates and dropped her monthly payments significantly.

She couldn't stop herself from pausing by the windows to watch him working with a faint smile. And when he came in smelling of clean sweat after a hard day in the sun, Molly felt something in her core stir dirty thoughts about the two of them at the most inopportune moments. And despite his seeming a little shy, she'd caught Alex staring at her when he didn't think she'd notice.

A week after Alex started the fence project, Molly had the kids in the kitchen making their own pizzas for lunch when Alex came in through the back door.

"Daddy! I'm makin' a pizza with marshmallows and pineapple!" Hannah had flour all over her hands and face from rolling out the dough. Her small pizza was covered with sauce, cheese, and topped with her less traditional ingredients.

"Wow, that sure looks… interesting," Alex said with a helpless smile at Molly.

"I tried to talk her out of it, but she's determined," Molly whispered to him, leaning closer to enjoy his masculine scent. "I'll keep an eye on hers to make sure the marshmallows don't catch fire."

Alex stepped over to inspect the boys' creations. "And what have you two made?"

"Mine is an alien," Manny said as he pointed out the pepperoni eyes, olive nose, and hammy lips laid over its cheesy skin.

"I made a race car," Will said. "It's got tomato wheels and a pepperoni body."

"What about us?" Alex asked Molly with an easy grin.

"You and I get regular old pepperoni and cheese, unless you want to mix it up," she replied.

"That sounds wonderful," he said as he poured himself a glass of her sweet tea from the pitcher in the middle of the island. "I never used to like sweet tea, but something about working in the sun all day makes me crave your tea now."

Molly blushed from the compliment as she watched him drain the first glass and pour another.

"Alright kids, let's get these pizzas in the oven so you can help me clean up."

While the pizzas cooked, Molly handed out wet paper towels for the kids to wipe off the flour on the island and the floor. She grabbed the mixing bowl and other utensils and started washing them in the sink. "How many posts did you get in today?" she asked Alex over her shoulder.

"Four so far. I'm kinda surprised the fence line is still mostly straight." He sat down at one of the stools with his tea.

"I'm not," she said as she gave him an encouraging smile, then turned back to washing the dishes. "Hey, I heard back from Roger about using his range. He's happy to have you over anytime. While we were chatting, he mentioned his grandkids are up for another visit and wanted to go swimming in the creek this afternoon."

"I wanna go!" Will cried. "Can you guys swim?"

"Dad, please? I know where my suit and floaties are!" Hannah cried out as Manny jumped in place behind her with his hands clasped under his chin.

Molly turned to watch Alex waiver under the triple assault of pleading children while she dried her hands on a dish towel. Alex was a bit overprotective, but Molly had been working on him to loosen up. "Roger and I will be in the water the whole time and it's only about waist deep on them."

Alex's cell phone rang, interrupting them. When he saw the screen he frowned and walked out of the kitchen without a word. Molly had noticed he got calls at odd times and was never in a good mood afterwards, so she didn't think he would agree to a swim in the creek after this one.

To keep the kids from being too disappointed she said, "It's probably gonna rain this afternoon anyway. Maybe we can have Roger's grandkids come over here later and watch a movie. Let's finish cleaning up and set the table."

By the time Alex came back, the disappointed children had put out napkins, cutlery, and the grated parmesan cheese to shake on the pizzas. Alex sat back at his place and took another sip of tea, then stared out the kitchen window with a faraway look on his face. Molly got the pizzas out of the oven while the kids argued about which superhero was strongest.

"I think I'll take the afternoon off and join you at the creek if you don't mind," Alex said with the same kind of determined look he'd often had about the fence.

The kids went completely nuts while Molly tried to read his expression. It was almost like he was facing a firing squad instead of spending the afternoon splashing around the creek with a bunch of kids.

"Good," she whispered, drawing his attention away from the gleeful shouts of the kids. When their eyes met, she saw the shadow was still there inside him and resolved to do something about it. She told the kids, "Now eat fast so we can get changed into our swimsuits and go."

When she placed his pizza down in front of him, he looked up into her eyes and whispered, "Thank you. For everything."

Molly felt her heart skip a beat. He wasn't thanking her for lunch or her help with the kids, that much was clear. She reached over to touch him for the first time since they shook hands the day they met. When her hand brushed his shoulder electric sparks shot between them. He leaned his face over to rest his cheek on her hand for a moment, then released a slow breath.

When the moment was over, he turned his attention to Hannah who was pretending to like the gooey, melted mess of a pizza she'd made. Molly pulled her hand back and sat down to eat her own pizza, her heart fluttering like a bird in a cage.

Chapter 6: Alex

Alex wasn't going to let them win. For three years he had been hounded and harassed, but the calls had never gone beyond unnerving him. His plan to move to the country was to provide his kids some kind of a normal life. He'd built the house to withstand any reasonable threat and even his SUV was hardened against attacks, but if he was too afraid to allow his kids to go swimming in their own backyard creek, he might as well move back to the city.

While he dug out the kids' swim gear he considered the gentle touch Molly had given him. He was sure she was just being polite, but it awakened something inside of him that he hadn't felt since before Maria died.

Working with her all week had been as easy as breathing. Her help with the kids and around the house made him realize how lonely he'd been. The hardest part of every day was watching her leave to get Will in bed and work her night shift on the phones. Despite being exhausted from working each day, he'd stand in his patio with a cup of tea and stare at the lights shining through the windows of her house with a longing he couldn't, or maybe didn't want to, put into words.

He helped the kids get started with their swimsuits and floaties before he went into his bathroom to change clothes. Pulling up his swimming trunks, he caught sight of his farmer's tan in the mirror. His red face, neck, and arms coupled with a fish-white belly made him frown, but he had to admit he'd lost some weight since he began his fence project the week before.

Pulling on an old t-shirt, he stepped into his sandals, and grabbed towels out of the linen closet for them all. "You ready to swim?" he called out as he went into the kitchen.

"Yay!" Hannah danced around in her princess one piece swimsuit and floaties.

Manny had on red trunks and a super hero life vest that helped keep his head out of the water. "Look at my muscles!"

"Ooo, you're getting stronger," Alex said as he felt Manny's flexed arm. "You both need sandals or flip flops. We can't walk all the way to the creek barefoot because of the stickers in the grass."

While the kids got their shoes on, he put their towels, some cold bottles of water, and snack bags of pretzels in a wide mouth canvas bag. Then they went out on the patio so he could lock the door and set the alarm.

"You set your alarm when you go out?" Molly asked as she and Will walked up. "Heck, we don't even lock the back door most days."

"Old habits," Alex said, then turned around and stopped dead.

Molly had on a frayed pair of cut-off jeans, old sneakers without socks, and a bright green bikini top. Her muscle definition and flat stomach made it obvious she worked out regularly. Her hair was still up in a loose pony tail but the bikini top allowed his eyes to follow the graceful curves of her neck down past her shoulders. Alex suddenly felt the urge to trail his lips from just below her ear all the way down to her fingertips.

Once again, he realized he'd been staring a few seconds too long and looked up to meet Molly's eyes. She was smirking, probably at his obvious reaction, but had started to get the kids moving in the right direction.

"You're gonna make me put on a t-shirt if you keep staring like that," she whispered, then poked him in the side.

"Sorry," he mumbled. "I… um."

"I know, *Mister I-Um*," she said as she poked him again. "I was *I-Um-ing* you all week while you were working."

Alex felt his mouth dry up at her comment, but before he could say anything, she was running through the field after the kids, laughing like there were fairies chasing her.

He followed with their bag at a more leisurely pace, a wide smile spreading across his face. *She likes me?* his thoughts buzzed. Molly kept glancing back as if making sure he was still following them. Her hair flipped in the light breeze. *And damn me, but I like her, too.*

He had only been to the creek a few times while he was scouting the site with Larry. While the swimming hole was apparently on land that belonged to Roger Dunlop, the creek wound its way across both his and Molly's property as well.

When the wild squeals of children playing reached his ears, he stepped up his pace. The trail wound around a rise where the creek made a big loop in the shadows of tall oak trees. He arrived just in time to see Molly holding Hannah and Manny's hands while they stepped into the water, the kids' flip-flops poking out of her back pocket.

Watching her with his kids made his heart thump in his chest. He had noticed how much his kids had taken to her and Will all week. "Let me give you a hand," he said as he took Hannah's hand. Will was already swimming hard across the creek to join three other kids and three adults playing near the far bank. Alex had to hold the bag up high to keep it from getting wet.

Hannah squealed. "It's cold and there's mud squishing in my toes."

"I know! Isn't it cool?" Manny exclaimed as he splashed along holding Molly's hand.

"Daddy! Pick me up!"

Alex reached down and picked her up one-armed while keeping the bag out of the water. "Hold tight to my neck."

An older man stood up out of the water as they approached. "You must be our new neighbors. I'm Roger Dunlop." He had a flat-top buzz cut and an unlit cigar in his mouth.

Roger took his hand. "I'm Alex Thompson and these two are Hannah and Manny."

"Let me introduce my son, Christopher and his fiancée Charlotte Guidry. And these three monkeys are my unofficial grandkids Noah, Jen, and Lisa."

"Unofficial?" Alex asked as he put Hannah down in a shallow sandy spot. She immediately chased her brother and Will to meet the other kids. Noah and Jen looked the same age as Will, but Lisa was closer in age to his own pair.

Charlotte stood up and gave Molly a curious grin, then extended her hand to Alex. "Christopher is Noah's guardian, but Jen and Lisa are my cousins even though they call me Aunt Charlotte. Your kids are adorable."

Alex liked her soft Cajun accent. Taking her hand he smirked and fake-whispered, "And don't they know it."

Her laugh was rich and made her chocolate eyes sparkle. Christopher was a very lucky man, although he was currently being drowned by kids hanging on his back and every limb.

"You need help, *sha*?" Charlotte called to Christopher.

"Whiskey! Tango! Foxtrot! I'm taking fire and being overrun!" The fact that Christopher could stand with six kids hanging on him was a testament to his strength and balance.

Charlotte and Molly splashed over and began scooping water at the kids causing shrieks of laughter while Christopher turned to bring them into the line of fire. Alex carried his canvas bag over to the sandy bank where Roger had a wooden picnic table.

"Do you mind if I unload here?" Alex asked Roger as they walked out of the water.

"Please do," he said as he sat on the bench with his back to the table to watch the kids playing. Alex joined him with a happy sigh.

"That's some house you built for yourself," Roger said.

"Yeah, it's been a dream for a while."

"I appreciate you doing it. Turns out we started building at the same time and I got the benefit of your contractor working out here."

"Oh yeah?" Alex asked as he gave Roger an appraising look. "I figured you'd been here for a while." He knew Roger had owned his thirty acres for decades from his reports on the neighbors.

"We used it as a hunting lease for years. I finally got my last boy out of high school and moved up here for good this summer."

"You liking it so far?"

"It's quiet most of the time, but the kids have been coming up every couple of weeks. They're the ones making it fun for me." He chewed on his cigar with a satisfied grin on his face. "What about you?"

Alex watched Molly splashing Hannah and Lisa with her hair hanging damp around her face. "I love it here."

"Daddy! Come splash with me!" Manny called from Charlotte's arms as she helped him stay upright.

"Go on," Roger said. "These years pass too quickly."

Alex nodded, then got up to jog toward the water when suddenly, a shot rang out.

Chapter 7: Molly

Molly was sitting on the sandy creek bottom playing with Hannah and Lisa. The girls were splashing and looking for pretty rocks when she heard the rifle shot. The woods had plenty of game, like feral hogs and whitetail deer, so hearing hunters shooting in the area wasn't very remarkable.

That was why watching Alex completely panic was so unexpected. He had just started jogging towards the creek to play with the kids when the shot rang out, but his face paled instantly under his ruddy tan.

"Hannah! Manny! Come to me right now!" He grabbed Hannah around her waist and tucked her into his chest while he splashed towards Charlotte and Manny.

"What's wrong?" Charlotte asked when Alex grabbed Manny from the shallow water and made for the opposite bank with both kids hanging onto his neck.

Molly looked around to see if she missed something. Christopher reacted as well, scanning the woodline around the creek with a confused frown on his face.

Roger stood up and called, "Alex, it was just a neighbor target shooting or hunting hogs. No one is shooting at us."

Alex stopped where the bank overhung the creek and turned around to stare at them all with wide eyes. Hannah's lip was trembling as she glanced around to find what had scared her father so badly.

Molly approached him slowly and touched his arm. He was reacting like someone in the grip of a post-traumatic stress event. "Hey, everything's okay."

Alex was shaking and taking fast, shuddering breaths as he continued to scan the area. "This was a mistake. I need to take the kids back home."

Molly noticed his pale skin was prickled like he was cold but there was sweat dripping along his face. Then he swayed for a moment like he was having trouble keeping his balance.

Charlotte came over and whispered to Molly, "He's about to pass out from shock. We need to get him warm."

"I'll take the kids, Alex. Let's go with Charlotte and sit down for a minute before we go home." Molly managed to pry Hannah from his arms while Charlotte pulled at him to follow her back across the creek. Christopher came by and took both Manny and Hannah to play before they reached the shore.

While Christopher and Roger distracted the kids, Molly and Charlotte got Alex to sit at the picnic table and put a dry towel around his shaking shoulders. Molly knew Charlotte was a registered nurse and trusted her assessment of his risk.

"Alex, I need you to listen to me. You've got to slow down your breathing or you're going to pass out. Take deep breaths for me, that's it." She kept her open hand on his back as her eyes scanned his face and body.

Alex slumped forward and rested his head on his crossed arms. "This was a mistake. We shouldn't have come," he whispered.

"We'll get you home as soon as we can, but you need to calm down and warm up a bit first." Charlotte gave Molly a worried look and gestured to his hands. Spotting the blue tint under his fingernails, Molly knew it meant he was low on oxygen. She caressed his hair and back.

Eventually he raised up on his elbows and looked at his shaky hands. "This has never happened to me before."

"Do you want to talk about it?" Charlotte asked.

He shook his head as his color returned slowly. "Not out here."

"Then let's get you home, okay?" Charlotte suggested.

Rather than walk back through the woods, Roger led them up the short trail to his house. He told the kids to pile in the back of his truck with Charlotte and Christopher. Molly and Alex got into the cab with Roger.

"Is this safe?" Alex asked, taking in his surroundings like a man waking from a deep sleep.

"We're only gonna be on the road for a minute. It'll be fine," Roger said as he pulled out slowly.

By the time they arrived back at his house, Alex had recovered some of his composure and invited everyone to come inside. Molly stepped up to help since she knew the house as well as he did at that point.

After everyone got settled around the patio and the kids disappeared inside to play, Molly handed out cold drinks while Alex put together a few bowls of chips and salsa. When he came out to join them on the patio, Alex refused to look anyone in the eye as he put the snacks out and sat down next to Molly.

"I'm sorry about what happened down at the creek," Alex said, staring down the neck of his beer.

Charlotte was still looking at him with the critical eye of her profession. "You've never had a panic attack like that before?"

Alex shook his head and took a sip of his beer. "It felt like an elephant was standing on my chest. All I could think about was getting the kids away."

Molly recalled the upsetting phone calls he'd gotten, his subtle paranoia with the kids, and how careful he was about setting the house alarm. "Alex," she said to draw his eyes to hers. "Are you or the kids in danger?"

He glanced down and to the right. "Not that I know of."

"But?" she prompted, knowing in her heart there was more to the story.

He tore the label off his beer bottle and looked at each of them in turn before answering. "I know Molly knows about what happened to my wife, but do the rest of you?" Charlotte and Christopher shook their heads. "It was in the news for a while. My wife, Maria, had a stroke late in her pregnancy and was kept alive with a respirator. The doctors found massive brain damage and said she'd never recover. After the kids were born, I turned off the respirator."

The only sounds were the wind and birds chirping in the trees for a long moment. Alex gathered himself before he continued. "Maria's parents didn't agree with the decision. They wanted to hire experts to try and save her, but Maria and I had discussed that exact situation when we found out she was pregnant. She had a family history of troubled pregnancies and didn't want to live as an invalid if anything happened. But, no matter what, she insisted that I save the kids first."

"I'm so sorry to hear that," Charlotte said as she took Christopher's hand. "Did you have living wills?"

Alex nodded. "There was nothing her parents could do to stop me, but they never forgave me. Connie and Rubin are really wealthy and sued me to get the kids after Maria passed. When they lost the case, things got really bad."

"Have they been coming after you?" Roger asked as he leaned in.

"Not directly. For the last three years, I've gotten threatening phone calls and letters from different anonymous people a few times a week. I hired a security firm when it started, but I'd go broke paying for twenty-four hour protection." Alex took a deep breath and let it out slowly. "It wears you down to live in the fear that someone could kill you or take your kids at any moment. When I finally got free of my work obligations, I moved here in hopes of giving the kids a chance at a normal life."

"God, no wonder you jumped at that shot," Christopher said with a sad shake of his head. "I can't imagine how you must feel."

"Actually, right now I feel a little better. I've never told anyone the whole story but Larry, my liaison at the security company. They keep tabs on us remotely and handle changing my cell phone number every month or so. We still don't know how they keep finding my number."

Molly leaned into his shoulder and looked him in the eyes. "So, how can we help you?"

Alex looked up surprised. "No, I couldn't ask any of you to put your families at risk for me."

Christopher and Roger both chuckled.

Alex looked at them, confused by their reaction. "What?"

Christopher glanced at Charlotte who wore a determined expression. Then he said, "You have two Marines, a decorated Army grunt, and one pissed off coonass sitting around this table with you right now. Between us, we have more combat experience than any other group of people for fifty miles. I'd be more worried about the strangers sneakin' around here than someone getting through to hurt you or your kids."

Alex looked at Molly in confusion. "You were in the service?"

She really didn't like talking about her time in the Army. "Yeah, but it was a long time ago."

"How about we take you out to my gun range for a little training in the morning?" Roger said, then tipped back his beer. "It might help with the panic attacks. And if there's one thing I know how to do better than anything, it's getting men ready to fight."

Chapter 8: Alex

"First, always point your weapon in a safe direction, which usually means the ground. Second, never touch the trigger until you are ready to fire. And third, a gun is always loaded, even when you're sure it's not." Roger had a pistol and shotgun on the rough wooden table at the edge of his private gun range.

Alex felt his stomach churn as he looked at the weapons and boxes of ammunition. He'd never shot more than a pellet gun and after his reaction to the gunfire the day before, he was nervous he'd embarrass himself again.

Roger ejected the magazine from the pistol and pulled back on the top to look inside. "I'm checking to see if there is a bullet still in the chamber. Look here." He pointed out the space at the opening for the barrel. "We're clear, but we still treat it like it's loaded. Here, feel the weight."

Alex took the pistol, careful to keep his finger away from the trigger. "It's heavy."

"And that's unloaded. The movies make it look as easy as pointing and firing, and boom, the bad guy goes down. The truth is most gunshot wounds won't kill you right away, and unless the bullet hits a bone or major organ, it may not necessarily stop you for a while."

Alex frowned. "I never knew that."

"I hope you never find out first hand, but don't assume being shot means you're dead. Now, I'm gonna focus on showin' you how to clean and fire this Glock 19 pistol and that Mossberg Thunder Ranch shotgun today because those are the best home defense weapons. I got a gun dealer stopping by later to sell us the guns, some ammo, and a gun safe for your house."

Alex was overwhelmed. "How much will it cost?"

"He's giving us a deal. Fifteen hundred for everything, including installing the gun safe."

"Will he take a check?" Alex asked.

"No, but I will. Trust me, you'll feel better when you know you're able to defend your family."

Over the next hour, Alex learned to take both weapons apart, how to clean them and apply gun oil, and then to put them back together before Roger let him fire them. Spending time handling the weapons allowed him to relax before it came time to load them with ammunition.

Molly, Christopher, and Charlotte were keeping the kids busy playing in the creek so Alex and Roger could have time without worrying about them. But Alex did worry. He trusted Molly more than he had anyone in years, but letting her take Hannah and Manny away had been a real test of his will. He realized his mind was wandering so he made himself pay attention to what Roger was saying.

"You load the Glock's magazine with fifteen bullets like this," Roger said and pushed the 9mm bullets into the spring loaded magazine. "Now you load this other magazine."

Alex took the bullets from the box and pressed them into the magazine until he counted fifteen rounds. "Now what?"

Roger picked up noise suppressing earmuffs and handed them to Alex. "Put these on, check the safety, then load that magazine. Remember to keep it pointed away from us. Then I want you to aim and try to hit that target over there against the berm."

The gun was even heavier fully loaded. His palms were sweating as he took the pistol in both hands like Roger had shown him. The target was about thirty feet away and looked like a cast iron skillet hung by its handle under a little swing set frame. He raised the pistol in both hands, his left palm under his right hand. He clicked off the safety, lined up the shot, then gently squeezed the trigger.

The report was loud even through the earmuffs and the kick of the pistol was more than he expected. When he saw the target swinging he felt a thrill roll through his stomach.

"Perfect shot," Roger said with pride in his tone. "Try it again."

Working a shot at a time, Alex managed to hit the target ten out of fifteen shots. When the magazine was empty, he set the safety and ejected it, then pulled back the slide to inspect the chamber. He placed the pistol and magazine back down on the table and picked up the Mossberg.

"This time aim at the metal target box in the middle of the berm," Roger instructed. "Show me whatcha' got."

Alex checked the safety, then loaded six rounds into the shotgun. Bringing the stock to his shoulder, he sighted the target and gently squeezed the trigger.

The shotgun kicked hard, but he was ready for it this time. The metal box smoked as the pellets hit the painted target inside. Without waiting for confirmation from Roger, he racked another shell into the chamber and fired again. This time all six shots hit the target.

Alex felt a sense of power and control he'd never experienced before as he checked the chamber of the shotgun and returned it to the table. As he took off his earmuffs, he saw Roger nodding.

"How'd that feel?" he asked with a knowing smile on his face.

"Empowering," Alex replied.

"You've got good instincts and a steady hand. All you need now is practice."

"Thanks for the help. I don't remember the last time I felt this good."

"Let's see how good you feel after you clean my guns again," Roger said with a chuckle, handing him the rags and gun oil they'd used earlier.

By the time Alex had cleaned the guns to Roger's satisfaction and helped put them away in his gun safe inside, they heard a truck pull up. Alex was excited about the prospect of buying his own guns now that he was more familiar with how to use them. He and Roger went outside to find Bubba Caldwell coming around the front of his truck.

"Mister Thompson," Bubba called with a wide grin. "I do believe I owe you an apology."

"You guys know each other already?" Roger asked, looking back and forth between the two men.

"Bubba, here, delivered my fence materials a week or so ago," Alex nodded at him.

"Yup," Bubba drawled with a grin. "And I been drivin' by watchin' you work on that fence all week. When you get it all up in a couple of weeks, Joshua and Isaac will owe me twenty bucks each for betting against you."

"You bet them I'd do it after talking to me like you did?" Alex said, still irritated about the way Bubba had treated him.

"You can't ride a bronc' without a thorn under his saddle," Bubba laughed. "Hell, Roger, if I know'd you was sellin' to Mister Thompson here, I'd a' quoted you cost." He crossed to Alex and extended his hand. "Welcome to the neighborhood."

By the time Molly came home with the kids, Roger, Bubba, and Alex were sitting on Alex's back porch drinking beer. Alex watched them make their way through the fields until his kids caught sight of him and ran the rest of the way. Christopher and Charlotte followed, carrying a cooler between them while Will, Noah, Jen, and Lisa ran around the yard.

"Daddy!" Manny said as he ran up. "Mister Christopher caught a bunch of catfish *with his hands*!"

"Did he?" Alex asked as his son and daughter climbed into his lap.

"Yes!" Hannah answered. "And he taught us how to free-lay them, too."

"It's fillet," Molly grinned. "Do you mind if I fry up some catfish for dinner?"

"We can do it out here if you want," Alex said, gesturing to the outdoor kitchen. "Let me get the cast iron skillet and oil." Alex gave both kids kisses, then got up to follow Molly inside. "Play nice with your friends."

"The kids were great and had so much fun. How'd you and Roger do today?" She opened the spice cabinet and grabbed a few things.

"It went really well and I feel much better now," he said. "I suppose I'm officially a Texan since I have a gun safe and everything." The cast iron skillet was hanging above the island on a pot rack built into the ceiling. He got it down and turned to face Molly.

"Good," she said. "I was worried about you all night last night."

Looking in her eyes he couldn't deny the attraction he felt for her. Even after spending a day playing in a creek, with her hair escaping the tail she usually kept it in, he wanted to lean in and kiss her. Judging from the look on her face, Alex thought she probably wouldn't object. When he stepped closer, he noted the corner of her mouth inched up. He hesitated a few more seconds, trying to determine if the look in Molly's eye was approval.

"So are you gonna kiss me or what?" she whispered with a smirk.

Before he could do anything, the back door flew open and Hannah ran in doing the pee-pee dance. "Daddy, I gotta go!"

"I'll meet you in the bathroom." Alex handed the skillet to Molly with a smirk. "And we'll continue our *discussion* later."

Chapter 9: Molly

Molly carried the skillet, oil, and other ingredients outside with a dreamy smile on her face. Alex was going to kiss her before the night was through, she was sure of it. She didn't know what would happen after, but she was looking forward to finding out.

Charlotte had taken the cooler full of catfish to the sink in Alex's outdoor kitchen. When Molly joined her there, Charlotte gave her a quizzical look while she rinsed the fish. "You look flushed. Are ya' feelin' okay?"

"Oh, I'm just fine," Molly purred as she sat the skillet on the burner. She put the bowl full of ingredients on the counter, then began to mix the flour, cornmeal, and spices to make the batter.

"Roger said Alex did really well today," Charlotte commented as she washed the fillets and handed them to Molly.

"He seems more relaxed than I've ever seen him," Molly said. "Definitely a good day."

"You and Alex seem to be getting along nicely," Charlotte raised her eyebrows a few times with a knowing smile on her face.

"Yup." Molly tried not to smile, but couldn't stop the blush. "Wow, it sure is hot out here."

"It sure is," Charlotte chuckled.

While the catfish fried and the group visited together, Molly found her eyes drawn back to Alex. He'd stood close by sipping a beer, being helpful without smothering her. He dealt with the little crises that arose when the kids fought over toys or played too rough. He seemed in his element with Roger, Christopher, and Bubba, smiling at the gentle ribbing he got for his determination to finish the fence by himself.

"Dinner's ready," Molly called as she finished the last of the catfish. There were a dozen good sized fillets, golden brown and crispy on the serving platter. Alex put out disposable plates and utensils for everyone while Christopher went to wrangle the kids to the table. Molly got some leftover potato salad and bags of chips to round out the impromptu meal.

"Eat up kids, we gotta get on the road back to Houston," Christopher said as he loaded up plates for Noah, Jen, and Lisa.

"I don't like potato salad," Lisa whined.

"I'll eat yours," Manny said and scraped hers off onto his plate. "Miss Molly's potato salad is the best."

"I like her cupcakes better," Hannah said.

"Oh, I know," Will moaned. "I wish we had some for dessert."

Alex grinned past her at the kids carrying on, then turned to glow at Molly. Charlotte kicked Molly's leg under the table to let her know she'd noticed, forcing Molly to look down to hide her embarrassed smile.

"Molly, you definitely have the touch," Bubba said. "My wife can either make catfish moist or crispy, but not both."

"Then her oil's not hot enough," Molly said. "My Nanny showed me how to cook it growing up."

"That's right, I'd forgotten you grew up with her after your folks passed." Bubba frowned at the memory. "Your daddy and I went to school together. He was a straight up guy."

"I don't remember much about him," Molly said. Her parents had died in a car accident when she was about Will's age. It was odd to miss people so much that you didn't really know.

"Well, he positively loved your mama, no doubt about that. They dated and carried on all through high school."

Will was watching the exchange carefully and turned to Molly. "I thought Nanny was your Mommy."

"No, sweetie, I've told you before, she's my grandmother," Molly said and gave him a comforting squeeze. "Keep eating."

Roger took the opportunity to change the subject. "Alex, I saw your house while it was being built and since we had the same general contractor I wanted to pick your brain if you don't mind."

"Sure," Alex said as he glanced the kids' direction. "Ask away."

"He said he never built a cinder block house before like yours. What'd he mean?"

"Well, you guys already know about my safety concerns. I had the architect design this place to be as safe as I could afford." He sat his fork down to gesture to the French doors. "All the windows in the house are a new kind of transparent ceramic material that can stop a bullet. The cinder block walls are reinforced with rebar and filled with cement all the way to the roofline. There's almost no wood in the house at all, and all the materials are fire resistant including the supports for the slate roof."

"Damn, I bet that cost a pretty penny," Bubba said.

Alex glanced at his kids. "But worth it to me. We're gonna live here for a long time." They were having their own conversation about movies, princesses, and toys.

"I'm glad," Molly whispered.

Under the table, Alex put his palm on her bare knee. The electricity sizzled between them as Molly covered his hand with her own. Alex squeezed her for a moment and said, "Me, too."

After the food was gone, Molly and Alex said goodbye to their guests. Bubba teased Alex about calling if he needed help finishing the fence. When Roger offered to stop by and help with the fence both Bubba and Alex protested. Bubba didn't think he'd win the bet with his boys if Roger helped and Alex really wanted to try to finish the job himself.

Once they were gone, Alex put the kids to bed, finally agreeing to allow Will to sleep over in Manny's bunk bed. The boys were ecstatic, but Hannah was in tears because she had wanted Lisa to stay over, too. In the end, Alex had to let her sleep with Manny to stop the cries of injustice.

When he finally got back to the kitchen, Molly had just finished washing the cast iron skillet and was heating it up with a touch of oil in the bottom to season it again.

"You didn't need to do all that," Alex said as he came back into the kitchen wearing soft shorts and a t-shirt. He crossed his arms and tried to look upset, but Molly thought he only managed to be cute.

She took in the view of his strong legs with a sigh and forced herself to look away. "I didn't mind."

After turning off the burner, Molly discovered she couldn't reach the hook to hang the skillet above the island again. Alex stepped close behind her and lifted it to the hook for her. She leaned back against his chest with a sigh.

"It seems to me we were having a discussion earlier that I'd like to continue." He spoke with a low voice in her ear.

"Me, too," she whispered.

His hands were warm on her shoulders. He seemed content to let her lean against him for as long as she wanted, but Molly wanted more.

She turned and placed her head against his chest, weaving her arms under his and around to his back. When he bent to kiss the top of her head, she had to shut her eyes. He still carried the faint aroma of burned gunpowder, fried catfish, and his own personal scent that drove her crazy with desire.

"Why are you hugging my mommy?" Will asked from behind them.

She was glad Alex didn't jump away. Instead he let go and turned, keeping his hand on her shoulder. "I was thanking her for all her help today. She took really good care of us all and sometimes it's important to let her know how much we appreciate her. Do you want to hug her too?"

Will grinned and ran at his mom's legs. "Thanks, Mom!" Then he stopped at the fridge long enough to fill his glass with water before running back to Manny's room again.

"Does he ever just walk?" Alex asked with a chuckle.

"I've never seen him do it," Molly answered. "Wanna watch a movie until the kids fall asleep?"

"I'm just gonna put the towels and swimsuits in the wash before they start to mildew. Go pick us out a good one."

Molly went into the living room and turned on the large flatscreen television. Alex had a satellite dish and a ton of channels to choose from. She was still browsing when she heard his strangled cry from the laundry room.

"Molly!"

She ran back to find him holding the canvas bag he'd brought to the creek the day before when they heard the gunshot. He was white as a ghost and looking at her in the grips of another panic attack. Then she noticed his fingers sticking through the two bullet holes in the sides of the bag.

Chapter 10: Vizcarra

"What do you mean, *you missed*?" Vizzy growled through the encrypted satellite phone.

"I had a clean shot, but he moved at the last second. Before I could line up another shot he'd grabbed the kids and gotten under cover. I had to withdraw before someone spotted me." Vizzy could hear the panic in the man's voice, threatening to overcome his professional demeanor.

Standing on the top of the wall surrounding his hacienda, he could almost see San Fernando through the dense trees. His thoughts drifted for a moment. When Vizzy had started working for the cartel he now controlled, someone would have put a bullet in his head for screwing up a simple job like this.

"I'm sorry I missed, but I can—"

"You can do nothing," Vizzy hissed. "This was part of a larger operation and you…" He paused to control the anger that rose in his voice. "You know the consequences."

"Give me one more chance," the man on the other end of the phone begged.

They always begged.

Vizzy paused as his frustration grew. Getting everything in place had been expensive and time consuming, but money wasn't the issue. He was running out of time. Ever since his attorney had discovered the flaw in his grandfather's trust, he'd been obsessed with exploiting it. But he had to be the guardian of Alex's mongrel offspring for a while to pull it off.

"Vizzy, please, give me one more chance. I can work this out."

"How? It was supposed to look like an accident. And from what you just said, he clearly knew you were taking a shot at him."

"No one else around him reacted, though. They all thought he was crazy. Just give me a few days and I'll come up with another plan. I swear I can fix this!"

Vizzy took a moment to control his thoughts and let the man sweat for another moment before answering.

"One week. And if you fail me again, I'll have everyone you love killed before I kill you myself." Vizzy dropped the call.

The clock was ticking, but maybe he could still stop the remainder of the operation. He scrolled through the contacts, then pressed the screen.

"Ambassador Corelli's office," a low female voice answered.

"Is he in?" Vizzy asked as he walked slowly along the parapet. The sun was easing into the trees leaving the sky a deep purple and orange.

"No, señor de Cervantes," she answered with a warm tone. He remembered her, too, and felt his mouth twitch at the memory of what hers could do. "He's in route to Washington, but I can still reach him if you need to pass him a message."

"There's been an issue. Tell him to stop the delivery until he hears from me again," Vizzy sighed. It wasn't too late after all.

"I'm sorry, but the diplomatic pouch went over earlier today," she said, her silky voice hesitating as she spoke. "The Ambassador wanted to make sure it wouldn't be delayed. You had stressed the importance of the timing."

Vizzy looked up into the darkening sky and growled in frustration. "I understand. Ask him to call me when he gets to the embassy then."

"Yes, sir."

He hurled the phone against the concrete parapet and stomped the broken pieces. When he heard his sister's mocking laughter in his head, he screamed at the sky, "Shut up! You're dead!"

It wasn't the first time he'd heard her voice since he left her townhouse nearly six years before.

He'd been certain she was dying when he'd left, but by the time he got back to San Fernando his mother had left him a half-dozen voice mail messages updating him on the status of her coma. The last one was her tearful announcement that Maria had died but that he was an uncle to healthy twins. Healthy twins who stood to inherit his grandfather's trust.

In the midst of his parents' grief, it took almost nothing to convince them that Alex had killed Maria when he signed the order to remove her life support. Vizzy had claimed a specialist at the UCLA Stroke Center was convinced they could help her. A generous donation insured an expert was available to testify at the trial over her wrongful death. But in the end the judge had refused the request to grant his parents custody of their grandchildren.

Vizzy heard Maria laugh at him for the first time when he got the word of the trial outcome. After that failure, tormenting Alex had become a game he used to entertain himself. Anytime someone owed him a little money or a favor, he gave them a throwaway phone, a script, and Alex's phone number. He also loved using an app to disguise his voice so he could call Alex sometimes, like the night before he moved to the Texas hill country. Watching Alex waste his money on a security firm may have been petty, but it gave Vizzy a deep satisfaction.

But lately he'd heard Maria whispering to him more often, both awake and dreaming. Sometimes he dreamed of that gurgling noise she'd made just before he left the townhouse. In that dream, he was certain he knew what she had been saying, but when he woke it faded away. Other times he felt her breath in his ear, like she was standing over his shoulder whispering vile things. But mostly it was her mocking laughter when he failed at something important. Maybe when Alex and Maria were together in the land of the dead, she'd finally leave him in peace.

He knew why she laughed this time. He'd overplayed his hand. If he was lucky, Alex would assume the shot came from a careless hunter, especially if there was no other evidence. But if Alex found out about the actual motives, he would increase his security. Vizzy would have to wait until he let his guard down again, but waiting to possess what his grandfather should have left him chafed like a blister on his heel.

After passing an armed guard and descending the steps from the wall, Vizzy turned into the historic villa he'd restored using the traditional Spanish styles he loved. Fountains and gardens flowed around the grounds. Colorful tile mosaics framed every door and covered the thick stone walls that had kept the residents safe for hundreds of years.

He entered the library he used as an office and got another satellite phone from the array stored in charging stations on the shelf behind his desk. He had to call his parents before they found out what he'd done in their names from someone else. But first he wanted to calm himself, so he sat in the large leather chair behind his desk and pulled out a fat cigar.

His tech staff kept him on the cutting edge of security and communications technology. He destroyed his phones often enough for them to be disposable, but all of his data was continuously backed up to his private servers. He was too smart to use the same device for too long or to rely on commercial cell service.

His tech guys had devices that could monitor and intercept cell calls, which was how he always knew Alex's new phone number. Whenever Alex changed it, someone would park nearby with a laptop-sized device and watch the cellular traffic. Eventually Alex's new number would pop up in the logs when he called his office or friends. Then the harassment would begin again.

Vizzy needed to call his mother at their family island resort, but blowing smoke rings kept him occupied a while longer. The resort chain had been founded by his great-grandfather and passed down intact from one generation to the next. His grandfather had left the resort chain to be run by Vizzy's father, Rubin, but for the first time, he had split the stock between generations. His father still held enough stock to ensure his seat on the board of directors, but the majority of the family shares and other corporate assets had been missing since his grandfather's death.

Everyone assumed they were in the trust he left to Maria, but no one was certain. When Papi had cut Vizzy out of his inheritance, other changes were made that Papi took to his grave. The trust only referenced a safe deposit box at the central Banamex bank in Mexico City. One key had been given to Maria as the trustee, but the bank would only allow the trustee access to the box when ordered by a judge after certain conditions were met—she had to be older than thirty, married for ten years, and have had children.

Maria had just turned thirty when she died. While she'd had kids, she and Alex had only been married for five years. Coincidentally, it was that particular set of circumstances that provided the key Vizzy needed to escape his grandfather's conditions and take back what should have always been his. When he eventually inherited his parents' estate and combined it with the trust assets, he would finally restore the family legacy again, with him at the helm.

It was time to call. He crushed out the cigar and picked up the phone. It rang twice before he heard her familiar voice. "Mama, there is something you need to know."

Chapter 11: Alex

Alex couldn't believe the evidence in front of him. The holes in the canvas bag were opposite each other, but at an angle across the short side. He dropped it and grabbed the damp towels on the floor of the laundry room while Molly picked up the bag to examine the holes herself.

He held up a blue towel with similar sized holes in it. Holes that would probably line up if he folded it back the way it had been when they were at the creek. It was the towel Hannah had grabbed and wrapped up in when they left. He couldn't remember, but he thought Charlotte carried the canvas bag in.

"This has to be some kind of mistake," Molly whispered as her fingers poked through the holes.

"No," he said. "They finally tried to kill me. When I jumped up to go in the water, they missed their shot."

His mind raced while his body shivered from the adrenaline rushing through his veins. Thoughts fluttered like leaves in a storm, but one came through loud and clear. He pulled out his cell phone and pressed the number at the top of his frequent call list.

"Context Security," the male agent answered.

"This is Alex Thompson." He stopped because he couldn't make the rest of the words come out.

"Yes, Mister Thompson," the agent said while the sound of typing came through the phone. "How can I help you?"

"I need to report... I've been shot at." He had to cough the words out.

"Are you injured?" he asked without sounding ruffled. It felt wrong to Alex that the agent sounded so calm when he was losing his mind.

"No, they missed. It happened yesterday, but I only found the bullet hole today. At the time we thought the shot was just some hunters in the woods."

"Are you in a safe place?" he asked.

"I'm home with the alarm on."

"I'm contacting your security liaison and activating our incident response team now. They'll be in contact shortly to let you know when to expect them. Under no circumstances should you leave your home until the agents have arrived and verified your safety. Your safe phrase for the in-field team is *running water*. Can you please repeat the safe phrase?"

"Running water," Alex repeated tonelessly.

"If anything else happens, call immediately. Stay safe."

"I'll try," Alex said and hung up.

"We need to warn Roger," Molly said. "If someone is creeping around his property, he needs to know."

"Call him then," Alex said and stalked out of the laundry room to his bedroom. Just inside his walk-in closet was the new gun safe Bubba had installed and bolted down into the concrete foundation of the house. The combination was still fresh in his mind and it opened the first time he tried.

After a few minutes, Molly came to stand in the doorway, watching him with a fierce expression. "I'll take the Glock."

Alex handed it over with two full magazines after verifying the safety was on, then got the shotgun and box of shells for himself. "What did Roger say?"

"He was shocked at first. Then he thanked us for the heads up and is going to keep his eyes and ears open tonight. He'll call if anything happens. What did the security company say?"

Alex nodded and clenched the shotgun in his fist. "They're sending their incident response team. From what I remember of their procedure they'll investigate the scene down by the creek and provide temporary security for us. If they find anything, they'll also coordinate their investigation with local law enforcement."

"You mean the Barney One-Bullet we have in charge around here?" Molly asked as she chambered a round and set the safety back on. She slipped the shoulder holster over her head and put the pistol in the holster under her left arm. "If we're depending on Sheriff Jerry Hammer to save us, we're better off alone."

"We will be tonight," he whispered and looked away. "I'm sorry I got you involved in all this."

She touched his chin and turned his face towards hers. "I'd rather be here in your fortress with you right now than alone in my house. Hell, I probably wouldn't have even locked the door tonight."

Looking in her eyes, Alex realized he had more to worry about than his kids. Molly and Will were already closer to his heart than he ever expected. It was too soon to say what he was starting to feel, but he couldn't resist her anymore.

She shut her eyes just before their lips touched. Her mouth was warm and soft, but the kiss crackled with electric sparks that made his heart race. She deepened the kiss, leaning into him for a moment before pulling back to open her eyes.

"This is horrible timing to start something," she whispered, but softened the blow by touching his cheek with her palm.

"I know," Alex whispered back, then took a deep calming breath. "Let's go back to the living room. I wanna show you something."

They carried the weapons with them into the living room but left all the room lights off. Alex motioned for Molly to sit on the couch while he retrieved a tablet from its charging base next to the entertainment center. Sitting down next to Molly, he put the shotgun down on the coffee table before entering the unlock code on the tablet. Then he fired up the custom home security application installed by Context Security.

"The house is fully wired with night vision cameras, inside and out," Alex said as he swiped through views including one that showed them sitting on the sofa in the dark. Molly looked around to find the camera, so Alex pointed to the smoke detector on the ceiling. "The cameras are embedded in the smoke detectors inside the house. Outside they are hidden under the eaves or disguised in decorations."

"Show me the kids," she said.

Alex flipped to the view of them all sleeping soundly in Manny's bunk beds. "Better than a baby cam."

Alex flipped through the outside cameras until he got to the one that showed Molly's house. "There are optional motion alerts when I set the alarm. Anything moving within visual range of a camera pings my phone. That first night I ended up waking up a dozen times whenever hogs or deer wandered through the yard. I need to turn them back on tonight."

He flipped to the control screen and activated the motion detection again. Molly leaned back against the couch with a fearful look on her face. "This is why you tried to keep your distance from us initially."

Alex sat the tablet down next to the shotgun on the coffee table. "I thought I could do everything I wanted to do and keep the kids safe at the same time. Back in the city I managed just fine, but we stayed indoors most of the time and the security company was a mile away. I honestly believed that after three years of harassment, nothing would ever actually happen."

"That's probably what they wanted you to think." She turned slightly to look at him. "I'm sorry I didn't take you seriously yesterday. Your gut instinct was right and mine was wrong."

"So, the big talk around the table was just to make me feel better?" he asked with a wounded look on his face. "You guys thought you were humoring a nut."

Molly looked down. "Didn't working with Roger today make you feel better?"

"Except my kids were over at the creek where I'd been shot at and no one took the threat to them seriously," Alex said as his anger overcame his panic.

"My son was there, too! So were Noah, Lisa, and Jen. You knew there was a threat when you *moved* here, but didn't tell anyone until you had to!"

"Would any of you have believed me?" Alex said as he leaned into her face. "When I *did* tell you the truth, you didn't take me seriously until I found the bullet hole tonight."

"Stop it," Molly whispered as she looked down in her lap. "This isn't helping."

Alex realized he just wanted to fight with someone and that Molly was just as trapped as he was. "I'm sorry."

"Me, too." She leaned into his arm while she scraped her nail polish off with her thumb. "Hell of a way to spend our first overnight."

Alex smiled and put his cheek on her head. "Look on the bright side, it can only get better from here."

Chapter 12: Molly

The alarm on the tablet woke them up a few times during the night to watch deer or feral hogs trot through the yard, but nothing real happened until a black suburban pulled into the driveway around six in the morning.

Molly had to admit she'd enjoyed taking advantage of the snuggle time with Alex. When they did sleep, she loved the feeling of his strong arm around her shoulders, and his firm chest made a wonderful pillow. When he thought she was asleep, he'd kissed her hair or stroked her arm. Despite the circumstances, Molly felt her heart opening to him.

After Alex silenced the alarm, they walked to the front door and stood waiting until they heard a quiet knock.

"The safe phrase is *running water*," a man said through the closed door. Alex pressed a long sequence of numbers on the pad next to the door until a deep thunk sounded from around the door frame.

"Sorry to get you up in the middle of the night," Alex said as he opened the door. "Thanks for coming, Larry."

Molly spotted the black uniform bulging around ballistic armor and the matching boots looked to be military spec. The MOLLE belt at his waist had a holster for his side arm, extra magazines, and pouches for additional storage. Then she noticed him giving her the same kind of professional going over she'd given him.

"I'm Larry Hanover," he said to Molly as he extended his hand.

"Molly McDill," she said before Alex could speak for her. "I live next door."

Dismissing her, he returned his gaze to Alex. "So, give me the short version while our guys are clearing the area."

Molly followed as Alex explained what had happened, then he showed Larry the holes in the canvas bag and towel. Larry seemed skeptical at first and made Alex draw out a diagram of the swimming hole, picnic table, and location of the canvas bag. Molly made a few comments to add her point of view of events, including how she had initially doubted him.

"You think the shot came from this direction." Larry indicated a line on the diagram. "I'll need to go to the site of the attack to see if we can recover the bullet as well."

"I'll take you," Molly offered. When both men looked at her, she was struck by the difference in expressions. Alex looked worried, but Larry appeared annoyed that she was still around at all. Molly sighed at their hesitation. "Do you really want Alex walking around the woods? He can stay here to keep an eye on the kids and I'll introduce you to Roger so you don't get shot."

"Why would this Roger guy shoot me?" Larry asked with a frown.

"Because he's a retired Marine drill sergeant who can snapshot a dime at thirty meters and the swimming hole is on his land." Molly gave him a sweet smile like she was nothing but the cute country mom she appeared to be.

Larry rubbed Molly the wrong way like so many of the misogynist assholes she dealt with in the Army. Part of her responsibility as a sergeant and expert marksman was to train others to use their weapons. There were certain men who had trouble with a woman being more skilled than they were. Some responded by working their asses off, scheduling extra time at the ranges, and eventually gaining her respect when they matched or surpassed her skill. Others attacked her gender or slandered the way she achieved her rating, despite her regularly demonstrating her skill. Larry struck her as the latter.

Alex pulled her aside while Larry went outside to brief the men he'd brought with him. "I'm worried about you going out there."

"I'm glad you care so much," she said, trying to keep her mind on the compliment and not the insult in his statement. "But I promise it'll be okay."

"I know I'm being silly. You've got more experience in this kind of thing than I do."

"I'll be back before you know it," she said before giving him a soft kiss.

"Daddy?" Hannah whispered, her brows drawn down in confusion at their display of affection.

"Hey, baby girl, how about waffles?" Alex said as he swept her up in a tickly hug.

Molly grabbed the canvas bag before beating a quiet retreat to slip out the back door. First Will catching them hugging, then Hannah seeing Molly kiss her father. They were going to have to discuss where things were going before the kids got caught in the middle. She should have been worried about that discussion, but Molly couldn't keep the grin off her face.

When she reached the four men wearing black, Larry frowned as he glanced at the Glock at her belt. "I'd prefer you not be armed. We're trained to deal with threats and want to avoid friendly fire."

Molly grit her teeth and stared him in the eyes, placing her hands behind her back like she was about to conduct an inspection. "Sergeant," she growled.

"What?" he asked with a look of confusion.

She mocked his statement, "I'd prefer you not to be armed, *Sergeant.*"

The three other men were a little younger than Larry was and still had the reflexive response to authority the service ingrained into them. She noticed they stood a little taller and gave Larry an uneasy glance.

Larry raised one eyebrow. "Army, right?" he asked with a dismissive tone.

"Drop the attitude with me. You may work for Alex, but my kid's in danger, too. I'm not giving up my sidearm and I'm not gonna take any shit from you." She pushed past them and dug out her cell phone.

While she pressed Roger's contact she heard Larry sniff and mumble something to the other three guys, but no one laughed or responded with a comment she could hear. If they had, she would have been tempted to demonstrate some *friendly fire* to them.

"Hey," Roger answered. "What's up?"

"I'm coming over with four guys from Alex's security company if you want to meet us at the swimming hole."

"You sound pissed. Is everything okay?"

"You'll see when you meet us there," she said, trusting Roger to know what she meant.

Molly scanned the swimming hole with an eye to an ambush now. It was perfect. The tall bank on the far side of the creek and large trees gave a perfect view of the swimming area and picnic table. The fact that Alex had grabbed the kids and ran toward the far bank kept him out of view for a second shot.

She placed the canvas bag on the table the way they had recalled it, lining up the holes so the higher one faced the likely direction of the shooter. Before she could move to explore the likely spots for the bullet or spent casings, Larry stepped up with a laser pen on a flexible stand.

The red laser light shot out both ends of the pen, so he lined up one side to shoot through the two holes in the bag. She saw the red dot hit a big oak tree about a hundred meters away on the far bank. Two of the security guys headed that direction.

The other red dot hit the floor of the sandy clearing a few meters behind the table. Roger appeared from that direction carrying a scoped rifle slung over his shoulder and a metal detector in his hands.

"Thought this might come in handy," he said as he approached. "I'm Roger."

"Larry Hanover, Context Security," he said with his hand out.

Roger gave him a once over as they shook hands. "Let's see if this is as bad as Alex thinks it is."

Molly watched Roger sweep the detector over the area around the laser dot. Larry tossed away a few bottle caps and pull tabs before he dug out a mostly intact bullet from the sandy soil.

"Here it is," Larry said as he held the bullet up for Roger and Molly to inspect.

"Thirty-aught-six," Roger said and frowned hard. "The shot should have been louder if they were firing at our position from over there."

"You can find videos online to make a suppressor that would eliminate the muzzle flash and reduce the noise," Molly said. "Going with a subsonic round, we wouldn't have heard the crack when the bullet passed." She glanced to the tree where the other dot was. "The shot should have been close enough to handle the reduced accuracy except that Alex jumped up suddenly just before he fired."

"So this really *wasn't* an accident," Roger sighed with a weary shake of his head.

"Sir?" The two other guys were coming up after inspecting the tree where the shot originated. "There are footprints in the soil around the base of that tree. We didn't want to approach and contaminate the scene."

"I need to bring in local law enforcement now," Larry said as he bagged the bullet. "This was an attempted murder."

Chapter 13: Alex

"Where's Mom?" Will asked as he followed Manny and Hannah into the kitchen.

"She's helping some friends of mine and will be back in a bit."

"Can we go out and play after breakfast?"

"Why don't we watch a movie? You guys can pick the one you want and I'll put it on for you."

Alex kept his false smile up hoping to spare the kids his anxiety. He had his hands full making waffles and bacon for the three kids. Between pulling out the trays of bacon from the oven before they burned and making sure none of the kids touched the hot waffle iron, he lost track of time but couldn't shake worrying about Molly.

After the kids began stuffing breakfast in their mouths and arguing about what movie they wanted to watch first, his cell phone rang. Alex pulled it out expecting to see an *Unknown Caller* taunting him but was surprised to see his lawyer's name, Peter Jameson.

"Pete! What's up, my friend?"

"Alex, I'm sorry to call so early, but I've been contacted by the State Department and needed to let you know what's going on as soon as possible."

"The *State Department?*" Alex asked with an incredulous tone. "What do they want from me?"

"Your kids, ultimately," Peter sighed into the phone as Alex reeled from the news. "Rubin and Consuela de Cervantes got a judge in Mexico City to convict you in absentia for the manslaughter of their daughter. Then they somehow got the Mexican ambassador to the US to contact the State Department in some half-baked scheme to get custody of Manny and Hannah."

"Are you *shitting me*?" Alex spoke harshly into his phone, and the kids stopped eating to stare at him. "How the hell do they even have jurisdiction in Mexico?"

"Daddy," Hannah chastened. "No potty words."

"Sorry, baby," Alex said as he stepped into the laundry room and closed the door enough to prevent the kids from overhearing. "Peter, they can't really take my kids, can they?"

"No, they can't, but if anything were to happen to you, they could theoretically use this to get standing in a custody fight, no matter how tight we've got things buttoned up in the trust we've set up. They are technically next of kin."

Alex felt his hair stand up all over his body. The timing was too perfect. "Someone took a shot at me on Saturday." Peter was silent on the other end of the phone. "It's a long story, but I had to call in Context Security. I'm still waiting for the results of their investigation."

"Alex, this can't be a coincidence."

"But why wait three years? If they had the connections to do this kind of thing, why the cat and mouse game with the harassment and threats?"

"Maybe I can find out. Let me bring that investigator back in that we used during the trial. I'll even spend a few hours chatting with a buddy of mine who's more familiar with the Mexican legal system than I am."

"Bill me whatever it takes," Alex said as he heard the alarm chime to indicate someone had come through the back door. "I gotta run, but call me if you figure anything out."

Through the laundry room door Alex heard Will ask, "Who are *you*?"

"Will do," Peter said and dropped the call.

When he stepped back into the kitchen, Manny and Hannah were bouncing around the kitchen asking a thousand questions of their *Uncle Larry*, but the expression on Larry's face confirmed what Alex's gut had been telling him. Will was looking around with a confused look on his face.

"Will, this is my best friend, Uncle Larry," Alex said as he crossed the kitchen.

"Is that a *real* gun?" Will asked, suddenly fascinated with the black uniform and sidearm.

"Keep eating, kids. I'll be right over in the living room talking to Uncle Larry for a minute."

When they got out of earshot, Larry whispered, "We found the bullet and some other evidence to indicate it was a deliberate shot rather than an accident. I'm calling in local law enforcement now."

Alex's heart pounded in his chest at the news, but instead of paralyzing him with fear, it pissed him off. He had no doubt Rubin and Connie were behind the attempt on his life.

He looked over at his kids and realized for the first time that no matter how careful he was, he couldn't really protect any of them from anything. All it took was one mistake and their lives together would be over. His rage burned white hot at the injustice for himself and his family.

Alex looked up at Larry. "Do what you need to do. I'm gonna go put up the rest of my fence."

"Are you sure that's smart?" Larry asked with a dubious expression.

"I'm sure it's not," Alex growled. "But I moved out here to have a life with my kids. I've only got one, but I'll be damned if I let them take it away from me before I'm dead."

"I'm gonna get the security team working in shifts to cover you for now, two on, two off, for the next couple of days at least. I want to see if we can track down anyone suspicious staying in the area motels and assist the police department investigation as much as we can."

"Thanks, Larry." Alex turned to address the kids eating at the kitchen island. "I'm gonna go change clothes. I want you all finished eating so I can start the movie when I come back. Okay?"

"Yes, sir," Manny and Hannah answered, prompting Will to echo them.

Alex went into his bedroom to take off the clothes he'd slept in. That brought to mind the oddly sweet night he'd spent with Molly on the couch. She made soft puffy snores when she slept. He'd taken advantage of her sleeping to squeeze her close and kiss her hair. It had felt good to show affection to someone again. It felt even better knowing she welcomed his attention when her response was to snuggle into his chest.

He had just gotten on his work clothes when there was a tap at his door. "Come in," he called expecting it to be one of the kids.

"Are you decent?" Molly asked as she peeked around the door.

"Yeah, just changing into work clothes." He was sitting on his bed tightening up his steel toe boots.

She looked at him with a frown. "You're not seriously gonna go out and work on that fence today, are you?"

"Yes, that's exactly what I'm gonna do." He finished tying his work boots and stood. "I hope you're willing to continue our arrangement, but I understand if you want to take Will and run as far away from me as you can."

He knew he was in trouble when she scowled and stomped up to get in his face. He wasn't much taller than she was, but he set his jaw, crossed his arms, and waited for her to unload on him.

"We found a thirty-aught-six slug in the ground. The fact that none of us heard the crack meant it was a subsonic round purchased specifically to kill you. Based on where the canvas sack was hit and the likely location of the shooter, we estimate he was going for a chest shot while you were seated and still. If you hadn't jumped up to run into the creek, you'd be dead right now. Your kids would have watched you bleed out next to the picnic table before we could get help. Is that what you want their last memory of you to be?"

"No," he growled as his own temper rose to match hers. "But I've spent the last three years hiding them away. I realized today that there is no way for me to stop it from happening. No matter how hard I try, I'll eventually make a mistake like I did on Saturday and give them another chance at me. But I refuse to go back to hiding and let them steal what's left of my life before I have a chance to live it."

Her face had grown softer as he ranted and she stayed quiet for a moment before saying, "But I just found you. I can't lose you now."

Alex felt his heart contract at her words. She had no way of knowing how deeply she'd just cut him. He whispered, "I said almost the exact thing to Maria right after her stroke."

Molly's hands flew to her mouth. "I'm so sorry."

Alex's stance softened as he unfolded his arms and he shook his head slightly before wrapping his arms around Molly's waist. "If these are my last days on earth, I can't imagine anyone I'd rather spend them with." And then he kissed her as if it could be the last time.

Chapter 14: Molly

Molly kept looking out the window to assure herself that Alex was still alive. The kids kept her from going crazy worrying about him. Her lips still burned from the kiss he'd given her; it had lasted minutes and his unshaven skin had rubbed her raw. She brought her fingers up to feel the heat while Alex set another fence post.

"Miss Molly?" Manny asked. "The movie's over."

"Y'all want to watch another one?" Molly asked as she turned her attention back to the kids.

"I'm hungry," Hannah whined. "Is it lunch time yet?"

Molly glanced at the clock. "It's only ten. How about we have a snack and play a game in the kitchen?"

The kids argued about which board game to play while Molly got them some yogurt with fruit in it. She had just gotten started playing with them when Larry came in the back door. "Molly?"

"Will, would you play my turn until I come back?" Molly asked her son as she got up.

"Okay," Will said without looking up from the board where Hannah was moving her piece, counting one square at a time.

Larry motioned for her to come outside where she found Sheriff Jerry Hammer talking to Alex. He was a big man who had gone fat over the years, with loose jowls and eyes just a bit too close together. Molly always thought he looked vaguely porcine, which given the slang term for the police was ironic enough to make her suppress a smirk.

"So, let me get this straight," Jerry drawled to Alex in his deep Texas twang. "You move out here and a couple a' weeks later you say someone took a shot at'cha. Then you brung in these here fellas to tell me how to run a 'vestigation in my county?"

Alex rubbed his forehead. "I know it's a lot to take in, but if you'll just take a look at the evidence Larry and the guys found—"

"Hell, it was probably someone huntin' hogs too close to the Dunlop place." Jerry slid his department issue hat back long enough to scratch his thinning hair. "Unless there's more goin' on here than you're sayin'…" He trailed off and gave Alex a squinty eyed look of suspicion.

"Hey, Jerry," Molly said. "You know me from way back. I've seen what Alex and Larry are talkin' about. Why don't we take a quick walk and let me show you what we found since I was there when it happened, too."

He stared at her chest instead of her face while she spoke, but eventually looked up and shrugged. "Fine. Lead the way, but I'm still bettin' this is a snipe hunt."

"Alex, you'll stay with the kids?" she asked over her shoulder.

"Sure will," he nodded, then mouthed *thank you*.

Larry followed along, but allowed Molly to speak for them as she pointed out where they recovered the bullet, the placement of the canvas bag, and the likely location of the shooter.

"So why'd someone want to take a shot at this guy?" Jerry said as he hooked his thumbs in the belt loops around his broad leather belt. "What's really goin' on here?"

Molly glanced at Larry who shrugged like he didn't have a suggestion. *Some help you are.*

"I don't know if you remember, but there was a big news story about Alex losing his wife, Maria, when their kids were born. She'd had a stroke and only lived long enough to give birth. Maria's parents are crazy rich and blamed Alex for her death."

"Wait, *he* was the guy those Mexican grandparents sued?" Jerry laughed and shook his head. "Shit, like any Texas judge would take them kids from their daddy."

"Exactly," Molly said. "Since then he's been gettin' anonymous calls and letters threatening to kill him and take his kids. It looks like someone tried to make good on the threats."

"Even if they did, you guys shoulda called me in to 'vestigate it." Jerry had the petulant look of a child picked last for a team in a ball game.

Larry finally spoke up. "We're all licensed private investigators and we followed proper evidence collection procedures. I've got signed affidavits from my guys that are just as valid to the courts as your own paperwork."

Jerry frowned at Larry, shaking his head. "Y'all don't know our judges out here. Look, I'll open a case, but I ain't promisin' it'll go anywhere with Judge Randall."

Molly frowned and was about to say something else when Larry put his hand on her arm.

"That'll be fine, Sheriff Hammer," Larry said with a sly smile. "I'll give you my cell number. Please call me with the case number, when you can, for our records."

By the time they got back to Alex's house, Molly could smell burgers grilling. Alex had the kids sitting at the large outdoor table watching a cartoon on the flatscreen mounted from the patio ceiling.

It was amazing to her that Alex could appear so relaxed under the circumstances. He bopped along to the song playing in the cartoon, putting on a little dance number for the kids who snickered at his silly behavior. When he looked up and saw her, the smile that spread across his face made her think naughty thoughts.

"I've got enough burgers for everyone if you guys want to stick around for lunch," Alex offered as they walked up.

"Naw, I got all this paperwork to do now," Jerry said as he eyed the burgers on the grill.

"Let me make you a couple to-go then," Alex replied and got the first smile out of Jerry since he'd arrived.

"That's mighty neighborly. Just mustard and cheese if you don't mind."

While Jerry and Larry went through the evidence and discussed the paperwork Jerry needed for the case, Molly started slathering mustard on a pair of buns. Alex put sliced cheese on the patties to melt for a minute then placed them on the waiting buns with a grin at Molly.

"How you holdin' up?" she asked him quietly.

"It's weird," he said as he began loading the remaining burgers into a serving plate. "Now that I've accepted I can't do anything about it, I'm not afraid anymore."

"I'm glad *you're* feelin' okay," she mumbled, her face pinched from the tension she felt.

Looking at the fields and trees surrounding the house, she felt that haunting sensation of being watched again. It was the same feeling she'd had so strongly before her unit had been hit with mortars and gunfire. The helplessness to do anything productive ate at her guts like acid. She had no problem facing an enemy openly, but her own time behind a sniper scope made her aware of just how vulnerable they all were.

Alex took the serving plate to the table for the kids while Molly wrapped the two burgers in napkins and put them on a paper plate. Jerry had put all the evidence in his car and was coming back up for the food.

"Here ya go, Jerry," Molly said.

"Thanks," he said. "I'll give y'all a call if somethin' turns up."

Molly watched him waddle back to his squad car without much confidence. Larry was grinning as he sat to make a burger, so she sat next to him.

"How can you smile after that fiasco?" she asked as she pulled a plate over to start her burger.

"We only needed him to officially open the case for us. Phase two is already underway," he said mysteriously. "Thanks for your help, by the way."

His compliment felt dismissive, but it was better than the contempt he'd shown her until then. "You're welcome."

Alex brought out juice pouches for the kids and soft drinks for the adults. "Thanks so much, Molly. I think that cop decided he didn't like me when he got out of the car. If you hadn't worked your magic on him he'd have turned around and left."

"He probably isn't going to do anything to help." Molly shrugged as she made a burger with cheese and mustard.

"We're gonna do his job, don't worry," Larry said. "Alex, I need to call into the office after lunch to start the PR guys moving."

"PR? Like public relations?" Molly asked around a bite of hamburger. When Larry nodded, she asked "What does a security firm need for public relations?"

"How else can we leak news of the investigation?" Larry asked her with a laugh.

Chapter 15: Alex

When Molly insisted she clean up after Alex had cooked the hamburgers, he returned to his work on the fence. He'd only gotten four holes dug before Sheriff Hammer showed up, so he carried over the fence posts to each hole next. After checking the depths with the posts and securing them with supports, he got the wheelbarrow, picked up two bags of concrete, and headed over to the hose at the side of the house.

When his cell phone rang, Alex's body immediately tensed, and he shut his eyes for a moment to prepare for another threat. When he saw Peter Jameson's name, he relaxed and answered immediately. "What's up, Pete?"

"Hey, I've been contacted by a news network looking to interview you. What's going on?"

"Larry thinks I need to get the attempted murder story out to scare off Rubin and Connie from killing me."

"Okay," he said in a long drawn out way that implied he wasn't sure it was a good idea.

"Look, if I go public with the harassment from the last few years, describe being shot at, and end with being contacted by the State Department about the kids, it would look pretty damning if I end up dead next week. Right?"

"Actually, that's not a terrible idea," Peter responded with a note of surprise in his voice.

"So, can you write me up some talking points so I don't end up accidentally slandering anyone during the interview?" Alex asked as he rubbed his sweaty face.

"Of course, I'll email you something in a bit." Peter paused to laugh. "Wow, you're really gonna do this?"

"Why are you so surprised?" Alex asked him, returning a laugh while he watched Molly through the kitchen window. She gave him a little wave then pantomimed to ask if he needed a drink. He nodded with enthusiasm and mouthed, *Yes*.

"You just sound so… different," Peter said. "Honestly, I haven't heard you sound this good in years."

Watching Molly pour him a glass of her wonderful sweet iced tea, he suddenly realized why. "While I was busy trying to stay alive, I forgot to live. And now I'm remembering."

"Well, let's see if we can keep you alive long enough to enjoy your new outlook. I'll call you back when I've got some more info from the network."

"Feel free to send them out as soon as they can get here. There's no point in delaying things."

"You got it."

Alex ended the call just as Molly showed up with the glass of tea.

"Here you go," she said as she handed him the glass, then glanced back the way she came. He emptied the glass in a few deep swallows, then she stepped closer to take the glass with a saucy grin.

"Thanks." He leaned in to kiss her quickly once, then again slower. She flicked the tip of her tongue against his lip and broke the kiss with a giggle.

"You're all sweaty," she said as she backed away. "But I think I like it."

"So, why are you running away?" he chuckled.

"Because I've discovered our kids can sense when we think naughty thoughts." Molly shrugged. "I think it's their super power."

Just then Manny came running around the corner. "Miss Molly? Will won't share the remote control car!"

"See?" she said to Alex and they both laughed.

"What's so funny?" Manny asked them, forgetting his complaint for a moment.

"Let's go see about that remote control car." Molly took Manny's hand to lead him to the back door. "Text me if you need anything!"

Alex was still chuckling about the exchange while he opened the bags of cement in the wheelbarrow. He turned on the water to fill it up while he mixed the cement with a shovel. The muffled sound of the children's voices kept him company as he let himself imagine, for just a little while, what could be.

There was no denying his attraction to Molly and his affection for her son, Will. The pieces of their broken families seemed to fit together like a puzzle, and the picture it made left him feeling more complete than he had in years.

He turned off the water and turned the heavy wheelbarrow to push it back towards the waiting fence posts. He and Molly needed to talk about things before he got his hopes up. For all he knew, she was only interested in an occasional friendly hookup while Alex dreamed of more. His fantasy life filled up the rest of the afternoon while his body was busy with the fence.

Just as Alex was securing the last post before dinner, a blue sedan and news van pulled into his driveway. He looked down at his filthy, sweaty clothes and shook his head. Before he could take a step, Peter called him back.

"Guess who just pulled up?" Alex said as a greeting.

"Damn, that was quick. I just got off the phone with the producer. She must have already been driving there. I've sent you an email with the talking points you asked for. The main thing is to avoid saying *anything* about Maria's parents. The producer has all the background I could give her on the case so she knows the story. I told her you'd be focusing on the facts you are directly aware of and not speculating for her ratings."

"I wished you'd called sooner. I look disgusting right now. If this doesn't work out, I'm blaming you."

"Go ahead, I'm billing you enough to cover my guilt," Peter laughed. "Call me after they leave."

By the time Alex got to the front of the house, Larry had already greeted the newcomers and given them a quick look over. There were two people in the car, an older guy who drove and a lovely blonde woman who looked vaguely familiar. Larry was leaning into the open side door of the van while its large antenna was rising into the late afternoon sky. As he got within earshot, he raised his hand in greeting.

"Hi, I'm Alex Thompson."

"Before we lose this light, can I get you to go back and work some more on the fence?" the blonde woman asked Alex as she strode toward him. A skinny guy ran up from the van aiming a large camera in his direction.

"Uh, sure…" Alex said and immediately turned to lead them back to the area where he'd been working.

"I'm Jenna Banks, by the way, and I'll be interviewing you for the network. Ron, see if you can get some shots of him running that drill thingy or carrying heavy logs or something." She turned back to Alex and pointed where the next post was marked to be placed. "Go do something over there."

Alex shrugged and grabbed the post hole digger. He'd become more confident after planting so many posts. He ignored the camera as much as he could while he placed the bit and began to drill it down into the sandy soil. Keeping his profile towards them, he pulled the drill back out of the hole and sat it on the ground. He had left a few extra posts nearby, so he picked up the heavy treated wood and lowered it into the hole with a thump.

"Perfect!" Jenna called over to him. "Lift some more things! Look manly!"

Alex tried not to laugh as he lifted the post and pounded down the loose soil below. He got the wooden spikes, bracing boards, and his hammer to quickly level the post. He didn't know how much she wanted him to do, so he got the wheelbarrow and hefted a bag of cement into it. They followed him to the house as he mixed the cement with water, then back to the post hole. After lifting the wheelbarrow, he used the shovel to scrape the thick concrete into the hole.

"That should be enough for the B-roll," Ron said to Jenna.

"Okay, great," she yelled and clapped for Alex like he'd been performing for her. "Ron, can you get some exteriors of the house and the area while Alex and I chat?"

"I'm on it," he said as he began walking around taking sweeping shots with his camera.

Manny and Hannah came running out of the back porch towards him while Molly and Will came running after them. Molly was yelling at them to stop and come back into the house. Eventually she gave up and shot Alex an angry look as she slowed.

"I tried to stop them," she said as the kids hugged his legs. "But your *superheros* must know something I don't."

"Let me guess, you're Hannah and you're Manny," Jenna said to the kids, purposely confusing their names.

"No, silly!" Manny laughed. "*I'm* Manny. Who are you?"

"My name is Miss Jenna and I'm gonna talk to your daddy." She glanced up at him with a mild look of distaste. "After he cleans up a little."

"He *is* pretty stinky," Hannah agreed as she let go of his leg to wave under her nose and laugh. Then she gave Jenna a shy look. "But you're pretty."

Alex was grinning at the exchange until he caught the heat Molly was directing at Jenna. "Molly, this is Jenna Banks. Jenna, this is my good friend and neighbor, Molly McDill."

"Nice to meet you," Jenna said and extended her hand. "You live around here, too?"

"Next door." Molly nodded to the house on the hill. It was obvious that she still hadn't cooled off enough to smile, but Alex couldn't figure out why she was so upset.

"Kids?" Alex said to get their attention. "Why don't you go play on the patio while the grownups chat about some boring stuff."

"Race ya!" Will called and took off running with the other two following at his heels.

"So, how do you know Alex?" Molly asked Jenna as she crossed her arms under her breasts.

The look on her face finally clued Alex in that he'd made a big mistake by not sharing his plan with Molly ahead of time.

Chapter 16: Molly

Good friend. Molly glared as the attractive woman gave her the same kind of pitying smile she always got from the popular girls back in high school.

"Alex and I just met," Jenna said. "I'm here to interview him for the network."

Molly had instantly recognized Jenna Banks from her nightly newscast out of San Antonio. Her ex-husband, Troy, had drooled over Jenna on television every weeknight. Seeing Alex fawning over her like she was a celebrity made Molly grit her teeth.

When Manny and Hannah had both run out the back door, Molly's cute comment about their kids detecting naughty thoughts came back to haunt her. It killed Molly to see Alex smiling at Jenna in the way she'd come to think of as hers alone.

"Larry hoped getting the story out would help," Alex explained without meeting her eyes. "They wanted to get some outside shots before it gets dark. After the kids are in bed, I'll talk to Jenna about what's been going on."

Molly was being ridiculous and she knew it, so she took a deep breath and forced her agitation away. "I'll get the kids fed while you clean up, then Will and I will head home."

"Thanks, Molly," he said, looking at her at last. "I can't thank you enough for all your help."

"What else would a *good friend* do?" she said as she turned back to the house. Molly immediately regretted the dig, but it slipped out before she could stop it. *Why did it have to be Jenna?*

"Miss Molly?" Hannah asked as she stepped into the patio. "Can we have a taco night?"

"And eat out here?" Will asked. "And watch a show?"

"Why not?" Molly grumbled as she went into the house to get dinner started. She was standing on her tip toes reaching for the cast iron skillet hanging above the stove top when Alex came in.

"Let me get that for you," he said as he reached above her. Jenna was dead wrong about Alex's smell. The musky scent Alex had after a hard day of work was intoxicating.

"Thanks." Molly took it from his hand without looking at him.

"I don't really know how you feel, Molly, but you're more than a good friend to me." Alex put his warm hand on her back as he said it, then turned toward his bedroom without waiting for a response.

Molly watched him walk away with a small smile. His jeans were getting loose, she noted as her eyes drifted down past his waist. Tearing her eyes away, she put the skillet over the hot burner as she opened the package of ground beef.

Larry came in the back door with Jenna and her crew. "Take a look around," Larry said. "Alex suggested the living room in front of the fireplace for the interview, but it's your call."

Molly ignored them as they invaded the house, but could hear them talking as they walked around. She was stirring the spices into the ground beef when Jenna came over to stand across the island from her.

"So, Molly, what's going on here?" Jenna asked.

Molly looked up, startled at her blunt question. "What?"

"I'm not stupid," Jenna said as she leaned over the island. "And I'm not interested in Alex."

"I never said you were." Molly was so befuddled and embarrassed, her mouth ran on its own.

Jenna gave her a significant look while crossing her arms across her chest as if to say, *Really?*

"My ex used to drool over you on television and seeing Alex —" She clamped her mouth shut as her eyes burned.

"He's crazy about you," Jenna said. "It's totally obvious." She grabbed a chip out of the bowl on the island and grinned. "When you ran up, it was like he lit up inside. I may need you to stand behind the camera so he'll light up like that again during the interview." She ate the chip and raised her eyebrows.

Molly couldn't stop the silly grin that pushed out as she stared at Jenna. It took a minute for Molly to realize that Jenna wasn't a threat. "Sorry I was a bitch."

"It's fine," Jenna shrugged. "So, how long have you known Alex?"

"It's hard to believe, but it's only been a few weeks."

"So then you only met him when he moved in here?"

"Yeah, but it's been a pretty intense few weeks."

Molly chatted with Jenna while she finished cooking and setting the table for the kids, suddenly feeling more relaxed about Jenna being there. Sitting apart from the kids while they ate, she found herself opening up about her life, telling more details to Jenna than she had anyone except her grandmother. When she realized that, it became obvious why Jenna had gotten into the news business.

Alex came out to the patio dressed in khakis and a blue dress shirt to find Molly and Jenna laughing together with beers in their hands. His expression of confusion at the scene made both women laugh even harder.

Shaking his head, Alex said, "Kids, if you're done eating, take your plates into the kitchen and put them next to the sink."

"But Daddy, the show isn't over yet!" Manny whined.

"Bedtime waits for no man," Alex intoned ominously, then he paused the show. "It'll be waiting when you wake up."

Molly and Alex picked up the leftovers while the kids shuffled into the house with their plates. Jenna drained the last of her beer and got up to follow the kids.

"I'll go make sure things are ready for the interview," Jenna said as she went into the house. "Nice chatting with you Molly. I'll give you a call next week about that interview."

As soon as Jenna went into the house, Alex turned to Molly with his eyebrow raised.

"What can I say?" Molly chuckled as she walked towards the back door. "She's good."

Alex followed with the rest of the dishes and glasses. "You're better."

When Molly glanced over her shoulder, Alex was gazing at her ass. The hungry smile on his face made her mind wander.

"Mom, can I spend the night again tonight?" Will asked through the doorway.

"How do they always know?" Alex chuckled to Molly.

"Sorry, Will, we're heading home tonight. I've got to work and Mister Alex has something he needs to do with his visitors."

"Fine," Will said with a long sigh.

Molly and Will cleaned up and did the dishes while Alex helped Hannah and Manny get ready for bed, Alex reappeared with clean, pajama clad kids and a book to read. Jenna had set up the living room for the interview with cameras and lights, but Alex ignored it all to pull the kids around him on the couch.

While he read about Max and the Wild Things, the kids snuggled into his lap. Molly was standing near the doorway watching her son, Will, snuggled right next to Manny and Hannah with tears in her eyes. Alex didn't just read the words, he changed his voice to bring the book to life for them. The kids were rapt as he read, resting against him and studying the pages as he turned them.

"You are one lucky woman," Jenna whispered to Molly as she stepped next to her.

"Not yet," Molly whispered back. *But I hope I will be.*

"When the time comes, make sure I get an invitation," Jenna chuckled as she returned to talk to her crew.

Alex finished the story with Max getting his hot supper, then hugged all three kids goodnight together. His two headed down the hallway to their rooms while Will came up rubbing his eyes and yawning.

"You gettin' sleepy?" Molly asked her son.

"Yeah," he said and took her hand. "Can we come back tomorrow?"

"Yeah, we can." Molly and Alex smiled at each other over his head. "Goodnight, Alex."

"Goodnight, Molly. Larry's gonna keep an eye on your place tonight, so rest easy."

"Thanks," she said giving him one last look. "I'll see you in the morning." His eyes followed her until she closed the back door.

Chapter 17: Alex

After Alex tucked his kids into bed, he returned to the living room ready to tell his story. Jenna was sitting on the couch looking in a hand mirror to touch up her hair and makeup. When she saw Alex come back, she waved him over to join her.

"I need to put some powder on your face," she said as she patted the couch next to her.

Alex sat at the edge of the couch feeling nervous about the lights and cameras pointing at him there. Now that the moment had arrived he was feeling much less sure about Larry's plan.

"Do you have to?"

She cocked an eyebrow at him as she tucked tissue around his shirt collar. Then she began using a soft sponge to spread the powder on his cheeks and neck. "Relax. It's just you and me talking like we've been doing all evening."

Alex forced himself to take a deep breath and shut his eyes while she powdered his forehead and eyelids. "Am I doing the right thing?" he whispered.

Jenna thought for a moment before she spoke. "My job is to tell compelling stories. I can honestly say that what you've been through is going to make an *amazing* story when we're done. But is it going to help you avoid getting killed?" She stopped and waited until he opened his eyes again. "I hope so, Alex, but who knows. I agree with Larry that national attention might scare them off so I'm going to do my best to get us there, but there are no guarantees."

"I know," Alex said as she finished with his ears and neck. "Thanks for everything."

"Now," she said as she plucked the tissue from around his collar. "I want you to do me a favor."

"What?"

"Think about Molly." Jenna watched his face as Alex first grinned, and then chuckled at the absurd request. "I knew it."

"Are you gonna explain that?"

"During the interview I want you to think about her. It makes your face light up." She tugged the the last tissue from around his collar and looked over at Ron. "Are we ready?"

"I'll be in the van keeping an eye on things," Ron said as he picked up his phone and turned to go.

After he left, Alex and Jenna settled back on the couch. "Remember we're going to be editing this down, so just relax and be yourself."

Jenna started with easy questions that allowed Alex time to get comfortable. The transition to more difficult questions was so smooth Alex didn't even notice. He forgot about the cameras as Jenna made him feel like the most interesting man in the world.

When he got emotional discussing Maria's death, she eased off for a bit to focus on his happy memories with the babies. She touched on the lawsuit filed by Rubin and Connie, but stuck strictly to the objective facts of the case and its inevitable outcome. Alex kept his tone even and didn't give into the rage he felt boiling under the surface when he thought of his in-laws and everything they had put his family through.

Eventually she got into the current mess he found himself in. She started with his decision to move out to the Texas hill country to give the kids a normal life. Since Larry had already shared their evidence with her, including pictures of the swimming hole, the bullet, and the holes in the bag and towel, Jenna focused on his immediate reaction to protect the kids, painting him as noble. Inside, though, Alex felt pathetic for having such a strong fearful reaction.

The final part of the interview focused on the news about the State Department. His lawyer Peter had provided her the official documents, so she kept her focus on how it made him feel and what he intended to do going forward. Alex lost his cool for a bit, but Jenna calmed him down to give him another chance to answer.

"I loved my wife Maria and part of me died with her, but our kids don't deserve to lose the only other parent they've ever known. I just want to give Hannah and Manny a normal life. I want them to have the chance to go to school, play sports, grow up, and fall in love." He thought of Molly and Will with a smile. "Maybe have another brother or sister someday."

"I hope you can give them that," Jenna said. "I think I've got everything I need."

Alex felt himself relax and let go of the weight his shoulders had been carrying since the interview began. "Thanks for coming out here and spending the evening with us."

"It was my pleasure. Seriously, this was almost like a vacation for me."

"Well, considering how well you and Molly got along, you're welcome to come back anytime you want a weekend off." Alex was still in shock over Molly's sudden change of opinion about Jenna and curious about what happened between them while he was in the shower.

Jenna gave him a secretive smile. "You two make a good team, you know."

Alex nodded. "It's different than Maria, though. She grew up with a lot of money. She wasn't snobby about it, but she had this… softness about her. Molly is different though, she's been through more. She's scrappy. Tough. She makes me want to be a stronger man. A better father."

"I'm gonna do a story on her. She's a genuine hero and now she answers the phone for a credit card call center to make ends meet. I think she deserves better."

"Good," Alex said as he stood. "Going through all that again drained me. I'm wiped. Plus I think I slept about four hours the last two days."

"I'll get my guys out of here as soon as I can." She stood and started towards the front door.

Alex was exhausted, but his brain wouldn't shut off. He went to the kitchen as the news crew started taking down the cameras and lights. After grabbing a beer from the fridge, he went to the kitchen window and looked out toward Molly's house.

Her lights were still on. She was working, he knew, so he only texted her. *All done. It went okay.*

He sipped on the beer while he waited for her to have time to respond. He smiled to himself as he remembered how her lips felt. That last little nip she had given him earlier made his stomach tight. He wanted so much more. His phone buzzed and he glanced down to read her response.

I'm worried about you. Do you want me to watch it with you tomorrow night?

Her sweet offer made Alex's chest tighten up until he sighed. *I'd like that.*

While he stood at the window he saw her shadow moving around in her kitchen. He knew Larry had guys out watching her, but he worried anyway. He'd feel better if she were inside his house, and preferably, in his bed.

His phone buzzed again. *I see you.*

Grinning at her shadow in the window, he raised his hand to wave. She waved back, then turned to go back into her house.

"We're all done," Jenna said from the entrance to the kitchen.

"I'll walk you out," Alex said as he joined her.

The night was dark without a moon. The air was crisp and clear. Alex watched them load the last of the equipment into the news van as the antenna lowered to rest on its roof. Then Jenna turned to him on the porch and extended her hand.

"Hang in there," she said. "I'll call you tomorrow once we have our time slot."

"Thanks again." Alex said as he shook her hand. She left without looking back and both vehicles pulled out of his driveway. Then he went inside, shut the door, and set the alarm.

Maybe it would be okay, he thought as he went in his dark bedroom. His phone buzzed in his pocket and Molly's message said, *Saw your lights go off. Sweet dreams.*

He sighed and typed back, *All about you. Thanks for everything.*

CHAPTER 18: MOLLY

Molly slept in the next morning, but kept her phone on the nightstand with her text messages to Alex open. His last text said he was going to dream about her and she couldn't help doing the same. But her dreams had chilled her heart with worry despite the warm morning light.

She was startled awake after seeing Alex shot and bleeding on the floor, with Will inconsolable at her side. There was no way she could risk Will's growing attachment to Alex, despite her own, more adult interest in being with him. She had to slow things down. Even if it didn't work out between them for more ordinary reasons, she had to be sure. She couldn't let Will be hurt again like he had when his father had left.

Will hadn't adjusted well to her ex-husband's decision to leave and had hated moving from San Antonio to Nanny's house in the country. In his mind, she'd ripped him away from his preschool friends and their comfortable apartment. She could no longer afford living on her own with Troy's sporadic child support, but Will blamed her for everything.

In an odd twist of juvenile psychology, the man who'd abandoned them both was somehow innocent in Will's eyes. The injustice of it burned her heart, but she never spoke badly of Troy. Will would have to learn who his father was all on his own. Some lessons can only be learned the hard way.

But the last few weeks with Alex, Manny, and Hannah had broken through the tough shell Will had worn for the last year. Suddenly her old Will was back, along with nightly hugs, sweet endearments, and the excitement in his eyes she'd missed so much. She wanted to preserve it for as long as possible, but the truth was if something *did* happen to Alex, it could be like Troy leaving them all over again. And Molly didn't know if she had the strength to go through it twice.

"Mom?" Will asked from her bedroom doorway.

She rolled away from staring at her phone to look at her son. His face bore Troy's stamp, but she could also see her grandmother in his eyes. "Wanna come snuggle for a minute?" she whispered.

He gave her a sheepish grin, like he thought he was too old but couldn't resist the temptation. She opened the sheets to let him climb in wearing his cartoon themed pajamas. His warm body curled into her arms and she savored his little-boy smell. It wasn't always pleasant, but it was familiar and uniquely his.

"You need to scrub under your pits a little better," she said, then kissed his messy hair. "You're starting to smell like a man."

"Yes, ma'am," he said. Even his manners had improved hanging around with Alex's kids. After a long moment he asked, "Mom, is Mister Alex gonna die?"

Molly was shocked to silence, especially given her morbid dreams. She and Alex had been very careful to keep what was happening away from the kids, but obviously they had not been careful enough. "Everyone dies eventually."

"I know *that*, but why would someone want to hurt him?"

Her heart raced as she scrambled for something to say. "Where did you hear that?"

"Mister Larry was talking to that TV lady on the porch." He gave her a guilty expression. "I didn't mean to listen, but we were playing there already when they came up."

Molly took a deep breath to stall. She tried never to lie to Will, but some adult things were too hard to explain to him. "It's grown up stuff, but you don't need to worry. Mister Larry and his friends are keeping a close eye on things. Did Hannah and Manny hear them, too?"

"Yeah," he sighed. "They said their *abuelos* probably did it. What's an *abuelos*?"

"It's Spanish for grandparents. Their Mommy's parents." Molly ground her teeth as she imagined breaking the news to Alex that his innocent little ones knew much more than he'd assumed.

"I heard Nanny say that she wanted to kill Daddy one time." It was barely a whisper, but it cut her deeply to hear the pain in his voice.

"Oh, baby, she didn't mean it like that." Molly held him tighter and kissed his hair again. "She was just mad that Daddy left us."

"But he didn't want to! He got that good job in 'ganistan. He promised he'd be back for my birthday." His tone was neutral, but Molly died a little hearing his disappointment voiced so plainly.

"I know he wanted to come," she lied. "But he was halfway around the world. I told you before, it takes a whole day just to get there. And we had fun, didn't we?" Molly had taken him into San Antonio to a huge water park for the day. She had emailed Troy the information weeks in advance but he had never even responded. Will kept looking at all the tall men hoping Troy was going to show up and surprise him.

"Do you think Mister Alex and Manny and Hannah could come with us next time?" Will looked in her face with a longing that resonated in her own heart.

"I don't know. We'll have to wait and see," she said, telling herself as much as Will.

After they got up to shower and dress for the day, Molly and Will walked around the fence where Alex was already up and working.

"Hey, you two," Alex said as he stopped to lean against the shovel in his hands.

Molly looked at his wet shirt and dirty hands, fighting the compulsion to push him down in the grass and climb on top of him.

"Hi, Mister Alex! Can I go and play?" Will asked as he already started edging toward the house.

"Sure thing," Alex said giving him an indulgent smile as he took off running. "They're on the patio watching a movie."

"I need to tell you something," Molly said as soon as Will was out of earshot. Her arms crossed under her breasts as she braced to share the bad news.

Alex looked back to her and his smile faded. "What's wrong?"

She relayed what Will had told her about overhearing Larry and Jenna talking on the porch. When she mentioned his kids speculation about their grandparents, Alex looked down and let out a long sigh.

"They were always clever," he whispered without looking at her. "I'm surprised it took them this long to figure it out."

"Didn't they ask about their mother or her family?" Molly asked.

Alex nodded. "They always knew Maria had died and just accepted it. I did all the family stuff with my sister and parents. It was our normal. Then after Rubin and Connie went after me in court, I never trusted them enough to lift the restraining order. When the kids asked about them, I just said they lived far away."

"What a mess," Molly said. "And I thought things were bad with me and Troy."

"You've never really mentioned him," Alex prompted, clearly inviting Molly to share more.

Molly took a deep breath. "Troy and I met in the service. After we got out and got married, he wanted to go back overseas as a consultant. I was against it because we had a baby to raise here, but he wasn't ready to settle down and couldn't walk away from the money."

"He's an idiot. Will is a *great* kid." Alex looked over toward the house and got a determined look on his face.

She paused to consider how to break her decision to Alex. "Will's better now, but it was so hard on him after Troy left. I never want to put Will through that again." Alex must have heard something in her tone because he turned to search her face with a frown. Molly took a deep breath. "Which is why I need to cool things off between us."

Alex flinched like she'd hit him, but then pinched his lips and nodded. "I see."

"Will's getting really attached to you. Watching you read to him and your kids last night brought it home." When his face fell, she felt the need to explain. "If it was only me—"

"Just stop, I get it," he growled and picked up his shovel. "Let me have today to find someone else to keep an eye on the kids for me and you're off the hook."

"No, wait, I still want to help you with them!" She panicked as she realized he'd misunderstood what she meant. "Will won't understand!"

He turned to glare at her. "Like my kids will?" he shouted. "They're getting attached to you, too, Molly!" He put his dirty hand over his face and let out a sad chuckle. "You know what? Forget it." He shook his head and grit his teeth. "Just get Will and go home. I've got some calls to make and I obviously need to have a long talk with my kids."

"Alex, no," she pleaded. "Wait!"

"Just go," he said as he threw the shovel down and stalked back toward the house.

Chapter 19: Alex

"Alex, don't do this!" Molly pleaded as he stalked away.

His heart was pounding so hard that his vision dimmed in time with the beats. He knew what her real problem was. He couldn't blame her for wanting to spare her own child what he couldn't spare his own. He knew he shouldn't be mad at her for wanting to get her kid away from his mess of a life, but it was so unexpected that he couldn't help it. He felt Molly grab his arm then she pulled hard enough to turn him.

"Damn it, Alex, this isn't what I meant!"

He had never seen her really angry before. Molly's eyes flared over her flushed red cheeks as her lips compressed into a thin line. A shock of desire cut through his pain at the sight of her, but he pushed it away. "You say you're worried about Will getting attached to me and then say you want to cool things off between us. What the hell am I supposed to think?"

"You're *supposed* to think I'm too crazy about you to think straight." She punctuated her statement with a stiff finger poking his chest. "You're *supposed* to think that I need to keep Will first in my life." *Poke.* "You're *supposed* to think that you've been a better father figure for my son in these last few weeks than his own father has for years." *Poke.* "And you're *supposed* to think that I'm terrified for you… and for Will… and for me." Her eyes brimmed with angry tears. "Just leave things the way they are and let me have some time. That's all I'm asking for."

Damn all crying women. Her raw honesty cut him to his heart, but her rejection still bruised. "I don't know how to cool off what I'm feeling towards you."

"Okay, how about this," she said with relief. "No more kissing for a while. It messes with me too much." She gave a short laugh as she looked him over. "Hell, just watching you work out here messes with me."

She tucked a stray hair behind her ear, her short pink nails caught his eye and he suddenly imagined them scratching down his chest. He blinked away the vision and swallowed. "Okay, I can do that. What else?"

"Step back a little with Will. He's soaking you up like a wilted plant in the rain. Don't hurt him or anything, but maybe save your bedtime stories and cuddling until after we've gone home."

Alex nodded, hiding the sting he felt at her request. Will was a great kid and he pulled hard at Alex's fatherly instincts. "What else?"

Molly took a deep breath. "I'll do my best to keep from teasing you, but let me know if I do something that sends mixed signals. I'll do the same. The kids are so perceptive I bet they already know how we feel about each other." She looked away. "For the record, I'm not just worried about something happening to you. We don't know each other very well yet. We may end up fighting and I don't want the kids caught in the middle. Will has to be my first priority."

"Now *that* I totally understand. I feel the same way about mine. It's the main reason I haven't been with anyone since Maria died." Alex watched her look back at him with her eyebrows raised.

"It's been *five years* for you?" she asked with an incredulous tone.

Alex shrugged. "Constant paranoia's a real buzz kill."

"Wow," she said as pink spots appeared on her cheeks. "I can't even imagine how hard *that's* been."

Alex smiled at her understatement. "You're actually the first woman I've even felt attracted to since Maria. And it's been so long since someone just touched me or held my hand. The other night on the couch was…" He suddenly noticed his own cheeks warm and his pants tighten. "Never mind. Okay, let's change the subject. I think I need to shoot something this afternoon. Mind if I call Roger up and go practice for an hour or so?"

"That'll be fine. I need to go grocery shopping for a few things for both of us. How about I drop you off on the way and pick you up on the way home."

Alex forced his fear down. Molly was probably better prepared to protect his kids than he was. "I guess the kids would want to go shopping with you."

She smiled at him and said, "Relax. I've got a concealed carry permit and will be bringing my baby Glock G42. We'll be fine."

Alex went back to work after watching Molly walk up to the house. She was right, he realized. They had no idea what was underneath the strong attraction they felt for each other. It would take some time to figure out if it was an infatuation or something deeper, but it was enough that Molly was interested in taking the time to find out.

Roger was happy to have Alex come over when he called, so they made plans to get together after lunch. After Alex finished the next set of posts, he cleaned up at the hose and went into the patio to cool off for a while. The kids had covered the huge slab table with race tracks and were making the little metal cars do loops and speed around tight curves. He grabbed a sports drink from the outdoor fridge and spent a little time playing with them.

"I've got sandwiches and chips for lunch," Molly announced from the doorway. "Come eat at the kitchen island. You can leave the track out there for now and go play again after we go to the store."

Alex couldn't help looking at her slim body with an ache in his chest. She was even beautiful after a busy morning with the kids. The spaghetti strap top and tight jeans she wore left her smooth curves open to inspection. A few strands of hair dangled down her neck to touch her shoulders. He felt a compulsion to kiss those shoulders and up her neck to that soft spot just behind her ears. Shutting his eyes to shake off his arousal, he got up to follow them inside.

"I don't like turkey," Hannah whined as Alex entered the kitchen.

"There's roast beef and ham as well," Molly said as she moved the meat and cheese plate closer. "You can make your sandwich any way you want."

"Mister Alex?" Will asked to get his attention. "Why does someone want to hurt you?"

The question silenced all the discussions and his own two twins looked up with guilty expressions. Molly looked like she was about to say something, but Alex subtly shook his head.

"Have you ever met a bully at school?" Alex asked Will.

"Yeah," Will replied with a sour look on his face. "Jamie Hammer always says he's gonna tell his grandpa to arrest me if I don't give him my lunch money."

"What?" Molly's shrill tone split the air. "That little—You tell me if he ever does it again."

"Yes, ma'am," Will said instantly, then looked back to Alex for his answer.

"I'm sorry to say that when you grow up there will still be bullies. Some people think they can make you do what they want because they know important people, like Jamie Hammer, or because they have a lot of money, or sometimes because they say they'll hurt you." Alex was explaining to his own kids as much as Will so he had to be careful what he said. "My wife, Maria, got sick when Hannah and Manny were still in her tummy. She died right after they were born. Her mommy and daddy thought it was my fault when it was just a sad thing that happened for no good reason. They are still mad and want to bully me now, so I asked Uncle Larry and Miss Jenna to help me."

"Why can't you just tell them it wasn't your fault?" Manny asked.

"I did, but they blamed me anyway." Alex saw the confusion in his kids' faces. "I wish I could explain it better, but sometimes grown up stuff just doesn't make sense."

"Are you gonna be okay, Daddy?" Hannah asked in a trembling voice.

"Yes," Alex said with more confidence than he felt. "I'm gonna be just fine. You'll see."

"Okay, the first one finished with their sandwich gets an extra cookie!" Molly winked at Alex as the kids stopped talking and immediately started eating.

After lunch, Alex got his shotgun, pistol, and ammunition before setting off with Molly and the kids to Roger's house. Alex insisted Molly drive his SUV, and after he pointed out the solid rubber tires, armored exterior, and bullet-proof glass, she agreed. When she drove off, Alex made his way over to Roger's gun range.

"Howdy neighbor," Roger called out as he ran an oily cloth down the barrel of his pistol. "How'd the interview go?"

"Okay, I think. We'll find out tonight," Alex said as he placed the guns and ammo on the table at the head of his range. "Thanks for letting me come over again. I cleaned these like you said but you should probably double check me to make sure I didn't screw something up when I put the parts back together."

Roger gave them a quick check and nodded with satisfaction. "Looks good to me. Let's see how your aim is today." He handed Alex a pair of noise reducing earmuffs.

Placing them over his ears, Alex took his Glock 19 in his right hand and snapped in a full magazine. After pulling back the slide, he gripped the butt with his left palm and lined up on the target. Firing one shot after another, he pinged the target fourteen times, only missing once.

"That's better than last time," Alex said as he ejected the spent magazine and checked the chamber.

"You wanna try a little quick draw practice next?" Roger asked.

Alex slapped in another full magazine. "What do I do?"

"Hold the gun down at your leg, then when I say go you aim and fire as quick as you can."

"Show me?" Alex asked and Roger got his own pistol off the table.

Roger fired off his entire magazine in a series of smooth motions. He went from a relaxed stance to firing faster than Alex would have believed if he hadn't seen it himself. Each shot didn't just hit the swinging metal target, it pinged the exact center of the target each time.

"The trick is to get the muscles in your arm and hand to aim where you're looking without having to think too much about it. I've been shooting almost everyday for twenty years, so it may look easy when I do it."

"No, it looks like fucking magic," Alex laughed as he got in the same kind of relaxed starting stance Roger had used.

"Go," Roger commanded and Alex raised the pistol too high and missed the target entirely. "Don't rush yourself. The trick to speed is to only move as fast as you can and still hit the target. Speed will come with practice." He waited until Alex was ready again. "Go!"

Alex pinged the very bottom of the target. "I think I see. Call it again."

They worked their way through two magazines a shot at a time. Roger kept suggesting improvements to his technique, and by the end, Alex could snapshot the target most of the time. By the time Molly came back to get him, he was feeling better.

"Thanks again, Roger," Alex said before climbing into the passenger seat of his SUV.

"Why don't you plan on stopping by after lunch for the next couple of weeks and let me work with you? You've got a great natural eye for someone who hasn't shot before."

Alex loved the powerful feeling that shooting gave him. It reduced his stress and seeing his improvements made him more confident. "I think I will."

"Don't forget to clean your guns tonight." Roger gave him the instructor's eye that said he'd be checking it was done to his satisfaction.

"Just as soon as the kids are in bed," Alex promised as he shut the passenger door to the SUV.

"How'd you do?" Molly asked as she waved goodbye to Roger.

"At least Roger doesn't think I'm hopeless," Alex answered as she pulled out of his driveway. He turned in his seat to look back at their children. "Did you kids behave for Miss Molly?"

"Yes, sir," they all answered and Manny added, "She even let us have a cookie!"

"Well, I have some more fence posts to set before dinner so I want you to stay on your best behavior. You hear me?"

"Yes, sir," they answered again.

After he locked up the guns and ammo in his safe, Alex returned to setting posts. He had completed the side that ran along Molly's property line and made it halfway along the back of his property before he ran out of steam. Wiping off the mud at the hose outside the patio, he left his dirty boots by the back door and went inside.

"Daddy, can Will sleep over tonight?" Manny asked with a pleading expression on his face.

"Not tonight," Alex said, avoiding Molly's eyes. "You kids say goodbye and we'll see Miss Molly and Will in the morning."

"Aw, Dad," Manny complained as he and Hannah gave Will a quick hug goodbye.

"I forgot I promised I'd watch the news with you," Molly whispered to Alex.

He looked up with a sad smile. "Go on home. You've done enough for me today."

"Are you sure?" she asked.

When Alex opened the kitchen door, she stepped through pulling Will after her.

"I'll be watching if you want to call and talk before my shift," she said. Her hand almost reached out to touch his chest, but she pulled her fingers back at the last second with a wince. "Sorry."

"It's fine. We've got time to work it out. I'll see you tomorrow."

He kept up the stoic expression until they were outside and he shut the door, then his face fell to reflect how lonely he suddenly felt. "Kids, go get ready for bed. I've got to clean my guns."

CHAPTER 20: MOLLY

The interview was heartbreaking. Between Molly's close feelings for Alex, and Jenna's skillful narrative, she watched the whole thing with tears streaming down her face. The real punch in the gut was when she watched Alex snuggled up reading a book to Will, Manny, and Hannah while Jenna dispassionately described how someone carefully set up the shot to kill him, only missing because he happened to move at the last second.

At the end of the story she sat stunned as the newscast credits rolled past on the screen. She generally knew what had happened to Alex and had even read some of the details online, but watching him talking about it brought the story to life in a way that nothing else had. Her most traumatic experiences never left her feeling as helpless as watching Alex suffering.

She picked up her phone and texted Alex. *Are you okay?*

When she didn't get an immediate response, she stepped over to the kitchen window to look toward his house. Alex was out on the patio, outlined by the lights inside his kitchen while having an animated conversation on his phone. One hand pressed the phone to his ear while the other was making emphatic gestures and waving at Molly's house. At one point he slumped his shoulders and shook his head, then let his hand holding the phone fall away from his ear.

Alex looked up at her house as he ran his hand through his hair. It had gotten longer since he'd moved in. He didn't look like a clean-cut investment banker anymore, but Molly couldn't help imagining her fingers running through his longer waves. She watched as Alex touched his phone briefly and lifted it to his ear. A second later, Molly's phone rang.

"Hey," she said as she watched him across the fence.

"I'm so sorry Jenna put Will in that couch shot without your permission," he said with a burr of anger in his tone.

In the midst of her emotional distress for Alex, Molly hadn't considered the implications. "Oh, shit, I didn't even think about that."

"She said she'll send you a release form via email. If you sign it and don't sue the station, she'll send you a check for five thousand dollars."

"What?" Molly froze as the words struggled to organize themselves into a coherent thought.

"She broadcast a minor on primetime television without his parent's permission! I just rang her bell about it."

"She's gonna pay me five grand because she accidentally put Will on television for, what, fifteen seconds?" Molly couldn't hide the giddy sense of joy at the thought of the money. "Holy shit, Alex!"

"So, you're not mad?" he asked.

"No!" Molly exclaimed. She realized that Alex was so rich he had no idea what it was like to live under the pressure of constant debt. Even what he'd paid her to help with the kids felt like finding buried treasure. That was the first time Molly felt an odd disconnect in their different points of view. "Thank you for your concern, though. Tell Jenna that will be fine if you talk to her again."

"She said she'd call you tomorrow after they get the paperwork for you to sign." Alex sounded calmer as he leaned against the patio wall.

"Jenna did a great job telling your story." Molly suddenly felt uncomfortable at the thought of admitting that she'd cried the whole time.

"Yeah," he sighed. "I'd hoped moving here would make things better. I'm sorry I've brought my troubles to your doorstep."

"But there's a silver lining in that cloud," Molly teased. "I'm glad we met." He didn't respond for a moment.

"Today was hard," Alex whispered to her. She needed to keep some distance between them, but she felt the same longing that was present in his voice.

"It was for me, too," she said. "But thank you for giving me the space I need."

"By the end of this week, the fence should be halfway up. I think I can wrap it up in another couple of weeks." The unspoken question of what would happen afterwards hung between them. She wouldn't have an excuse to come over everyday anymore.

"Do you know what you want to do next?" she asked, tempting fate while she watched him pace outside his patio.

"Not yet," he said, then laughed. "Probably get some goats and build a chicken coop."

"I know the kids would love that." She could just imagine Manny and Hannah fighting over who would get to feed the chickens or pick up their eggs.

"I need to order a gate," he said as he stopped pacing to stare at the fence between their property. "You're gonna have to walk along the road to get here before I'm done."

"A little arbor gate would be nice." She wanted to say so much more, but knew it was too soon. They had lived such different lives, and he didn't know her as well as he thought he did.

"Thanks for talking to me tonight. Watching the interview was harder than I thought it would be."

"Don't worry about the thing with Will. Anyone who knows him lives around here anyway."

"Jenna said she's already got a call from the network. The interview will be recut for a segment on their national news broadcast tomorrow."

That chilled Molly, but she couldn't say why. "So, the story's getting picked up? Jenna must be over the moon."

"Yeah, she is. And hopefully it'll rattle Rubin and Connie enough to back off."

"I hope so too." She suddenly wanted to kiss him and feel his arms around her again, but she pushed the craving away. "I've got to get on my computer for my call center shift."

There was a long moment of silence. She could see Alex staring up at the sky. "Molly…"

The ache in his voice frightened her. "Goodnight, Alex."

He sighed and said, "Goodnight."

Molly dropped the call and turned away from the kitchen window to get him out of her sight. Walking back to the kitchen table where she had her laptop ready to work, Molly took a seat and put on her headset. When she clicked the button to join the pool, she immediately got a call.

"Card services, this is Molly. How can I help you?"

While her mouth and fingers were on autopilot, Molly let her mind wander. Alex's need called to her, but she didn't know if what was growing between them was real or just convenient. She had made the same kind of mistake with Troy, confusing proximity with fate.

They had been in the same army company escorting refugees through the mountains of Afghanistan when they met. She was riding in the middle of the convoy when the first mortars hit. The air was instantly filled with the sound of screaming children and the smell of smoke.

Her squad spread out to provide suppressing fire to keep the insurgents from closing in on the stalled vehicles. Troy's squad rolled the damaged vehicle blocking the road down the mountain and herded the surviving refugees away from the ambush.

While Molly's squad continued to fire, someone had called in a strike against the mortar's position and a couple of Apache helicopters turned the craggy point above them into a flaming torch. Then an enemy sniper began to pick off anyone still in the open. Molly grabbed her M24 sniper rifle out of the Humvee and sprinted up the mountain with her spotter to flank the sniper's position.

It was an hour long game of cat and mouse, but her spotter finally caught a break and saw the suppressed muzzle flash across the mountain from their position. Molly waited until the sniper came up for another shot and splattered his brains against the rocks behind him. Two more shots took care of his support team, allowing the surviving soldiers and refugees to escape the area.

She and Troy met each other that night at the camp and fucked until the sun came up. They had both survived the ambush without a scratch and she had thought that meant they were fated to be together. He claimed to feel the same way, but in the end, he never got over the excitement of being in combat. He craved the danger like a drug and it became his mistress, drawing him away from her to risk himself for a private security firm.

Alex was nothing like Troy, but her experience made it hard to trust her feelings again. She found herself in another dangerous situation, feeling that same sense of fate with Alex. She needed to know more before she would risk her heart and her son. She had to *know* this time. And that meant taking whatever time it took to be sure, even if she risked losing Alex in the process.

Chapter 21: Alex

Wednesday morning after the interview broadcast, Alex was back out at dawn working on the fence. His frustration over nearly every aspect of his life drove him to work even harder than before. He couldn't stop the bullet that might end his life. He couldn't make Molly understand he was serious about being with her. He couldn't make Rubin and Connie stop their insane pursuit of his children. But he could damn well put fence posts in the ground. So, that's what he did.

Molly came over around nine o'clock looking subdued and tired. Will barely said hello as he ran around the fence towards the house to play with Manny and Hannah. Alex resisted the urge to start a pointless conversation, so he kept working after he greeted her but couldn't help noticing her swaying walk up to the house.

She brought him a big glass of sweet tea around ten, but he just drained it quickly and kept working. She watched him for a moment, then nodded to herself and went back in the house. Alex felt bad for not talking to her more, but he couldn't muster up the energy to start a conversation that was headed nowhere. Working was the only thing that seemed to keep him sane.

By the time he began to run out of steam just before lunch, Bubba's truck pulled into the driveway with his two boys in the back.

Alex walked over to greet them, wiping his hands on the dirty towel he kept around his neck. "Hey Bubba," Alex said as he shook hands and lifted his chin towards the boys. "Joshua. Isaac. What can I do for y'all?"

"Well," Bubba drawled as he moved his hat back to scratch his head. "The boys and me been talkin'. They see you got this fence going up just fine and decided since I'm gonna win the bet anyway, we might as well come help you out some."

Alex blinked at Bubba's words. "That's really nice of y'all." He was trying to figure out how to politely decline when Roger pulled in driving his truck. "Are they with you, too?" Alex asked, nodding at Roger and a lanky older guy getting out with their work clothes on.

"Yeah," Bubba said as he avoided Alex's eyes. "I mighta mentioned somethin' to Roger and Grant over't the ice house last night."

An old sedan pulled in and parked next to Bubba and a matronly old woman got out of the passenger side with a covered plastic bowl in her hands. She walked carefully across the river stone driveway and looked Alex up and down.

"And maybe Terry, too," Bubba admitted before she spoke.

"You must be Mister Thompson," the old woman said in a firm, steady voice. "I'm Alice Mayberry and this is my grandson Terry." She nodded to the sour faced man who had driven her over. "He's here to help you complete your fence."

"Call me Alex, please," he said as he looked at the growing crowd. "We're neighbors after all."

"Yes," Alice said, giving him a penetrating look. "We *are*. You may call me Alice."

Molly came out with the kids at that point and seemed to take over the whole affair. In moments, she had a lunch feast laid out on the slab table in the patio. Roger had brought some sliced brisket he'd smoked. Alice had brought an amazing German potato salad. Bubba and the boys brought some fresh baked rolls to make barbeque sandwiches and soon they were all talking and eating like this kind of thing happened everyday.

It was the interview, Alex realized part way through lunch as the shock began to wear off. His neighbors were rallying around him like he'd lived there his whole life. There were sweet moments when he had trouble swallowing from feeling overwhelmed. Molly seemed to pick up on it and would reach under the table to squeeze his leg and give him a smile of encouragement.

That afternoon, the men managed to put down nineteen fence posts, the last one being the corner post opposite where he started. By sundown the fence was officially halfway done, with eighty-three posts set and eighty-one more to go. Alex passed out Shiner Bock from the outdoor fridge to celebrate the milestone while the men sat around the slab table in the patio.

"Not a bad day's work," Bubba said, then drained half his beer and let out a loud belch. "Pardon."

"At this rate we could have it done before the weekend," Roger said. "So, Alex, what're you gonna do after you get the yard fenced?"

Alex drank a long pull of his beer to give himself time to think. "You guys already figured out I don't know what I'm doing, but I thought I'd start with some goats to get out of mowing the four acres around the house." They all laughed at that, but nodded like it was a good idea.

"A side benefit of having goats is my smoked cabrito recipe that'll make your mouth water and stomach smile," Roger said as he raised his bottle to drink.

"Maybe then I'd plant a vegetable garden with the kids." Alex shrugged and looked to the other men. "What do you guys think I could do to make it out here?"

"Well," Grant said to get his attention. "How many acres do ya' have all totalled?"

"Thirty-two. My land runs from the corner near Molly's place down the road about a quarter mile to where your fence line starts, Grant. It's only two acres across to the creek at this end, but at the other end it runs about a half-mile into those woods we share with Roger."

"So about half of it is wooded with the creek running through the middle," Grant clarified and Alex nodded. "I do okay with organic farming, but my land has been cleared for farming for a hundred years. Terry, you do pretty well with cattle, don't ya'?"

"Yup," he said through a lower lip swollen with snuff. He spit some tobacco juice in an empty cup before continuing. "I got good contracts with some upscale barbeque and hamburger joints, but we're scrapin' by. They can charge more because they use local meat, but if we have a drought like we did a few years ago when all the creeks dried up, it'll all be over for us."

"I bring in hunters sometimes to camp on my land," Roger said "I've got too many hogs and deer along that creek, so it helps keep the population down. You could do it too with all that wooded land you've got."

"What about raising horses?" Alex asked, chancing to mention his secret dream.

"You need a couple of acres for each horse to rotate grazing," Terry said. "If you had 32 acres of open land, that would only be sixteen horses. It's not really enough unless you're gonna raise thoroughbreds or some other specialty breed. And training horses isn't something you can learn from a video like planting fence posts."

They all smiled at that comment and sat quietly for a moment. Working all day had given Alex time to get to know each of them. Alex hadn't felt this close to a group of men since college. Even the silence was comforting.

Alice came out of the back door on Molly's arm with Will yawning behind them. "Terry, it's time for us to say our goodbyes."

Alex stood to shake Terry's hand. He had come to realize that Terry's sour expression was just the way his face sat and didn't reflect his good heart and wry sense of humor. "Thanks for your help today."

"I'll be back in the morning after I finish my usual routine," Terry said and glanced to his grandmother.

Alice stepped forward to take Alex's hand in both of hers. "Your dear children were a treat to spend time with. Would you mind if I stopped by to visit you all again?"

Her genteel country accent made Alex feel like he was in an old movie. He glanced at Molly who was giving Alice a sweet smile. "I'd be delighted to have you over anytime."

"You probably already know that Sheriff Hammer is useless as teats on a boar, but I still have some influence in this town." Alice drew herself up and patted his hand. "I've made it clear that anyone who helps your security friends with their investigation will have my gratitude. I don't know if it will make a difference or not, but it's the least I can do for a neighbor in need."

Alex pinched his lips for a moment to let the tightness in his throat pass, then nodded. "Thank you, Alice."

The rest of the men stood as if Alice had been the force keeping them all there. Handshakes went around along with plans to return to help the next day. Alex walked them out to their cars with Molly and Will and stood waving while they each drove away.

"Did you have anything to do with that?" Alex asked Molly.

"Nope," she said. "It's just something neighbors do out here."

"I'm glad I moved here," Alex breathed without looking her direction.

"Me, too," she said. "Come on, Will. You need a bath."

"Aw, Mom," he whined.

"I can smell your pits from up here. I swear I'm gonna scrub you with steel wool if you can't get that stink off by yourself," Molly said as she pushed him towards the edge of the fence. "Goodnight, Alex. We'll see you tomorrow."

"Goodnight, Molly. Goodnight, Will." Alex watched them walk all the way home in the dusky light, wishing the whole way that they didn't have to go.

Chapter 22: Molly

The national broadcast of the shorter interview made reference to the full interview online which sparked a viral interest. It made Molly uncomfortable when the world's attention briefly focused on her next door neighbor, especially with her son appearing in his video. While Molly worked her call center shift, she monitored the story as it exploded across every major news and gossip website overnight. Reading the discussions and comments between her calls showed nearly universal support for Alex and his situation.

Some enterprising users on a site called Reddit began compiling public information on Rubin and Consuela de Cervantes hoping to find a link to Alex's attempted murder. They had a handful of unlikely theories going. Her two favorites were that the deed to their private island had been lost and that the family secretly controlled an army of mercenaries, but the site administrators abruptly removed the thread for violating the rule about posting personal information. Molly didn't think the information would actually be useful, but she copied the last update on the post and sent it off in an email to Larry just in case.

The next morning, Jenna called early and woke Molly up to apologize for putting Will in the video without her permission. She promised to send Molly the check as soon as Molly faxed back the signed release form. When she and Will went next door later that morning, Alex took a break to help her fax it from his home office. The idea that Molly would soon be able to completely pay off one of her credit cards put her in a wonderful mood.

The neighborhood men were as good as their word and returned to help Alex with the fence again by mid-morning. Molly had enjoyed spending the day with Alice and was happy to have her back to help keep the kids busy while she prepared lunch for them all. As she cooked, each child colored Alice a special picture and presented it to her, explaining what the colored lines and shapes represented. Alice received the gifts with grace and praised each child for their artistic skills making Molly suppress a laugh. The retired elementary school teacher hadn't lost her touch.

When lunch was ready, Molly and Alice brought out platters of buttery grilled cheese sandwiches and bowls of potato chips, along with a few extra pitchers of Molly's sweet tea to wash it all down. Alex ate three sandwiches by himself and announced they were the best he'd ever eaten. Molly laughed it off at the time, but his compliment warmed her heart.

When the men returned to work on the fence, Molly washed the dishes from lunch and cleaned the kitchen. Alice kept watch over the children playing, then she joined Molly in the kitchen after they started a movie.

"You seem to fit right in around here," Alice said as she filled her glass with more tea.

Molly looked over to see Alice giving her a cheeky grin. "Like I said yesterday, Alex may be paying me to keep an eye on the kids, but I'd be happy to do it for free. His kids keep Will occupied so *I* can actually get some things done."

"I've watched you both around each other," Alice said as she leaned against the kitchen island with a knowing smile. "He seems very taken with you."

Molly felt uncomfortable discussing something with Alice that she didn't understand herself. "We've only known each other a few weeks."

"Sometimes it doesn't take very long to know." Alice stared out the window with a faint smile, like she was remembering something bittersweet. "My husband and I met at a dance for the returning soldiers just after the second great war. He always said he took one look at me and knew I was the one for him." She looked at Molly again with a coy smile. "Of course I didn't tell *him* I felt the same way. One mustn't let a man win too easily or he won't learn to value you. So many young women today fail to realize that."

Molly chuckled. "Don't worry, Alex and I are taking things slowly."

"So there *is* an 'Alex and you'?" Alice pronounced with a satisfied sigh. "Good, I'd hoped so."

Alice reminded Molly of her Nanny Gerry before dementia stole her wits. The temptation to open up to the older woman was too hard to resist. "Please don't say anything. I'm not sure where things are going yet. I rushed things with Will's father and regretted it. I don't want Will hurt again."

"Well, at my age, I'm a fair judge of character. Any man who loves his children the way Alex does is worth taking a chance with." Alice sipped her tea, then leaned in to whisper. "And when he doesn't think you're looking, he gives you the most wonderful glances. I can't remember the last time a man looked at *me* that way."

Molly felt her face heat at the comment. "We still need to know each other better."

"No doubt that will happen in God's good time." Alice took her glass of tea to the living room and left Molly to finish up in the kitchen.

Just as Molly joined Alice and the kids on the couch to watch the movie, her phone rang. Pulling it out of her back pocket, Molly saw Larry's name on the screen and frowned.

"What's up?" she said as she accepted the call.

"There's a yellow and black Camaro pulling into your driveway. Anyone you know?"

"Shit," she muttered and got off the couch to walk to the kitchen. "I bet it's my ex." Her heart started pounding. Troy always talked about getting a Camaro, and she couldn't think of anybody else that would drop by for an unexpected visit.

"That would be… Troy Moore, right?" Larry asked. "Were you expecting him?"

"Nope," Molly sighed as she looked out the kitchen window toward her house. The yellow car had just stopped and Troy got out to look around the front yard. "It's him. Thanks for the heads up, Larry. I'll go find out what he wants."

She rang off and looked back to the living room. "Will you keep an eye on the kids, Alice? I need to run home for a minute."

"We'll be just fine," Alice said with Hannah drowsing in her lap. "You go on."

Molly made her way out the front door and down the road as Troy walked up to her front door. Looking at his expensive new car made her grit her teeth. She knew he made good money, but he kept it in banks outside of the US to avoid paying her child support. It was his way of punishing her for divorcing him, but Will was the one who paid the price.

Troy had left Molly no option but divorce when he abandoned them to work a six month security contract in South America. After three months without any word or support from her husband, and no way to work with a toddler at home, she ran out of cash. An attorney friend helped her file the paperwork to dissolve their marriage and claim sole custody of Will.

Since she couldn't afford their expensive townhouse and the lease was only in Troy's name, Molly left everything there but her clothes and guns and took Will to live with her grandmother who was already struggling with the onset of dementia.

Troy tracked her down when he got back to the states, explaining there had been a screw up with his paperwork and begging her forgiveness. When she wouldn't take him back, he asked where his things from the apartment were. She thought he was going to hurt her when she said she'd left everything behind.

Since then, Troy made almost no effort to keep in touch with her or Will. He'd occasionally send a gift for Will at Christmas or his birthday, but other than infrequent phone calls or brief weekend visits, Molly had raised Will alone for two years.

She was walking up her driveway when Troy saw her.

"Where's my son?" he growled.

"I'm fine. How are you?" Molly growled back. "Did you lose your invitation to Will's birthday at the waterpark? I don't recall seeing you there."

"Cut the shit, Molly," Will said as he stalked towards her. "You put my son in danger! What the fuck was he doing with that rich asshole on TV?"

"As I recall, Alex was reading him a bedtime story." She put her fists on her hips. "Have *you* ever read him one?"

"This isn't about me, it's about you letting my son hang out with a guy who has a target on his back."

"Don't try to play me. What do you really want?" Molly asked as her McDill family temper roared to the surface.

"I want my fucking son!"

"*Now* you want him?" she shouted as she got into Troy's face. "Not when he needed you! Not when he cried himself to sleep at night missing you! Not when he had to leave you voicemails on his own birthday! And now that I've met someone who actually *wants* to spend time with him, *now* you want your son?"

Troy backed up a step, his face flinching from her verbal assault, but he still had some fight left in him. "You fucked up, Molly," he hissed. "When a judge hears how you've put him in danger, I'm gonna get him back."

His words were like ice water down her back. "You wouldn't dare."

"You just try me," he whispered as he put his nose an inch from hers. "I've already called my attorney. You may have divorced me while I was out of the country and couldn't defend myself, but I'm back now and I want my son."

"Wait," she said as his words filtered through her anger and fear to make her think. *He has to be living in San Antonio again to have gotten here so fast.* "You believe a judge is going to give you custody of Will after you *abandoned* us?"

"We're gonna find out… unless you let me see Will right now."

She cooled herself down and looked at him through squinted eyes. He was definitely up to something and Will was just a piece in his game like usual. "Fine. He's playing with Alex's kids. You stay here and I'll go get him."

"No, I'm going with you," Troy insisted.

"No, you aren't," Larry said as he stepped around the corner of Molly's house with his hand on his holstered sidearm. "Are you okay, Molly?" he asked without taking his eyes off Troy.

"Yes, I'm fine," she said as she watched Troy squirm under Larry's cool scrutiny. "Troy is going to wait right here until I get back with Will. Aren't you, Troy?"

"Fine," he muttered. "But hurry up."

As she walked away, she heard Larry speaking into his throat mic. "Code yellow at Sarge's place standing down. T-L-three until further notice. All eyes stay on Dad."

He made my codename Sarge, she smiled to herself. *Maybe Larry isn't such an asshole after all.*

Chapter 23: Alex

"Okay, last one for the day," Alex announced as he pulled the auger out of the hole.

The fence was complete on three sides, leaving just the side along the road to finish. Alex could barely believe it as Isaac slammed the last corner post down into the hole and held it to let Grant and Roger insert the split rails into the openings on the post. Then Bubba leveled it and hammered in the supports to keep the post vertical until the cement set.

"Pour it in, Josh," Isaac said to his brother.

Tipping the wheelbarrow, Joshua fed the thick cement into the hole while Isaac and Bubba spread it evenly around the post. With the post set, all the men stood back to inspect their accomplishment with satisfied expressions.

"It's straight as an arrow." Bubba looked back down the fence line.

"Who wants a beer?" Alex offered.

"Hell, yeah," Joshua answered, then grabbed the handles of the wheelbarrow to go rinse out the wet cement before it set. The men walked together in a group to follow Joshua around to the back of the house.

"Hey, I wonder who that is over at Molly's place?" Bubba asked, directing Alex's attention to the yellow Camaro in her driveway.

Just then Alex's front door burst open and Will ran out yelling, "Daddy! Daddy!"

Molly followed Will at a jog to keep up while Alex clenched his jaw. Her request to cool things off between them sprang to mind, making him wonder if she knew her ex-husband was coming to visit.

"Come on, that beer is sounding better and better."

Roger gave him a frown, but Alex ignored it on his way to the outdoor fridge in the patio. He handed beers out to each man, then got two for himself and sat down at the table. He drained the first bottle in six long draws, then let out a earthshaking belch.

"Pardon," Alex said, imitating Bubba close enough to make his boys laugh.

When Alex's phone rang, he stepped away to answer Larry's call. "What's up?"

"Got an update on a few things when you get a sec."

"Go ahead, we're done for the day. I'm just drinkin' beer now." Alex felt the hot tendrils of jealousy working their way into his head and he needed the distraction anyway.

"So far no one in town saw anyone out of the ordinary the day of the shooting. The three hotels in the area were full of the usual families, workers, and truckers you'd expect traveling through the area. Whoever it was got in and out through the woods, which means they are either local or well trained."

"I can't imagine anyone local trying to kill me," Alex said as he stepped into the back yard. His eyes were drawn to the sight of Will in his father's arms as Molly stood nearby with crossed arms.

"We can't find anyone local who'd have a motive anyway," Larry said.

"What about Molly's ex?" Alex suggested through clenched teeth.

"We're still looking into him. He wasn't in the initial round of background checks because he doesn't live here. I've got the main office running him now, but it may take a while since he's been working out of the country for the last three years or so."

"Yeah, Molly mentioned they met in the service and he was working as a security contractor." The jealousy pulled his thoughts in ugly directions. *Maybe I'm not really her type and she was just playing along for the money.* He felt unclean immediately after thinking it and pushed the thought away.

"He looked the type, but he's out of practice. I got the drop on him without even trying when Sarge was tearing him a new one." Alex heard a touch of admiration in Larry's tone when he used Molly's code name.

"So, it didn't seem like she was expecting him?" Alex asked, trying not to sound pathetic.

"No way. He was going off about how your interview put Will in danger somehow. He's working an angle, though. There's no way I'm buying that he drove out here for the kid."

Alex immediately felt horrible for what he'd thought moments earlier as he watched Will bouncing around Troy's feet. They were heading into Molly's house when she looked back toward Alex. He couldn't read her expression from so far away, but her body language was tense and angry.

"Keep an eye that direction if you can. I've got a bad feeling about this."

"Way ahead of you, boss. We're working three on, one off as long as he's here. I've got a twitchy feeling about him."

"Thanks, Larry," Alex said as he returned to the patio and dropped the call. "Who needs another beer?"

When he brought out another round, Alex sat down to join in the conversation. Roger was still frowning at him, like he wanted to say something but didn't know how to start.

"Spit it out, Roger," Alex whispered to him with an amused grin.

"Troy is bad news. Molly knows it," he announced in his no-bullshit way of cutting to the heart of things.

Alex nodded. "I hear ya. Larry's keeping an eye on things over there just in case."

"So, I'm thinkin' we're gonna be done tomorrow," Bubba declared to the group.

"And I was thinkin' of having a party to celebrate on Saturday afternoon," Alex replied. "Y'all wanna come back for some free booze and burgers? Bring some friends with you and we'll call it a housewarming party, too."

"Hell yeah." Isaac raised his beer. "This patio was made to party, man. I'll bring a cooler full of beer."

"I'll get up early and see if I can take down a yearling hog near the creek. If not, I'll grab some pork ribs at the store to smoke," Roger said.

"I've planted some early corn this season," Grant chimed in. "Ain't nothin' like fresh boiled corn cobs in butter."

"I know Nanny'll wanna come," Terry said. "Hell, if you let her, she'll have half her women's circle from church here with every casserole and side dish they know how to make."

"Good!" Alex grinned at the idea of having his new neighbors and friends over for dinner. "The more the merrier."

"I got horseshoes and a couple of cornhole boards I can bring to keep things interesting. Maybe we can do a few hands of penny ante Texas Hold'em after dinner," Bubba suggested.

"Good idea, Dad," Joshua said to Bubba, then turned to Alex. "I got my kids this weekend. Mind if I bring 'em?"

"You know we've got plenty to keep kids occupied around here." Alex smiled as his two children came outside with Alice.

"The kids are gettin' hungry," Alice said. "And Molly had something to take care of. Want me to feed 'em?"

"It'll only take a few minutes to grill some burgers. You're all welcome to hang out if you want."

Bubba and his sons had family plans, and Alice had a Thursday night Bible study that Terry had to take her to, but Roger and Grant stayed for dinner. The twins entertained the group with stories of what they did while the men were working.

Alex even made a few burgers for Larry and the guys, over Larry's objections, and sent plates out with cold soft drinks. By the time Roger and Grant left, the kids were in bed, and Alex had cleaned up the kitchen, it was well after eleven.

He was sitting on the back porch trying not to fixate on the fact that Troy's Camaro was still parked at Molly's house when his phone rang. He hoped it was Molly, but was almost as glad to see Jenna's name on the screen.

"Good evening," Alex said before tipping his beer back for a swallow.

"Hey, I know it's late, but wanted to let you know that I got the release pushed through corporate and picked up Molly's check. I tried calling her but it just went to voicemail, so I figured she might be over there."

"Nope, her ex-husband showed up today and they've been over at her house since after lunch." Alex was proud he said it without the jealousy he still felt leaking through.

"Oh," Jenna said with a touch of surprise in her voice. "I thought you and Molly… I mean, I thought he was out of the picture?"

"Not my circus, not my monkey." He frowned at the bitter tone that slipped out with the words.

"You okay?" Jenna asked, her tone quiet and sympathetic.

"Yeah, I am," Alex lied. "After our interview broadcast, some neighbors showed up to help me finish the fence. We'll actually be done with the whole thing tomorrow. So, Saturday I'm throwing a party to celebrate. Wanna come?" He really only asked because he never expected her to say yes.

Jenna was quiet for a moment and Alex took another sip of beer. "I could bring Molly her check if I went out there." His skin prickled as he worried that she might have the wrong idea about the invitation.

"I've got a spare room down the hall from the kids. It's even got its own bathroom." He'd added it for when his parents or sister visited.

"Perfect," she breathed. "I'll come after my broadcast Friday night and stay through Sunday. Is that okay?"

"That'll be fine," Alex said. He felt like he was making a mistake, but he didn't know how to correct it.

"Oh, it's been forever since I had a weekend off and I absolutely *loved* your house and the kids. What can I bring to the party?"

"Anything, really, it's just going to be a casual potluck with the neighbors."

"I know just the thing. It'll be late when I get there. I'll call when I get close tomorrow night so Larry won't panic. I can't wait!"

Alex felt his skin tingling after they hung up. He couldn't decide if he should be excited or worried. If Molly called, he could tell her so she wouldn't be surprised when Jenna just showed up. And then Alex could find a way to ask about Troy without looking like a jerk. Surely she would come over in the morning and they could find some time alone to talk then.

Larry walked up out of the shadows with the dirty plates and trash from the meal Alex sent out to them.

"Hey," Alex said. "Jenna's gonna come by tomorrow night and hang out for the weekend."

Larry's brow wrinkled as he walked to the trash. When he came back over, his mouth was moving around like he had something to say. Finally he settled with, "Are you sure that's a good idea?"

"I'll tell Molly tomorrow. It'll be fine."

"I don't mean about Molly. I had some time to talk to Jenna while she was here. I've known field agents who knew less about psychological operations than she does."

"You don't trust her?" Alex gasped. "That story she did might have saved my life!"

Larry looked down while he crossed his arms and shuffled his feet. "She seems nice, but it's her job to seem nice and it's my job to protect you. Her background check is clean, but she wants to go national. Ambition like that means she doesn't necessarily have your best interests at heart. All I'm saying is to be careful."

"I hear ya," Alex said and took another sip of his beer. "I'll keep that in mind."

After Larry went back out into the darkness, Alex drifted off in the chair on the patio with his feet up on the ottoman. When he woke before dawn, Troy's car was still parked at Molly's and all her lights were off.

He rubbed his face and tried not to think about what his jealousy forced him to imagine. As he stumbled away to shower off Thursday's stink before Friday's work began, he decided to focus on the fence. It would finally be done so Molly could go back to her life and he could get on with his.

Chapter 24: Vizcarra

"Hey, Jefe, we got a hit on one of the news alerts."

Vizzy looked up from his laptop with red eyes. The technician who had interrupted him worked in his operations center, but Vizzy couldn't remember his name.

"You said you wanted to know right away," the technician stammered, shifting uncomfortably at the office door.

Vizzy's sleep had been haunted ever since his attempt to kill Alex had failed. The whispers woke him constantly until he finally gave up on sleep altogether. Instead, he sat at his desk reviewing the reports from the people running the day-to-day business of his cartel. It was easy to get lost in the details, but nothing would shut Maria up.

"What?" Vizzy asked.

"There's a news story breaking out of Texas that hit on both the *de Cervantes* and *Alex Thompson* keywords."

"Shit." Vizzy rubbed his face. The silence that had followed the report of the missed shot should have warned him something was up. "Send me the link."

The technician nodded, then turned to jog back out of the office.

Vizzy stared at the laptop screen without seeing it, his hands clenched into fists. Alex must have figured out the shot had been meant for him and managed to convince others to believe him as well. Hopefully the news story was a blurb or short piece that would disappear like a pebble in a pond.

His incoming email alert beeped and he clicked the link. It opened his browser to the website for a television news station in San Antonio. From the first frame of video, Vizzy could hear Maria chuckling.

Alex looked rugged and ruddy, much better than the pale figure Vizzy had last seen at the trial. Hearing Alex share his perspective of the failed attempt on his life made Vizzy's blood boil. Even if his employee hadn't lied about the sequence of events, he'd obviously underestimated Alex and his security team.

Vizzy was forced to admit that the news story was compelling. In one scene, the twins and some other boy were all snuggled up on a couch while Alex read them a bedtime story. Watching them all together while the reporter described the attempt on Alex's life created a poignant juxtaposition, if you didn't know how badly Maria had squandered their birthright.

The one bright light in the report was that Alex apparently still thought Vizzy's parents were the ones behind the harassment and attempt on his life. The story didn't come out and say it to avoid slander, but the implication was clear. He would have to alert his parents before they caught wind of the news report to keep them from saying the wrong things.

If Alex were killed now, after the news story had aired, the world's attention would focus straight to Isla de Cervantes. The island was the flagship of their family resort chain and the home where he and Maria grew up. That home was a part of the legacy Vizzy had lost because of a few youthful indiscretions. It was time to take back what should have been his.

He smirked as a new plan sprang to mind. Once he had Alex's children in Mexico, he could arrange for evidence of the murder to lead directly back to his parents. Then loving Uncle Vizzy would volunteer to raise his sister's twins, aghast at what his parents had done to their father.

It fit the narrative of the news story perfectly, and a convenient murder-suicide would release his inheritance from his parents as well. Dealing with the trust assets and disposing of his sister's ill-conceived children could happen anytime after the public spotlight moved on to the next news scandal.

New hope steadied his mind and made up for all his nights of lost sleep. His employee in Texas had failed him so far, but perhaps a little more *incentive* would help him finish the job. Unlocking his phone, VIzzy texted a brief message through the secure satellite network: *Time's up! You and everyone you love will be dead on Monday.*

Next, he dialed his mother's cell phone. He would have to be cunning, because his father was as ruthless in his own way as Vizzy was.

"Vizzy," his mother crooned to him. "You've been too busy to call your Mama?"

"I'm calling now," he said with a smooth tone that contrasted with his haggard appearance. "I've missed you."

"You should come for a visit. You only stayed one night on my birthday and that was months ago." Her tone was soft, but Vizzy wasn't fooled. Connie was anything but sentimental. Her life revolved around herself and her desires more than anything else. And what made her happiest was making people do what she wanted. He was counting on that to make his plan work.

"I'm sorry, Mama, just too busy." Shifting in his chair, Vizzy changed the subject "Look, I'm calling to talk to you about something serious."

"Oh, *serious*," she mocked lightly. "Are you finally going to give me grandchildren I can actually *see* sometimes?"

The comment made Vizzy grit his teeth and swallow the rant that rose like bile in his throat. "No, but it *is* about your grandchildren. I think Papa may have tried to do something to Alex."

"Surely not," Connie sighed. "Rubin promised me after the trial that he'd let things go. I've even sent them birthday and Christmas cards every year to ask Alex to let us visit."

"Watch this video." Vizzy selected the link to the news video and sent it to his mother's phone. He heard the tinny sounds from the video and watched along with her with his sound off.

"*Oi*, my babies," Connie cried when the children were shown. "She looks just like Maria and he's got my brother Ramone's eyes. Look how big they are!"

Vizzy rolled his eyes and leaned back in his chair as he waited for her to finish watching.

"It wasn't Rubin," she declared. "There's no way he would do something like that, especially right in front of the twins."

"Then who, Mama?" Vizzy purred as the lies coiled on his tongue. "I don't have the connections to get a judge to rule against Alex, but Papa does. I don't have the money to hire an assassin, but Papa does. My manufacturing business is doing well, but not well enough to influence the Ambassador to the United States." Vizzy leaned forward to whisper the last. "And how often do you nudge him to do something so you can see your grandchildren?"

He waited patiently as his mother was quiet, then she sniffed. "Too often."

"Just be prepared for some hard questions, but don't let Papa figure out you know the truth."

"I don't know, Vizzy," she said with a waver in her voice.

"He was the one who tried to sue Alex to begin with," Vizzy said. The lies were mixed with enough truth to make them plausible to her. "I told you I tried to talk him out of it, but he wouldn't listen."

"You did," she sighed.

"Keep your ears open, Mama. I need to know what he's going to do. I don't want the kids getting caught in the middle and ending up in foster care."

"No," she cried. The tinny sounds of the video started again in the background. "I want to see my babies. Maria's babies."

"Then trust me," Vizzy pleaded. "I'm going to go see Alex this weekend. He doesn't have a restraining order against me. Maybe I can help somehow."

"Oh! Let me send some toys for the twins!"

"I'll take care of that. You just keep close to Papa and let me know if he does anything that worries you. And don't show him the video until he stumbles across it himself. Watch how he reacts."

"You're such a good son, Vizcarra. Rubin's father never saw you like we all did."

"It doesn't matter now," Vizzy said. "All that matters is keeping Maria's children safe."

It took Vizzy five more minutes of loving assurances to finally get her off the phone. While he was stuck on the phone, he used his computer to order his pilot to plan a flight to San Antonio for the weekend and alerted his most trusted bodyguard, Raul, of their impending trip. It was time to take matters in his own hands.

Maybe the murder attempt had rattled Alex enough for him to simply sign over the trust? He would still kill Alex, of course, but it would be fun to toy with him in person for a change. To give him hope and then steal everything away. Vizzy grinned as he realized Maria had finally shut up. Her silence was as welcome as his bed would be. He shut his laptop with a click and padded out the door toward his suite.

Chapter 25: Molly

"Where the fuck have you taken my son?" Molly screamed into her cell phone.

"Calm down. We're at the diner getting breakfast so you could sleep in a little," Troy replied with the hint of a smile in his tone.

"You do *not* get to take Will away from me without my permission," she growled. Of course he'd only done it to piss her off. "Don't go *anywhere* until I get there. You don't have his booster seat and he's not big enough to ride with just a seatbelt."

"Want me to order you something?" he asked like nothing was wrong.

She dropped the call without answering and stormed to the closet. Her hands shook as she pulled up her jeans, muttering to herself. "Think you can just sweep in here like you never left."

She took off the long shirt she'd slept in and grabbed a bra out of the dirty clothes hamper, sniffing to see if she could get one more day out of it.

"Will is so desperate he'll believe anything you tell him and you know it, you sonovabitch," she continued muttering as she pulled a t-shirt on over the bra and stomped into the bathroom.

Three quick brushes later she had most of her hair up in a tail. The dark circles under her eyes would take too long to cover up, so she just splashed some water on her face and dried off on her hand towel. Then she ran downstairs, stepped into her sandals, threw her keys and phone in her purse, and stormed out the front door.

As she drove to the diner, her heart rate began to slow. Troy had used every dirty trick to weasel his way into the house. First it was a drink of water, then how about dinner, then let's watch a movie, always keeping Will around so if she threw Troy out *she'd* look like the bad guy. Will was so happy to have his daddy around that Molly found herself delaying until she had to start her call center shift. When she checked on them during a break, Will had fallen asleep in Troy's lap.

After Troy carried Will to bed, he went back to the couch and fell asleep himself. There was no point throwing him out when her shift was over, so she just went to bed. It wasn't until she was just about to fall asleep that she thought of Alex, but it was too late to call him and explain.

When she arrived at the diner, she parked next to his Camaro and hurried inside to find Will grinning and bouncing in his seat over a plate of funny-face pancakes. "Mom! Daddy let me have *two* breakfasts!"

"I can see you haven't finished the second one yet," she said as she scooted into the booth next to her son.

"I'm gettin' full," he confessed. "Wanna share?"

"Sure," she said, giving Troy a dirty look as she slid her son's plate over. "Next time Daddy decides to take you somewhere and I'm asleep, be sure to wake me up so I don't worry, okay?"

"Okay, Mom," Will said before sipping the last of his orange juice and grabbing his father's smart phone.

"I was just trying to be nice." Troy gave her that infamous hangdog look of his. When they were married it was his way of apologizing without actually apologizing. When she felt herself slipping under his spell again, remembering the pain he'd caused made it easier to fight it off.

"You haven't earned the privilege of being nice yet," she whispered to Troy across the table. "You've been gone too long and too much has happened."

"Look, I never thought I'd say this, but I missed you," he said with apparent sincerity. "And I'm sorry."

In all the years they'd been together she could count on one hand the number of times he'd said he was sorry without it being sarcastic or a purely selfish gesture. She really looked at him and tried to filter out her own feelings and preconceptions. He was still handsome, but now he had a haunted look in his eyes. And despite getting more sleep than she had the night before, he looked far worse than she felt.

"Tell me the truth. Why are you *really* here?" she asked, then watched his eyes flicker to Will who was playing a game on his father's phone.

"I screwed up," he admitted without looking back at her. "I got caught up in what I was doing and lost sight of what was important." As he stared at Will, Troy kept nodding to himself with a pained expression. Then he leaned closer to look in Molly's eyes and whispered, "I don't expect you to just forget everything I've done wrong, but you've got to let me make it up some to Will."

Molly wanted to believe him. Troy looked so broken it would have been easy to convince herself what he was saying was true, but the paranoid itch she'd been feeling returned with a vengeance. The hairs on the back of her neck stood like a sniper was lining up a shot at her while she sat in the diner.

"I don't *have* to let you do anything," she said. He was definitely up to something and she needed to find out what it was before he sprung it on her. "But I guess we can take it a day at a time." Molly took a bite of Will's second happy face pancake while he continued to play on Troy's phone.

"So, can we do something together today?" Troy asked. "I mean, like something fun with Will?"

"Alex is paying me to watch his kids," Molly said as she realized she was already late. "Which reminds me, I need to call him."

Troy frowned. "So, you and him..." Molly raised one eyebrow at him and lowered her chin. "Never mind. None of my business."

"I like him," Will said as his attention on the game never wavered. "Can Manny and Hannah come with us to do something fun?"

"Good idea," Troy said, breaking into a wide grin at his son's suggestion. "I bet Mommy can get Mister Alex to let us take them."

"You obviously don't know Mister Alex," Molly muttered as she dug out her phone and touched Alex's picture.

She'd taken it when they had dinner together that first night with the kids. Will had told them his favorite new joke: *Where does the king keep his armies? Up his sleevies of course!* Alex was still laughing when she snapped the picture and just seeing his happy smile lowered her stress level.

"Molly?" Alex answered. "Are you and Will okay?"

"Yes," she said emphatically. "But things are just a little... complicated right now."

"I see," he said and took a deep breath. "If you need some time, Alice is here again today and offered to help with the kids."

"Tell her I said thanks," she sighed with relief. "I'll explain everything later."

"No, you don't need to explain anything to me," Alex said, but his voice was odd. "The fence will be done today anyway."

"That's wonderful," Molly exclaimed, but then realized what it meant. "Wait... oh."

"I'm throwing a little party tomorrow afternoon to celebrate. Bring Troy and Will if you want. Jenna will be here, too, since she's staying over for the weekend. She said she'd bring your check from the network."

No, it's not supposed to happen this way! Molly felt her skin prickle as her thoughts seemed to float above her head. Alex should be with her. Jenna even promised she wasn't interested in him! Then her lip quivered as her eyes snapped to Troy who was watching her with an eager smile.

"Okay. I'll talk to you later," she whispered to Alex, then dropped the call without waiting for his reply.

"So, can his kids come out with us?" Troy asked with a bright edge to his voice.

"No." Molly tried to figure out what went wrong between her and Alex. Then it hit her.

After she'd asked Alex to cool things down between them, Troy showed up and his car had been outside her house all night. Then Molly hadn't shown up at Alex's house that morning to help with the kids like she'd promised. And now that the fence was done he wouldn't need her to come over everyday anymore.

Somehow, in less than twenty-four hours, she'd managed to ruin everything without even trying.

"Mom, can we go to the water park today since Dad is here?" Will asked.

"Why not," she whispered as she looked down at the remains of his smiling pancake. Half of its face was missing, as if a sniper had taken it out with a head shot. Her mouth was too dry to eat another bite.

Chapter 26: Alex

Alex had blown it. His jealousy forced the words out about Jenna coming before he could stop them. And once they were out, he didn't have time to explain before Molly hung up on him. And she *had* hung up on him, no doubt about that. Stuffing his phone back in his pocket, he lifted the post hole digger and carried it down to the next marked spot.

He'd gotten an early start after getting the kids breakfast and putting on one of their favorite morning cartoons. While he waited for the other men to arrive he'd started drilling the remaining thirty-nine holes.

He had five done when Terry showed up with his mother, Alice, who came just to spend time with the kids. Terry had some work of his own to do and promised to return around noon. Alex had eight holes done when Roger and Grant showed up to place fence posts in each hole and drag over the split rails. When Bubba and his sons arrived, Alex had nineteen holes dug and they began bracing and cementing the posts Roger and Grant had already set.

Then Molly had called and Alex drilled a hole nothing could fill. He looked over at her empty house as he started the auger digging into the dry soil. His shoulders and back ached from the weeks of effort, but he had to keep working or he'd go crazy.

The mental image of her and Troy being together made him nauseous but it had become a compulsion, like poking a bruise or tonguing a sore tooth. Maybe it was better he cooled things off with Molly before they really began. Maybe Troy had changed and wanted to be a good father now. *Yeah*, Alex thought, *and maybe monkeys are gonna fly out of my butt.*

Alex stayed ahead of the others, drilling holes by himself so he wouldn't have to act like nothing was wrong. After each new post hole, the compulsion to call Molly and explain died a little. He started an unhealthy mental routine while drilling; he'd tell himself that what they felt for each other was real, but then the poisonous jealousy would eat away at his confidence.

Shortly after their phone conversation, both Molly and Troy drove back to her house. Molly didn't look over as she stomped up the stairs and into the house. Troy followed carrying Will over his shoulder like a laughing sack of potatoes.

A few minutes later, they all came out wearing swimwear and carrying towels. Molly had on her green bikini top and blue jean shorts. It stopped Alex as he took in her lean legs, breasts, and flat stomach. Then Molly headed to the passenger side of Troy's Camaro. Just before she opened the door, Alex thought he caught her looking at him. Before he could be sure, she opened the door and climbed into the car next to her ex-husband.

When Troy sped past his house, Molly pierced him with an anguished look. The electric jolt reminded Alex of what might have been and broke his heart all over again. The car was out of sight in moments, but Molly's expression was burned into his retina. Something was wrong, but Alex had no idea what it was or what he could do about it. Even if he knew, he wasn't sure he had any right to get involved. Molly had to live her own life, just like he did.

By mid-afternoon, the last hole had been dug and his friends set the last four split rails before bracing the final fence post. As Alex watched Isaac and Joshua tamp down the cement, the sense of accomplishment and security he expected to feel rang hollow. Now that he looked around the enclosed property, he wondered why it had seemed to matter so much.

The fence had started as a dream, a summer project to do with his kids. He'd underestimated the amount of work and overestimated how much his kids could help, but Molly had come to his rescue so he could still fulfill his dream. After the attempt on his life, finishing the fence had become a talisman of sorts, and the hard work was a useful antidote to how helpless he felt.

Now that the fence was complete, Alex looked over at that first post he'd set with Molly and the kids. It made his eyes burn to realize he'd finished the task, but somehow lost the dream in the process. Without Molly and Will, it felt just like a bunch of wood and wasted effort. He wiped his face with his dirty towel until he could get himself under control.

"Well, we got 'er done," Bubba announced and patted Alex on the back. "Now lemme see if I can track you down a few goats. I got a buddy that keeps some around for the milk 'cause his little girl has allergies."

"Thanks, Bubba," Alex said as he schooled his face. "I need to read up on raising them and maybe talk to your friend about what they need before we get 'em."

"I'll give him a call next week then." Bubba turned to his boys. "Let's go get cleaned up. Your mama wanted us on time for dinner later."

"Looks good, man." Isaac rolled the wheelbarrow over to the hose to rinse it out. "Lookin' forward to tomorrow."

"Me, too," Alex said with a false grin across his face when they shook hands.

After Bubba and the boys left, the other men helped pick up tools and clean up the bits of wood and strapping around the yard. After everything was cleaned and stored back in the garage, they retired to the patio for a beer.

Alex kept the conversation focused on guns, hunting, and sports until they each made their exit. Roger looked like he wanted to say something again, but since he drove Grant over, he left with it unsaid.

Terry and Alice were the last to go. Alice brought the kids out to play so she could join them and steal a few sips from Terry's beer. She made small talk until Terry went to use the restroom, then the look on her face made Alex's stomach twist.

"I heard from Molly a little while ago," she started without preamble. "I know it's none of my business, but she mentioned you're havin' that news reporter stay over this weekend." It was clear from her hard expression what she thought of the idea.

"Jenna is staying in the guest room. Hell, she's coming to see Molly and the kids more than me."

"Did you tell Molly that?" she asked with a softening tone.

Alex looked down and tore the label off his beer bottle. "No. I didn't get the chance before she hung up on me."

"Maybe you should've called her back," Alice said firmly, and then she finished the last of her grandson's beer.

"She's with her ex, Troy." The bitter jealousy leaked out in his words.

"He'll always be her boy's father," Alice sighed. "But he's not her *husband*. Not anymore."

Alex nodded, unable to meet her steely gaze.

Terry came back out of the restroom that opened into the patio. "You ready to go, Nanny?"

"I believe so." She slowly levered herself up. "We'll see you tomorrow afternoon. You sure it's okay I invite my women's circle to come?"

"The more the merrier." Alex nodded as he rose to hug the fiery old woman. "Thanks for everything, Alice. I'll talk to her tonight."

"Good," she said, then stood back as Terry gave Alex a back-slapping hug.

"Thanks again for your help, Terry," Alex said.

"If you wanna return the favor this fall, I'm digging out a bigger pond for the cattle and could use some help," he grinned.

"Just say the word and I'll be there," Alex said, feeling proud to be asked.

After they'd gone, Alex brought the kids in and got them started eating the tacos Alice had left warming on the stove. He showered quickly and put on clean clothes, then snuggled on the couch with his kids to hear all their adventures and read a story. When they started yawning, Alex helped them get ready for bed.

"Dad?" Manny asked as he got toothpaste on his superhero toothbrush. "I miss Will and Miss Molly."

"Me, too," echoed Hannah as Alex brushed out her hair. "Why couldn't they come over today?"

"Will's daddy came to visit and they spent time together as a family today." Alex loved brushing Hannah's hair. It was a lighter version of her mother's wavy brown. He kept the brush moving through it until it shined, then tied it with a scrunchy to keep it from getting tangled at night.

"I pretended that you were Will's daddy and he was my big brother," Manny said after he spit out the toothpaste.

"I always wondered what having a mommy was like, and now I know," Hannah said. "I wish Miss Molly was our mommy."

"Miss Molly and Will are very nice." Alex fought to keep his tone even. "But being a family is more than just playing together. You have to share everything, even when you don't want to. And I wouldn't have as much time to spend with just you two like I do now."

That made them both get quiet, but Alex could hear the wheels turning in their heads as he tucked each of them in bed and kissed them goodnight.

It was getting darker out when Alex went into the patio and turned on the financial news channel. He got a beer and sat in the comfortable chair he'd slept in the night before. There were lights on at Molly's house and the Camaro was again parked out in front. A familiar name on the broadcast caught his attention and he turned the sound up a little.

"Rubin de Cervantes, CEO of Lujo Jugar, the international resort chain, released a personal statement today on behalf of his family," the reporter announced over pictures of Rubin at his flagship resort. "He denies any involvement in the recent attempted murder of his son-in-law, Alexander Thompson, and repeats that he and his wife only wish to be a part of their grandchildren's lives.

"That statement seems to be at odds with their prior claims that Alexander Thompson killed their daughter, Maria de Cervantes, during a nasty court battle following her death five years ago. Both the case and its appeal upheld that Maria's advanced directives took effect when she was rendered brain dead after a stroke due to preeclampsia, and that Alexander had no responsibility for her death when life support was removed.

"The State Department has now confirmed that Rubin and Consuela de Cervantes recently attempted to assert custody over their two minor grandchildren using an unorthodox conviction in absentia against Thompson by a Mexican judge. We also have unconfirmed reports that the FBI are now looking into the attempted murder after a recent interview with Thompson made the case public."

Alex sat back and sipped his beer while he waited for Jenna to arrive, but his mind wouldn't let him rest. *I have to do something or I'm gonna lose her*, he thought. Then he picked up his phone and sent Molly a text before he could talk himself out of it.

I miss you. Call me when you can.

Alex's text message threw Molly off as she tried to enter the details of the support call she was on.

"Could you repeat that?" she asked the angry man who'd had his identity stolen.

While she typed his information into the form on her computer, ignoring his profanity, her mind tried to align the hopeful text message to the bruise she'd carried in her heart all day. After their phone call at breakfast, she felt like there was no chance with Alex and the regret felt like a wound.

Spending the day with Troy and Will at the water park had been bittersweet. Watching her son bask in the attention of his father was heartwarming, but the nagging sense that Troy was up to something kept her on edge. She joined in the fun, putting on a good face to keep things upbeat for Will's sake, but the breakfast phone call with Alex replayed in her mind endlessly.

When they got out of the water for a lunch of hot dogs and frozen drinks, Troy kept trying to engage her. It was like when they'd first gotten together, with him cracking jokes and making subtle passes at her. The only difference was that she now saw his hollow tactics for what they were. Troy could charm the birds from the trees, but he had all the substance of the cotton candy they'd eaten for dessert.

Alex was *solid*, and seeing Troy again had underscored that conclusion. It dawned on her that Alex wasn't solid because he was rich. He was rich because he was solid. He kept his word. He worked hard. He loved his kids and put their welfare above his own. She had slept with Troy the day they met, but now weeks after meeting Alex, she could kick herself for hesitating to build a stronger relationship with him.

After lunch, Troy had encouraged Will to play with some friends he'd made at the water park and turned his full attention on Molly. He had asked about her life as if he cared, but she noticed he kept circling back to Alex and his kids eventually. When he brought up Alex's television interview again, she remembered Troy's long-time crush on the reporter, Jenna. And that reminded her who Alex might be sleeping with while she was working her call center shift that evening. *Fuck!*

Filled with a momentary insanity, she had pulled out her cell phone to blast Alex with her anger and frustration but at the last second clicked on Alice's contact instead. Chatting with the sweet old woman about how Manny and Hannah were doing gave her time to come to her senses, but she had still made a misstep. Without meaning to, she had let it slip to Alice that Jenna was coming to stay the weekend with Alex. Alice seemed surprised and an ugly part of Molly hoped she had dressed him down after the call.

The rest of the day passed in a fog after her rage had burned out what little energy she had left. Troy drove them back, stopping at a drive-in for burgers and the frozen cherry-lime drink Will loved so much. As they drove past Alex's house, she'd noticed the fence was complete. Seeing his new gate closing off his driveway made her eyes fill. She stamped her pain down with anger at Troy and Jenna and fate.

It was a little after eleven when Troy began to snore on the couch. Molly sent a message to her remote manager that she wasn't feeling well and logged off the call center queue. It would cost her some money to miss the rest of her shift, but she couldn't stand the tension between her and Alex anymore. Since he texted her, Molly hadn't been able to concentrate on work anyway. So, she put on her shoes and checked on Will before slipping out the front door.

She was walking along the road in the moonlit darkness when Larry stood up out of a dry ditch near the corner of the fence. "Hey," he said as he stepped closer to the road and got a better look at her. "You okay?"

She put on her soldier face to keep him from seeing how much she was hurting and kept walking towards the gate. "Nothing I can't handle."

"Can I tell you something without you gettin' pissed at me?" he asked with his palms open.

She stopped and sighed. "Sorry, it's been a helluva day."

"It ain't been roses around here either," he said as he stopped next to her. "Look, Alex isn't just a guy I work for. Over the last three years I've seen him go through shit that would have *crushed* me and he still managed to keep things going for the kids. He ain't soldier tough, but he's metal where it counts, you know?"

"I know," Molly whispered.

"You are the first woman he's spent any time with as long as I've known him. He's never let anyone else take care of his kids before other than his family. Just be careful, okay? He's a good guy and I like him."

"I like him, too," Molly said as her chin started quivering and wouldn't stop. "Oh god," she whispered and wiped her eyes. "I think I fucked everything up, Larry."

"No, you didn't. He's on the back porch waiting for you." Larry gave her a hard pat on her shoulder. "Go on, I'll keep an eye on your house."

"Thanks." She sniffed hard and nodded, then on impulse she added, "I think Troy's up to something, but I don't know what."

"I have the same feeling. We've got the home office running a background check but it's taking a while because of the weekend."

"He's living in San Antonio again now," she said. "I get the feeling he fucked up his job and got canned. And seeing Alex with Will on that interview reminded him of what he's missing. I'm scared he's gonna grab Will and run."

"Not while we're watching he won't," Larry chuffed. "But if he says anything about who he worked for or what he's been doing, it could speed things up on our end."

"I'll see what I can find out," Molly said as she looked at Alex's house in the moonlight. "I need to go in there before I lose my nerve."

"He's fallin' for you, Molly." Larry had a serious expression as he searched her face.

She bit her lip and nodded, but couldn't get a sound past her tight throat. Larry opened the gate and let her inside before closing it again to return to the dry ditch.

Molly walked across the yard surrounded by the fence that Alex built. She recalled how silly it seemed when he started trying to put it up all by himself. She'd brought him a glass of iced tea that day and wondered what kind of idiot had moved in next door. Except he'd stuck to it. He had done much of it by himself through his sheer stubborn will, then was gracious enough to accept the help of his neighbors when they offered. *That's a rare combination*, she thought.

When she rounded the corner of the house, Alex was watching television on the patio with his feet up on the ottoman. He was night-blind from the bright television and didn't see her approaching until she entered the glowing ring of light.

"Molly," he whispered, then put his feet down and stood to greet her. Any other time they would have touched or hugged when they greeted each other, but Alex hesitated.

"I miss you, too," she whispered back.

That seemed to break the tension and they crossed the distance to hold each other. Alex buried his face in the hair around her neck and took deep shuddering breaths. Molly sniffed hard and blinked back the tears she felt pooling in her eyes. "We need to talk about this so it never happens again. I *hated* today."

Alex pulled back with his lips tight and his eyes focused on her face. "I know you said you need to cool things off, but I can't. I want to be with you, whatever that turns out to mean."

"Even if Troy is around more for Will?"

Alex nodded. "As long as we're both clear about the situation. I don't like Troy over there spending the night."

"And I don't like Jenna over here spending the weekend," Molly replied with real heat.

"She's staying in the guest room. I was very clear with her when she called and was going to tell you that before you hung up on me this morning."

"Troy's sleeping on the couch," Molly said as she looked away and shook her head. "He weaseled his way in by asking to stay in front of Will."

Alex pulled her close and kissed her hair. "I thought so many ugly things today. I'm so sorry."

"Me, too." Molly rubbed her cheek against his shoulder. "Are we okay now?"

"Yes," Alex said and tilted her chin up to kiss her.

His lips felt soft and warm as she pressed hers against them. The kiss went on slowly for a moment as the heat built between them, then she slipped her tongue along his lips to open his mouth. Feeling his tongue touch hers was like a spark hitting gasoline. She pulled him closer, running her fingers up his back to hold on.

Alex had his own fingers in her hair, rubbing them along her neck and shoulders as he kissed her deeper. The warmth in her core ignited and left her gasping for him. She wanted to feel his fingers everywhere, his hungry mouth on her bare skin. She was just about to reach for his belt when Alex's phone played a happy little song.

"Fuck," he muttered as he dug his phone out of the front pocket of his jeans. "It's Jenna. She must have made good time getting here."

"First the kids, then my ex, now our friends," she chuckled sadly. "We can't catch a break."

Alex grinned at her as he put the phone to his ear. "Hey Jenna," he said. "Molly and I were just talking about you."

Molly rolled her eyes and sat down on the loveseat, dragging Alex down with her. He was listening to the phone, but Molly was determined to keep his attention. She leaned in and took his earlobe between her lips to suck into her mouth.

"Th-that sounds g-great," Alex stuttered as he squirmed. "I'll let Larry know. See you in a few minutes!"

He dropped the call and pulled Molly into his lap to kiss her again. She could feel his erection under her butt, so she shifted around to make it harder on him. He gasped as they kissed, so she did it again.

"Damn it," he growled. "Why are you doing this now?"

"I want you thinking about *me* tonight instead of the woman in your guest room," she whispered in the ear she'd just had her tongue in. "And I want you more excited when Jenna leaves on Sunday than you are right now."

Alex shivered and tried to move away but Molly wrapped her arms around him and attacked his ear again. "If I get any more excited I'm gonna have to change my underwear."

Molly finally relented and pulled back to smile at him. "After she gets here, I'm gonna go lock myself in my bedroom tonight and *think* about you."

"Oh," Alex murmured as he got what she was really saying.

"I might even *think* about you two or three times." Molly leaned in to kiss him again. "Because I want you, Alex Thompson, and *nobody's* gonna take you away from me. Do you hear me?"

"Yes, Sergeant," Alex growled and kissed her back, sending shivers all over her body.

Chapter 28: Alex

Molly had found his most serious weakness. Every time she nibbled his ears, it sent jolts of electricity all over his body and turned him into a quivering mess. She exploited it mercilessly until Larry called to let him know Jenna was coming through the gate. Alex had barely composed himself and straightened his clothes before Jenna's car pulled up and stopped in front of the house.

Molly seemed unfazed as she stood to look down at him with a subdued smile. "Let's go welcome our guest."

Her use of *our guest* made Alex smile to himself as he followed her out the patio and around to the front of the house.

Jenna was still dressed for her broadcast as she got a couple of small bags out of the trunk. She smiled when she saw them both coming. "Hey! The fence looks great," she said.

Alex took her bags. "Thanks. I had a lot of help this week."

Molly gave Jenna a quick hug. "We're so glad you came."

"We?" Jenna's eyes were sparkling as she looked between them.

"Yes," Alex said as he smiled over at Molly.

"Yay!" Jenna clapped her hands and hugged Molly again. "I love it when things work out. Do the kids know yet?"

"No," Molly said. "We're not gonna make a big deal about it right now, but we both want to move things that direction."

Alex felt his heart thump hearing her announce their decision to Jenna. It felt more real said out loud. "Come on in, we'll get you set up in your room and then we can have a beer and catch up."

After Jenna had changed into shorts and a t-shirt, she joined Alex and Molly sitting together in the living room. She handed a plain white envelope to Molly before she took the beer Alex offered. "Thanks," she said as she sat and took a long pull.

Molly opened the envelope and sighed. "Thanks so much for bringing me the check."

"I'm just sorry we used that footage of Will without your permission. I had so much going on that day, I never even noticed until Alex called me after the broadcast."

"It didn't bother me until Troy saw it and showed up," Molly said as she tucked the check back into the envelope and leaned against Alex's side.

"Is he the ex that Alex mentioned?"

"That's him." Molly sipped her beer. "He showed up acting all upset that Will was in danger, but it was just an excuse to weasel his way back into our lives."

"He never wanted to be a part of Will's life before?" Jenna raised an eyebrow at Molly.

"Let's just say he had other priorities." Molly took a deep breath. "I still don't trust him showing up like this, but I can't deny Will the chance to know his father."

"How long has it been since he saw Will?" Alex asked. His worry for Molly and Will burned in his chest, but he tried to keep his voice level.

Molly tilted her head back and forth while staring up. "Nine months, maybe? He stopped by for a weekend a few months before his birthday. Before that was about six months."

"I can't imagine not seeing my kids for a *day*," Alex said as he shook his head. A selfish part of him wished Troy had never shown up so he could claim Will as his own. Realistically, he knew he had no right, but his heart didn't care.

Molly looked over at him with a wistful expression. "Neither can I."

"So, what was more important than Will?" Jenna asked.

Molly took a sip of beer and stared away for a moment. "Troy was always a thrill seeker. When we were in the service, he volunteered for all kinds of crazy missions. I was ready to settle down when I got pregnant with Will, but Troy wasn't." She looked down and shook her head. "I was an idiot and assumed he'd grow out of it once Will was born."

"Men don't change," Jenna said with a knowing nod. "As they get older they just become more concentrated versions of themselves."

"What does that mean?" Alex asked, unable to stop sounding offended.

"Take you," Jenna said as she gestured with her beer bottle. "You've got this stubborn streak that I bet you've had your whole life. You get a plan in your head and nothing can derail you. Right?"

"Well," Alex started as his face flushed. "Maybe I am a little single-minded."

"My point is that whatever your character is, it's going to stay that way. If anything, you get *more* stubborn when things get tough."

"But that's true for women, too," Alex said, trying to rationalize away the sting her comment left.

"Yeah," Jenna said, but then shook her head. "And also no. Most women I know like to work on their relationships and make changes to improve themselves and accommodate others. Now don't get defensive, I see you looking at me like you're going to argue about this. I'm just speaking generally. I know it's not very progressive of me to fall back to women being nurturers, but there are some real differences between how men and women view life."

"Ok, I guess I see where you're coming from," Alex grumbled, leading Molly to pat him on the leg.

"It's true though," Molly said. "I bent over backwards to work things out with Troy for years but nothing changed."

Alex studied her face and added silently, *And I've only known you for a few weeks but it feels like everything worked immediately.*

"My problem was I didn't see who Troy *was*," Molly continued. "I only saw who he could have been."

"I do the same thing all the time," Jenna confessed. "It's part of the reason I'm still single. Another beer?"

"I'll get another round," Alex said as he collected the empty bottles. He could still hear Jenna and Molly chatting about the interview as he got three more cold Shiners from the fridge. He walked back in time to hear Jenna gushing about the ratings and was reminded of what Larry said.

"I swear, I never dared to hope the story would do that well nationally, but the viral buzz online really pushed it out there," Jenna said as she took the cold beer from Alex on his way back to join Molly on the couch. "Thanks."

"Is this your first story that went national?" Molly asked as Alex sat and handed her a beer, then he pulled her closer to lean against his chest again.

"Not the first, but it's definitely the biggest." She took a sip and looked down at her lap. "I got a tentative offer this morning to work for the network's national news desk."

"Wow," Alex exclaimed. "That's awesome!" When she didn't react he asked, "Isn't it?"

"It could be," Jenna sighed. "I don't know if I prefer being a big fish in a little pond or a little fish in a big pond. Little fish tend to get eaten."

Alex thought he picked up something and went with it. "You've got a good reputation around here for reporting actual news instead of fluff pieces. There aren't many high profile female news reporters doing that on the national level."

"Exactly," Jenna said as she met Alex's eyes. "Promises are bullshit. I'm rolling the dice and hoping I won't end up doing recipes and celebrity interviews."

"Sounds like a tough decision." Alex took another drink of beer before continuing. "Selfishly, I hope you stay."

"Me, too," Molly nodded.

Alex had been afraid there would be more tension with Jenna staying at his house, but Molly's kiss had claimed him and left no room for any doubt. As they continued to chat, Alex couldn't keep his eyes off of Molly's expressive face. She was as fascinating as a movie all by herself. While his attention wandered, he missed something funny and when Molly laughed she glanced over and noticed his attention.

"What?" she asked him.

"He's been staring at you like that for the last five minutes," Jenna betrayed him with a grin.

"Sorry," Alex said as heat rose up in his face.

Molly looked in his eyes then studied his whole face before leaning in to kiss him again. Her lips opened long enough for the tip of her tongue to trace his bottom lip.

"And that's my cue to go to bed," Jenna giggled as she stood. "I'll see you guys in the morning."

Molly broke the kiss with her own flush rising. "Sorry, didn't mean to make you uncomfortable."

"Not uncomfortable, just envious." She made her way to the hallway. "I'll shut my door just in case."

Alex covered his face with his hand while Molly chuckled. "G'night!"

As soon as the door clicked shut, Molly pulled herself up to his lips and kissed him again. "Mine."

"I won't forget," Alex said.

"I need to get back home before I decide to stay here all night," Molly sighed as she sat up.

"Troy's there if Will wakes up. You sure you couldn't stay a little while?" Alex hadn't wanted anyone this badly since high school.

"And what if Manny or Hannah come climbing into your bed in the middle of the night?" she asked and stood. "You know they have radar when it comes to us. Hell, I'm surprised they haven't come out already."

"You're right," Alex admitted and stood up. "I'll walk you home."

"No need. Larry was keeping an eye on me when I came over and I'm sure he's still out there. Just kiss me goodbye at the door."

Alex followed her to the front door after adjusting himself when she turned away. Maybe a cold shower would do him some good. She waited as he opened the door for her, then stepped into his arms.

"I'm going to enjoy figuring this out," she said between kisses.

"We're having a sleepover as soon as our house guests are gone," Alex growled.

"I can't wait." Molly gave him one final, lingering kiss. "G'night."

CHAPTER 29: MOLLY

"So where'd ya go last night?" Troy asked while Molly washed the breakfast dishes.

"Who says I went anywhere?" she replied with a churning in her guts. Troy had no right to ask and knew it, but he loved pushing her buttons.

"I woke up after midnight when you came back in." He sat his coffee mug next to the sink, then turned to lean back against the counter to watch her face.

Molly grabbed the mug and dipped it in the soapy water to scrub it out. "You need to butt out." She looked over and pinned him with a hard look. "My private life is my own," she hissed and smacked the mug down in the drying rack.

"Not if it impacts Will," Troy growled back. "You've already gotten him too involved with that human target you live next door to."

"God, I wish you'd have stayed gone." The words flew out before her mind could reign in her mouth.

Troy froze with eyes wide. "I'm his father! I deserve a place in Will's life."

"Once upon a time that was true, but you gave it up when you *left us*. The only reason I haven't thrown you out is because I want Will to see for himself what kind of man you really are." The tingles of rage flew up the back of her neck raising hairs along the way. "Then we can both move on with our lives… without you."

She stormed away before he could reply, heading up the stairs and slamming her bedroom door shut. Steaming in the middle of the room, she rocked her head to crack the vertebra in her neck. *Breathe. Calm. Let it go.*

Luckily, Will was still in the shower and missed their fight. She had to keep her cool for Will's sake and always tried to prevent her personal feelings about Troy from influencing Will. Troy would screw up soon, she could feel it. And as much as she wanted to spare her son pain, some lessons could only be learned the hard way.

Molly showered quickly and put on work clothes. Alex wanted to have his house ready for the party, and she intended to be there for him. She mentally planned out what she needed to do to help. Cleaning the kitchen and living room, sweeping out the patio, and cleaning the table and counters outside. They needed to review what everyone intended to bring so she could make a shopping list of what else Alex wanted to offer.

Will was dressed and playing video games with Troy when Molly stomped down the stairs.

"I'm heading over to help Alex get ready for his party," she announced.

"I wanna come!" Will dropped the controller making Troy frown.

"Wait, we're almost finished with this mission," Troy said.

"Come with us! We can play with Manny on his system. Their TV is *so big*—"

"We need to get a move on." Molly grabbed her purse and headed out the front door, hoping Troy would decide to stay.

Having to take the road to get to Alex's gate felt wrong somehow. She had loved being able to amble through the field between their homes, stepping around thistles in the tall grass. Alex had suggested putting a gate between them. Molly had immediately imagined a lovely arbor gate with a curved trellis rising over it. Maybe they could plant a passion vine to scent the air as it grew to cover it.

The warm morning promised a hot day, and the sky was clear. Taking a deep breath, she let it out slowly as the sound of a pair of running footsteps reached her. There were quick steps as her son caught up and grabbed her hand, then the heavier ones followed that weighed down her mood.

"So, what's this party all about?" Troy asked from behind.

"Mister Alex finished his fence and wants to thank everyone who helped," Will said. "Right, Mom?"

"Yeah," she said. "But it's also a housewarming to give the neighbors a chance to get to know him and his kids better."

"Brave neighbors" Troy mumbled under his breath.

The gate across the drive was already open and while Molly couldn't see Larry or any of the other Context Security agents, she could feel their eyes on her. Oddly, knowing it was Larry watching didn't give her the sense of danger she'd felt recently. If anything, her ex-husband's gaze on the back of her head unnerved her more.

Will let go of her hand to run around the house to the back porch. She could hear the squeals of the kids before she rounded the corner herself with Troy catching up to walk at her side. Alex was outside with Manny and Hannah, sweeping off the porch while the three kids jabbered about the show playing on the patio television.

"I figured you wouldn't be far behind when I saw Will," Alex said. His eyes caught hers, then his gaze warmed the rest of her face until she smiled and looked away. She noted with amusement that he ignored Troy completely.

"What can I do to help?" she asked as she approached him. The impulse to touch him in some way moved her hand before she could settle it back to her side.

"The kids have cleaned up their rooms, but I'm afraid the living room is still wrecked. Don't do it for them, though. Hannah has been slacking lately and needs to do her share." Alex gave the kids an indulgent look and shook his head. "Jenna offered to clean the bathrooms and kitchen after she gets out of the shower."

"What about food? Do you need me to run to the store?" Molly asked.

"That would be a big help. Since I'm grilling the burgers for everyone we'll need to pick up the ground beef, buns, and cheese."

"I'll go," Troy said from behind Molly, obviously trying to nose his way in. She rolled her eyes since Troy couldn't see her face and steeled herself for the inevitable introduction.

"Alex, this is my ex-husband Troy Moore. Troy, Alex Thompson." Molly wanted to follow his name with *my boyfriend*, but the kids were too close and might overhear. Instead, she said, "My neighbor."

Watching them shake hands made Molly tense. Troy had the advantage of height and physical strength, but Alex had a calm charisma and bearing that won their subtle pissing contest. It was Troy who first looked away, almost like he couldn't stand to keep eye contact with Alex.

"Nice place," Troy said on the last shake.

"You've got a fine boy," Alex said as their hands fell away.

Molly nearly laughed. Both men had managed to highlight their differences perfectly. Troy's comment about Alex's house showed where his priorities were. He was all about toys and status, focused on the outward signs of success.

Alex lived for his family. He might have a nice house and car, but the priority was on security, not status. He had worked hard and earned enough money to impress anyone, but his love for his kids had won Molly's heart.

"Let me put a shopping list together for you. I appreciate your help," Alex said as he passed the broom handle to Molly and headed inside. As soon as the door shut behind him, Troy looked over and searched her face.

"So, it's you and him," Troy whispered. Emotions flickered on his face too fast to name, but Molly spotted his familiar sulk pushing its way through. "I figured you were going for that guard of his, Larry."

"Butt. Out."

Troy looked like he wanted to say something else, but wisely kept it to himself.

Molly attacked the pile of dirt and leaves Alex had swept up so far, then continued to clear the patio until Alex returned with the shopping list. By the time she had the debris in the garbage bag, Alex was discussing the items on the list with Troy.

After refusing Alex's offer of cash with a shake of his head, Troy called out to Will to ask if he wanted to tag along. Will was watching a show and didn't want to leave, so Troy gave him a wave goodbye, shot Molly an unreadable look, and jogged up the driveway back to his car at Molly's.

"That was unexpected," Alex said as he stepped closer to speak near Molly's ear.

"Yeah," she growled. "It was."

"Anything wrong?" Alex asked.

Molly pushed her frustration with Troy away to look at the man who warmed her heart. "Nothing you can't fix with a… smile." When she had hesitated, Molly glanced at Alex's lips and thought about saying a more satisfying word.

"I want to kiss you, too," he whispered with his eyes glued to her, but didn't make a move. They both needed to wait until things settled down.

"Dad, can we have a snack?" Manny asked as he tugged on Alex's hand.

"Go on," Molly grinned as Alex chuckled silently. The kid's super power to detect parental desire was still working like a champ. "Feed our superheroes and I'll start wiping down the counters out here."

Alex took the kids inside while Molly stood for a moment with the broom in her hands. Watching him through the kitchen window warmed her in ways Troy never could. They gathered around the island while Alex cut up fruit, smiling and telling them something that made them all laugh. His kids, her kids. Maybe, someday, their kids.

The sound of Troy's Camaro drew her attention to the road. She saw him clearly as he sped by. He was on the phone with someone and looked enraged. *His attorney*, she guessed with acid eating her guts. *Why won't you just leave and let me be happy?*

Chapter 30: Alex

The patio was filled with people talking and laughing while Alex stood next to the grill with a spatula in his hand. The flames made the burgers spit and hiss. He glanced over at Molly again. She was wearing a thin green dress that clung to her curves over a pair of white strappy sandals that showed off her red toenails. At that moment she was laughing with Roger, his son Christopher, and Charlotte.

Molly had been acting as his hostess all afternoon, welcoming the guests and passing out drinks. The grins that Roger had given them both implied he'd noticed something had changed between them. Even though Alex hadn't touched her once all day, he couldn't keep his eyes off her or the grin off his face.

Alex was flipping the burgers when Alice came to stand near his elbow. "It appears you had that talk with Molly," she said with a subdued smile.

"Yes, ma'am." Alex glanced Molly's way again and he felt his heart beat a little faster.

"Good," she said. "The ladies in my women's circle are all taken with your lovely home and delightful children. Perhaps when you've settled in a little more, you'll consider coming to speak to our group about your life and family."

"I'm not particularly religious," Alex said, hoping not to offend.

"God loves you anyway." Alice gave him a dismissive wave. "We've had all kinds of people come speak to us on all manner of topics. You're particularly interesting, I've discovered. I'd love to share you with my friends."

He felt a debt for her kindness and nodded. "I'd be happy to. Please let me know when you'd like me to come and I'll be there."

"Wonderful," she said and clutched his arm. "I'll find out and speak to you soon." Then she was off to mingle while Christopher and Charlotte both came up with worried grins.

"Hey, Alex! Great party." Christopher greeted him, hand in hand with his fiancée. "Look, I'm sorry I didn't believe you. On the way home, Charlotte kept telling me she had a feeling—"

"Something kept bugging me," Charlotte interrupted. "I don't know why. When Roger called about what happened—"

"If we'd believed you right away we might have caught the bastard," Christopher finished with a frown. "I'm really sorry."

"We both are," Charlotte said and touched Alex's arm.

"You've got nothing to be sorry about," Alex shrugged, strangely touched by their confession. "Hopefully getting the story out will scare off whoever took the shot and I can get back to living again." As he finished his sentence, his eyes wandered over to Molly and a smile crept across his lips.

Charlotte and Christopher followed Alex's eyes, noticing his smile. "Good. I hope so, too. Well, I need to find out what kind of trouble Noah is getting into," Christopher said as he pulled Charlotte away.

"Thanks for coming to the party!"

Jenna's laugh drew Alex's attention. He saw Troy standing with her at the edge of the patio. She had a gift to draw people out and make them feel interesting. From Troy's animated expression, he had fallen under her spell. Maybe she'd have better luck than Larry on figuring out what he'd been up to recently or gain some insight on what might make him go away.

Alex put the cooked hamburgers on a serving platter and pushed the selfish thought away. Will needed to know his father, he told himself, but the jealousy he felt at their connection surprised him. The boy was precocious and, like most kids his age, had an open nature that trusted easily. Alex could see Troy loved his son, but more as a trophy than the person he was becoming. Seeing the adoration in Will's face when he looked at Troy made Alex worry. Troy had the power to destroy his son's sweet nature with a few careless words or actions.

The platter of hamburgers went in the center of the table. He immediately set about making three plates for their kids. He knew how each one liked their burger. Manny had his with ketchup and cheese only, Hannah with mayo and lettuce, and Will with mustard and pickles. After adding a handful of potato chips he called the kids to the table.

"Thanks, Dad!" Manny was the first to arrive and took a bite of his burger. "Will and Noah and I are digging a hole to China!" Will ran up with a huge grin and a nod.

"How far have you gotten?" he asked with an amused smirk.

"Only knee deep so far," Will said as he sat down. "I hope we can get to some lava by this afternoon."

"Magma," Alex corrected. "It's only lava when it comes out of a volcano."

"Jen and I told him that," Hannah said as she joined the boys and gave Will a snotty look. "And you better not because my dad's shovel will melt."

"Don't worry, I can get another one." Alex ruffled Hannah's hair. "You did wash your hands after digging in the dirt, right?" All three kids presented their clean hands for inspection while chewing on big bites of burger.

"Eat up and I'll check on you in a bit," Alex said.

Stepping back, he watched others come forward to make themselves a burger. Troy followed Jenna up, his eyes glued to her ass. Alex shook his head and went inside the house to get himself a beer from the fridge. Three of the older women from Alice's circle were huddled around the coffee pot at the other side of the kitchen and looked up when he came in.

"Hi," he said to them as he opened the fridge. They nodded in greeting and smiled back at him. Grabbing himself a Shiner Bock, he used the bottle opener sitting on the island then pulled a deep swallow from the long neck bottle.

Molly walked in through the back door. "There you are," she said and stepped close to hug him around his waist. When she put her face against his chest, Alex kissed the top of her head.

"You havin' fun?" he asked her with an amused tone in his voice.

"Lovin' it! Thanks for feeding the kids." She released him then realized the older women were in the kitchen. "Oh!"

"Don't worry about us, dear," one of the women said as they all nodded with knowing smiles.

Alex's phone buzzed and when he pulled it out Larry's name was on the screen. "I'll be back out in a sec. Can you hold down the fort for me?" he asked Molly.

She held up her hand for a high five. "I got your back."

He slapped his palm to hers with a grin then stepped into the laundry room to take the call. "What's up?"

"We have a situation out front. Can you come out?" Larry's voice was tight.

"Be right there," Alex said and dropped the call.

He opened the door into the garage then pressed the button to open the large garage door. It opened on Larry and another of the guards holding their XCR assault rifles on a man standing next to a black luxury car. By the time the door opened enough to step through, Alex realized the man was his brother-in-law, Vizcarra Yermo de Cervantes.

Vizzy Cervantes was the twin brother of his wife, Maria, but they couldn't be more different. Where Maria had a certain joy of living, Vizzy only looked at the world for what he could wring from it. The last time they'd spoken was shortly after Maria passed away. Vizzy had started sniffing around because his grandparents' trust had automatically gone to the newborn twins. That was the first pebble in the landslide of lawsuits and acrimony that followed.

"What do you want, Vizzy?" Alex growled as he stormed towards the tableau.

"Alex," Vizzy exclaimed in a carefree manner, opening his arms wide like he wanted to give Alex a hug, ignoring the weapons pointed in his direction. "I thought it was time for us to have a little chat. Are you busy?" His soft Spanish accent reminded Alex of Maria's gently-accented English.

"The restraining order wasn't enough to keep you away?" Alex asked as he stopped between Larry and the other guard. "I don't think you're gonna like sleeping in our county jail."

"Diplomatic immunity," Vizzy said with a dismissive wave. "Besides you only have those orders against my parents. Not me. I checked."

"I'll fix that today." Alex hissed. "Diplomat or not, you're gonna leave right now."

"I understand from the news you've been having some trouble recently." Vizzy leaned back against his car while his eyes narrowed. "I wanted to offer to help make it stop."

The implied threat made Alex's stomach twist, then he gestured to Larry. "I've got plenty of help."

"I agree." Vizzy gave them both an amused smirk. "Quite formidable, but ultimately useless against a motivated assassin. Your security has to stop every attempt, where only one has to succeed. I believe I can eliminate the threat entirely."

Alex snorted. "At what price?"

"A single signature that ultimately costs you nothing." Vizzy made the offer with his hands open, like he had nothing to hide. "And the key to a safe deposit box."

The damned trust. All this over the trust Maria's grandfather left to her alone. Vizzy had been cut out years ago because his grandfather saw the kind of man he had become. Alex raged, but the fear of dying and leaving the kids without any protection left him frozen instead of pounding that smug look off Vizzy's face.

"Too much has happened for me to believe that."

Vizzy squinted and raised one eyebrow. "You have nothing to fear by signing. *When* the assassin succeeds, I'll get what I want anyway…after I get custody of my niece and nephew."

"Never," Alex whispered. His heart pounded hard enough to make his vision pulse.

"Suit yourself," Vizzy said and walked around his black car. "When you see Maria, tell her I tried."

"You'll be talking to her before I will." The bluff sounded false in his own ears, but Alex couldn't let Vizzy have the last word.

After his car turned onto the road, Larry relaxed and pulled out his phone. "I've got to call this in."

"And I've got to go back to the party," Alex muttered as rage and fear churned in his gut.

Chapter 31: Molly

Molly and Jenna spent Sunday afternoon sitting on the comfortable furniture on Alex's patio. The kids were inside playing video games with Troy and Alex. It had been odd watching the two men put aside the discomfort they obviously felt toward each other for Will's sake. Troy initially tried to be competitive, but Alex maintained a graceful distance until Troy eventually stopped.

"This is the life," Jenna said as she sipped her beer. "I'm gonna hate going home tonight."

"So, the kids didn't bug you?" Molly asked. Both ladies had their shoes off and feet up on the same ottoman.

"They are so adorable," Jenna smiled. "Hannah came in the guest room this morning with her princess dress-up clothes on. I fixed her hair and put a little color on her lips. She danced around all morning like she was at a ball."

"Oh, I always wanted a little girl," Molly sighed. "Maybe someday."

"I'd say that day's coming," Jenna said and leaned her head back. "It's obvious Alex is head over heels."

Molly didn't need the confirmation, but it was nice someone else noticed. "It was fun playing hostess with him yesterday. And thanks for keeping Troy occupied and out of my hair. I owe you big time for that."

"I hate to say it, but you really do." Jenna looked like she was sucking lemons. "What the hell did you ever see in him?"

Molly sighed. "I saw what he wanted me to see and never bothered to look past the surface."

Jenna leaned forward to take another pull on her beer. "I admit he's got a nice surface. Too bad he's such an ass."

"Did you notice the way Larry kept watching you two?" Molly asked.

"See? He doesn't like Troy either," Jenna deflected with a chuckle.

"I'm bettin' Larry would've looked at anyone spending time with you that way." Molly watched Jenna carefully and saw her cheeks color.

"I bet he has some interesting stories," Jenna whispered without meeting her eyes.

Molly suspected that was high praise coming from Jenna, but decided not to push it too hard. "So, have you decided if you're heading east?"

Jenna grinned and leaned back again. "I'm gonna roll the dice and see what happens."

"Wow!" Molly tickled her toes along Jenna's foot on the shared ottoman. "I feel silly saying it since I've only known you a week, but I'm proud of you. I bet you'll do great things at the network."

"Thanks," she said. "Since the story about Alex and the kids is still pulling in huge numbers online, they asked me for a human interest follow-up story."

"I'm sure he'd be happy to do it if it would help you."

"Would *you* be willing to be in it, too?" Jenna asked with a wrinkled nose, like she was worried about Molly's reaction to the question.

Molly opened her mouth to answer but then hesitated. She realized that the human interest aspect Jenna was referring to was the budding relationship between her and Alex. "We haven't even told the kids about us yet."

"They already know. Well, Hannah does anyway," Jenna said with a studied expression. "While we were playing dress up this morning, she asked if I thought you would let her carry the flowers when you married her dad."

"What?" Molly gasped with wide eyes. "Did you ask her why she thought we were getting married?"

Instead of answering immediately, Jenna sipped her beer with a sideways smile. "Sometime during the party yesterday, were you and Alex… affectionate?"

"Uh…" Molly scanned her memory and recalled hugging him in the kitchen while Alice's three friends looked on. Her Women's Circle had a legendary reputation for gossip. "Shit."

"Apparently there's a pool going around now for when he'll pop the question." Jenna tickled Molly's foot in return with an amused chuckle. Both women were silent for a moment while Molly frowned at her beer bottle.

"He hardly spoke to me last night," Molly admitted before she could filter her thoughts. She had been worried all night that Troy had done or said something to piss Alex off.

"He's had a lot on his mind lately. After you left with Will and Troy, Alex just put the kids to bed and disappeared into his room. I bet he was just tired."

"You're probably right." Molly peeled the label off her beer. "We haven't talked about anything seriously yet. It's too soon."

"Too soon or not, you guys are too freakin' cute," Jenna said. "I was so happy to see you together when I got here."

Molly smiled as she recalled attacking Alex that night on the same couch she was sitting on again. There was something attractive about his scent that haunted her ever since. Thinking about it again got her juices flowing and she let out a frustrated sigh.

"Jeez," Jenna chuckled as she took in Molly's flushed face. "Was it something I said?"

"Sorry, is it hot out here?" She fanned herself, unable to keep the smile off her lips.

"I understand it's new and you may not want to discuss the details, but it would really humanize his story to give a glimpse of this happy ending you're working on together."

"I'll talk to him about it." Molly could give her that at least. "I'm gonna get another beer. You want one?"

"I'll come with you," Jenna said as both women slipped on their sandals and walked towards the back door. Jenna opened the door and offered to take Molly's empty bottle.

"Thanks," Molly said and headed into the living room to see how the game was going.

"I'm winning!" Will announced to her as he bounced on the couch with the controller waving in his hands.

"Good," Molly said and roughed his hair. "Show me."

Will, Manny, Hannah, and Troy all had their controllers out as the race began again. Troy was obviously holding back and letting the kids fight it out between themselves. While they were all focused on the race, Molly couldn't resist stepping closer to Alex and touching his shoulder.

Alex was watching the kids with his eyebrows peaked and a faint smile on his lips. The combination appeared wistful and sad to Molly. She wanted to bring back that sparkle and smile he'd had before the party and drew his attention by tickling her fingers through his hair.

When he looked up at her with the same expression, she whispered, "You okay?"

"Yeah." He pinched his lips and nodded. "I just realized I never thanked you for your help yesterday."

"I had a great time," Molly said and sat on the arm of the chair. His open hand moved up her back to caress her with a tenderness that felt as natural as breathing. It made her arch her back against his touch when a spot above her shoulder blade began to itch. "Scratch up to the right."

He gave her a good scratch, bringing up both hands to dig in and make her sigh. "Oh, right there."

Jenna came over and handed Molly a beer, then sat down next to Hannah on the couch to watch them play.

"Miss Molly? When you marry my daddy, are you gonna live here with us?" Hannah asked with her eyes locked on the game.

Jenna, mid-drink, leaned forward and covered her mouth, suppressing an obvious smile.

"What?" Alex gasped as his hands froze on Molly's back.

Molly felt a chill crawl up from her stomach to encircle her heart. Her mind scrambled to come up with something to say.

"Will said he doesn't mind. Since we don't have a mommy, he said we could all share."

"And my dad can live in our old house, couldn't he?" Will suggested with a glance at Molly. "That way we could all have our dads, too."

Despite the warning Jenna had given her, Molly stared between Alex and Troy, unable to speak. Troy was pale for a moment before a flush ran up his neck to his cheeks, his face hardening as he glared at Molly and Alex sharing a chair.

Still frozen, Molly felt the first tendrils of panic claim her. It was too soon. Surely Alex would say something to defuse the situation. She needed more time to figure out what they had started working on together.

"I… uh… You might be jumping the gun a little, sugar," Alex said to Hannah. "Who said we were getting married?"

"Everyone," Hannah said with an exasperated tone eerily similar to Alex's way of answering obvious questions.

"Yeah, all the people at the party were talking about it," Manny said with a shrug. "Mister Roger said he bet you'll ask Miss Molly soon and then Mister Bubba said he'd take that bet. Then they started writin' down when everyone thought you'd ask her."

Molly tried to force her mouth to make words. Troy was staring at her now, his face a mask. She felt the hate radiating off of him like heat from a fire but she couldn't utter a sound.

Alex slumped in his seat and whispered, "Shit."

That drew her attention away from Troy and she turned to look helplessly at Alex.

Chapter 32: Alex

Everyone in the room was staring at them. Even Molly, who was perched on the arm of his chair, leaned back to give him a look as well. She hadn't said a word, but the shock on her face said enough. Jenna wore an amused smirk and Troy glared at them with a deep flush coloring his cheeks. The kids, oblivious to the destruction their curiosity left in its wake, stared up at him with identical expectant expressions.

After spending the last twenty-four hours obsessed with Vizzy's threat, Alex couldn't muster the energy to be upset about the kid's questions. What they described was close enough to his fantasy to force out a weak smile. Besides, if he didn't ask Molly soon, he might never have the chance. And in that moment he wanted to marry her more than anything in the world.

"What do you say?" he asked Molly in the silence. "Wanna marry me and live happily ever after?" The kids jumped up with excited smiles when he popped the question.

"No!" Molly jumped from his chair like it was on fire. Her response stilled the room.

Hannah's lip trembled for a moment, then she turned and ran towards her room. Jenna sat her beer on the floor before following Hannah with a frowning glare at Alex.

Molly trembled as she looked at Alex in horror. "What are you *thinking* asking that in front of everyone?"

"I'm thinking I want to marry you," Alex whispered. His dream popped like a bubble and left him empty.

"I thought we were on the same page about things!" She looked away and mumbled to herself, "I can't do this right now."

Troy suppressed a smirk as he stood. "I'll take Will home and give you a few minutes if you want."

Will looked up at his dad more confused than upset as they left.

Manny stood alone in the middle of the room glaring at Molly. "I *hate* you! I wouldn't want you to be my mommy anyway!"

Molly gasped at his reaction then covered her mouth to hide her pain. "Manny…I…"

Alex leaned forward to gather his crying son in his arms. "Don't be mad at Miss Molly. This is my fault, buddy."

That made Manny cry even harder as he buried his face in Alex's chest. Alex met Molly's gaze over his son's head as he pulled him into his lap. "I'll talk to you later."

Molly stepped backwards, then turned and ran for the door. Alex felt his own chin quiver as he looked up at the ceiling. In the hideous clarity of the moment, he wondered if it might be best to make a clean break after all. He couldn't spare his own kids, but maybe he could spare Will and Molly a little pain.

The new threat from Vizzy changed everything. Larry wanted to bring in the FBI, but the only evidence were his vague threats they'd recorded outside. Over the last three years, nothing could be tied directly to Maria's family, despite the certainty that the threats and harassment originated from them. And it appeared the recent publicity about the failed attempt on his life hadn't changed a thing despite his hope that it would.

When Alex became the twins' trustee after Maria passed away, he'd had Peter look into their trust. In a typical trust, the assets are disclosed as part of the trust documentation. In a blind trust, the beneficiary has no information on the assets that the trustee manages. The trust the kids had inherited was even more mysterious.

The assets of the trust would remain sealed until certain conditions were met. When Maria became the sole trustee and beneficiary just before her grandfather's death, he had required that she be married ten years and have a child before the trust assets would be turned over to her. When she passed away, her two children became the beneficiaries under the same conditions.

Despite being the trustee, Alex had never been able to determine what assets it contained. The trust referenced a safe deposit box at Banamex that only the beneficiary could access when the conditions had been met. Obviously Vizzy hoped to get control of the account and the contents of the box somehow.

Alex had considered giving Vizzy what he wanted. He could sign over his rights as the trustee and give him the key to the box, but he knew it would never be over. The kids were the rightful heirs and would remain in danger of Vizzy for the rest of their lives. There was nothing he could do to change that.

It may have appeared fatalist, but Alex realized an important truth over the past few months. There was *nothing* he could hold on to in life. Maria had died. His own life had been threatened. His kids would either live or die, and there was ultimately nothing he could do about it other than be careful. The lesson he learned wasn't to give up; it was to simply let go, just like he'd been forced to do with Maria.

While his son cried in his arms, Alex soothed him with soft words, rubbing his back until he stilled.

"Dad?" he whimpered.

"Yeah?"

"Why doesn't Miss Molly want to be our mommy, too?"

Alex sighed. *Let it go.* "I don't know, but I do know I'll always be your daddy."

Jenna walked back into the living room carrying Hannah. She had her face pressed against Jenna's shoulder and stared at Alex with red eyes. Jenna lowered Hannah to the floor and she ran to climb on Alex's lap as well.

"I'm gonna head out," Jenna said with a worried frown. "I'm so sorry."

"It'll work out or it won't. Either way we'll survive the best we can." Alex settled back with his arms full of his snuggling kids. "Have a safe trip home."

"Will do," she said as she went back to the guest room.

Alex and the kids helped her get her bags to the car and waved goodbye from the porch with Larry looking on.

Their dinner was subdued, with leftovers warmed in the microwave. They watched a movie until they fell asleep. Alex tucked them both into Manny's bed, then he kissed them goodnight.

Not ready to sleep himself, Alex locked up and set the alarm, then got himself a book to read in bed. He selected an old favorite, *Shabumi*, written under the pen name Travanian. The 1979 novel told the story of a skillful assassin who could kill his enemies with a drinking straw or fountain pen. Alex read the book late into the night, dreaming he had the same kind of skill.

He must have dozed off because the beep of his alarm being disabled woke him. It was still dark outside. Larry or one of the other guards would sometimes come in to use the bathroom, but they usually called out to let him know it was them. Feeling foolish, he still got up and stepped into the closet to open his gun safe.

"Larry?" he called as he reached in to get the Glock. Alex checked the safety and stepped back into the bedroom. After he cleared the room, he leaned into the doorway to look down the hallway.

When he saw the man-shaped shadow creep in from the living room, his heart pounded in his throat. He hesitated bringing the gun up a second too late. The bright flash and bang startled him into returning fire. Remembering Roger's lessons, he took aim and squeezed the trigger from a wide stance, using both hands and the door jamb to steady the gun as he fired.

The sound of gunfire in the hallway was deafening and the air quickly filled with acrid smoke. The slide jammed open when Alex exhausted his magazine, leaving a ringing silence as he staggered against the opposite door jamb. He was so scared he couldn't seem to catch his breath. In the confusion and weakness that followed, he heard Manny and Hannah crying, but couldn't make his legs move towards them for some reason.

When the gun slipped out of his grip, he looked down to see why. There was a bubbling red hole in his chest. *Molly will never be able to get that stain out*, he thought. He slid down the wall to thump on to the floor. If he could just catch his breath he would go make sure the kids were okay.

A moment later he saw Troy carrying Hannah and leading Manny through the smoke and darkness. Surely he'd keep them safe. There was blood on Troy's shirt. Why was there blood on Troy's shirt? Alex shut his eyes to rest for a moment.

I just need to catch my breath, then I'll get up to find out what happened.

Chapter 33: Troy

The chloral hydrate finally kicked in as Manny's jagged crying slowed to deep, even breaths. Troy pulled off the road and grabbed the duct tape rolling in the passenger floorboard. His left shoulder screamed as he stretched to open the car door, but he pushed the pain out of his mind to focus on securing the children before the drug wore off.

It was supposed to have been an easy job. Shoot a guy, take his kids, deliver them to Vizzy. He'd done operations for the cartel that were a hundred times more complex and involved dozens of men, but none of them happened next door to his ex-wife and kid.

Troy knew Molly's grandmother lived nearby when he and Vizzy started planning the job. In fact, Vizzy had decided to use him because he was familiar with the area. It wasn't until he got there that he realized Molly had moved into her grandmother's house with his son.

Seeing them again, even through high-powered binoculars, hurt like hell. He'd gotten so caught up in the excitement of running Vizzy's secret mercenary force that he'd never had time to dwell on what he was missing. When Molly had divorced him, he'd been furious and wanted to hurt her. But watching the quiet life she led with Will while he waited for Alex to move into the house next door had given him too much time to think. He could have been happy there.

Killing Alex should have been just another job. Emotions compromise operations, Troy had that fact drilled into his head over the years. But watching his ex-wife and son play house with Alex had created a level of jealous rage that completely overwhelmed him. By the time he'd lined up the kill shot near the river, he was unable to relax his pounding heart—and he'd missed.

With the kids legs and arms taped together, Troy slipped a few more drops of the chloral hydrate between their slack lips with shaking fingers. He needed them all out until after he gave the twins to Vizzy and collected his money. Then he and Will could disappear into South America. There were plenty of out-of-the-way places he could go. Places where a man with money could live a good life and raise his son in peace.

Slipping back into the driver's seat, he panted away the pain with his eyes closed for a moment before reaching across to shut the door with his right hand.

Fucking unbelievable. Troy had nailed Alex with a perfectly placed chest shot, but instead of going down, Alex emptied his clip and managed to break Troy's shoulder. At least the bleeding was slowing down after pouring on a handful of WoundSeal on the entry wound.

Grabbing his satellite phone, he pushed the only contact button. He had no idea what the number actually was because the phone had been designed and built to assuage Vizzy's growing paranoia. It even had a remote self destruct that would scramble the data and melt the chips inside on command.

"Did you get them?" Vizzy growled when he answered.

"Yes," Troy gasped. "I'm on the road now to rendezvous with you at the border."

"How did Alex die?" His voice hissed like a snake slithering over sand.

Troy puffed a laugh at the irony of being shot in nearly the same spot as he'd shot Alex. "Upper chest wound. When I left he was sitting in a pool of blood. Make sure you have my money."

Vizzy dropped the call without another word. Troy started the car and pulled back on the road towards I-37, heading south.

Alex had been Troy's last job. He'd been tempted to kill Molly as well, but the look on Alex's face when she turned down his ridiculous marriage proposal had changed his mind. Knowing Troy had taken away both her son and the man who loved her would pay her back in full. He wanted her to suffer like she'd made him suffer when she took away his son.

Troy glanced in the rearview mirror at his son sleeping in the back seat. He had to keep Will safe from Vizzy. No matter how tough Molly thought she was, Troy was one of the few who understood just how crazy that bastard was. When he threatened to kill everyone Troy loved, he wasn't kidding. If Troy had waited one more day to act, Will would have been dead. And Troy couldn't let that happen. Not to his son.

There were so many things he needed to make up for. He'd missed birthdays and holidays because of the job and Vizzy's paranoia, but now he could retire and focus on what was really important.

This job would bank him enough to live the rest of his life in luxury. And the best part, Will would only remember going to sleep at Molly's and then waking up in his new life on the road with his dad. He'd have to come up with a story to explain what happened to Molly, but the kid was six. What did he know?

The pain helped keep him awake and focused as he drove, but the vision in his right eye seemed darker despite the brightening pre-dawn sky. Blinking and shaking his head made the pain in his shoulder worse, but didn't help him see any better. He had no choice but to keep driving south, the cruise control set to the speed limit to avoid attracting more attention than a Camaro would on its own.

When he got to his family's hunting lease near the Mexico border, he needed to present a strong front to transfer the twins and get his money. If Vizzy sensed any weakness, he would kill him. Troy had planned to move Will out of the car somewhere to keep him safe, but with his left arm useless, that was going to be too difficult.

He drove and planned, ignoring the worsening vision in his right eye and the growing headache. His mouth was dry and chalky, but he couldn't stop for a drink without someone seeing the bloody gunshot wound. He only had a few hours to figure out how to pull off this plan with his life, money, and son intact. Glancing into the rearview mirror, he checked that his son was still okay. He had to be okay. He had to stay okay.

Chapter 34: Molly

The house was unusually quiet when Molly woke up. She wasn't in her bed. Giving a bleary look around, she realized she had been sleeping on the couch and was still wearing her clothes from the night before.

"…the hell?"

The beer bottle on the coffee table was only half full. That was all she'd drunk when she came home, which couldn't explain why she felt like she'd been drinking all night. Rubbing her face helped her focus enough to stand.

The predawn light coming through the windows showed no signs of Troy downstairs. She wondered if he went upstairs to sleep when she took over the couch he'd been sleeping on. Jogging up the stairs got her blood pumping and helped clear her head of the fog that persisted. When she peeked in on Will and only found an empty bed, her heart beat even faster.

"Will? Troy?"

Will's room, her room, the bathroom, and the junk room were all empty. The cobwebs began to clear as her panic grew. She ran downstairs again, almost tripping in the process, and looked out the front window. Troy's car was gone and it was way too early for breakfast.

"You fucker," she growled and ran out the door. Larry might have seen Troy leave if he had been on duty. Molly ran to the road and turned towards Alex's house.

She didn't want to think about his absurd proposal anymore, but couldn't stop herself. She and Troy had a whispered fight about it after Will had gone to bed. In a strange reversal, Molly found herself defending the option to marry Alex, even though she had just turned him down cold in front of everyone, crushing Hannah and Manny in the process.

As she approached the corner of the fence around Alex's house, Molly saw a booted foot sticking out of the tall grass in the ditch. Running closer, Molly gasped as she saw Larry lying in the ditch with his night vision goggles blown apart and blood all over his face.

"Larry!" she cried as she reached his side. Her military training took over as she verified he was still breathing and had a pulse in his neck. The goggles were only held on by a strap around his head, so she carefully removed it to get a better look at the wound on his scalp.

Larry moaned as she lifted the goggles off his head. The bullet must have hit the goggles just right and deflected up to split the skin on his scalp. She felt around his skull for any weakness or bone movement which brought Larry awake with a gasp.

"What happened?" he said when he realized Molly was in the ditch with him.

"Troy took Will." Her reply sounded emotionless, but she was barely hanging on to control. "I guess you got in the way."

"I can't remember," Larry said and pressed the switch on his throat mic. "Code red. This is not a drill."

He tried to stand, but Molly had to help him. By the time he was standing up, she noted the panicked look on his face as he pressed the switch again. "Code red. Respond."

Molly's eyes followed the direction of his stare and saw Alex's open front door. "Oh God, no!"

"Wait for me, someone could still be in there," Larry said, but it was too late.

"Alex!" Molly ran towards the house, gasping through her tears. "Alex!"

The lingering scent of sulphur led her to the bedroom hallway. The blood splatter on the wall made her throat close, but she turned towards Alex's bedroom anyway. She found him sitting on the floor near his doorway, leaning against the wall with a pool of dark blood spreading in a circle around him.

Kneeling next to Alex, she leaned his head back to reach his neck with trembling fingers. His pulse was thready and she hadn't seen him breathe yet. "Alex, baby, hang on," she whispered to him. Her voice broke when she called for help. "Larry! We need an air ambulance!"

Molly sat down in the blood with him to reach under his shirt and place her hand flat over the red frothing wound. Then she put her other hand over the similar wound in his back.

"Yes," she whispered as she felt him take a shallow breath. When he inhaled, Molly let the air escape from the wound with a wet burp, but tried to keep any air from going back into his chest cavity. "Yes," she repeated.

Larry found her there keeping a tight seal on the wounds with her hands. "I've got some vented dressings in the trauma kit in my car, hold on."

"Yes," Molly whispered against Alex's cheek. He took another breath and Molly wept. "Yes."

It felt like she stepped out of time. There was only her and Alex in the world as she kept repeating the affirmation that seemed to help him breathe. She kissed his cold face and shifted his weight to support him against her chest. The agony of feeling Alex dying and her terror for Will slowly pulled her to pieces.

She should have told him yes when he asked her to marry him. She should have dragged him to a judge in the middle of the night just to have the chance to say the words she needed to say. Feeling his breath leaking through the holes in his chest and back killed her right along with him.

"I called in a company chopper from San Antonio," Larry said as he knelt down next to her. "I'm gonna cut off his shirt, you keep the pressure on his wounds."

After cleaning the excess blood off around the wounds, Larry applied the vented dressing to help Alex inflate his lung again as he breathed. Then Larry collapsed next to Molly without warning.

"Gah, I can't even see straight," Larry gasped and wiped off the fresh blood dripping down his face. "That bastard gave me a concussion."

Molly kept Alex leaning against her chest by wrapping her arms around him. "Alex asked me to marry him last night," she whispered.

"That's a surprise," Larry replied as he pressed a wad of bandages on his scalp wound. Molly glared at him until he looked up. "Didn't he tell you what happened?"

"No."

"His brother-in-law, Vizzy, showed up in the middle of the party on Saturday. Turns out he's the one behind all the shit going on. He wanted Alex to sign over some trust that the kids got from their great-grandparents. Alex refused." Larry nodded at Alex bleeding out. "This is the result."

Molly had obviously noticed the kids were gone, but until that moment she hadn't seen the truth. "Troy took his kids. I guess we know who he's been working for now."

"Yeah," Larry muttered. "I screwed this all up."

"No more than I did." Molly brushed Alex's hair off his forehead and kissed him again. "I'm gonna go after our kids, Larry. No cops." She gave him a cold look that communicated her murderous intent.

"I wish I could go with you," Larry said as he reached into a pouch on his belt. He brought out a small electronic device in a rugged yellow case and handed it to her. "I stuck a GPS locator under Troy's car after he took off with Will the last time. Take Alex's SUV. It's fully armored."

"Can you keep the heat off me until I get back?"

"I'll do my best," Larry said and stared at her cradling Alex. "So, you gonna do it? Marry him, I mean?"

She looked down at Alex with tears in her eyes and whispered, "Yes."

Alex took another wheezing breath.

The heavy thumps of an approaching helicopter drew a sigh of relief from them both. Larry switched on his throat mic to give the incoming team a situation report.

Chapter 35: Molly

After throwing away her bloody clothes and taking a quick shower, Molly put on an old pair of comfortable jeans, a dark green t-shirt, and her old Army boots. She was hurrying to the basement where she kept her gun safe and reloading equipment when the doorbell rang. Pausing long enough to open the door, she saw Roger standing there.

"I heard the chopper this morning but the security guys over at Alex's place won't talk to me. What happened?" he asked with a sour expression.

"Troy shot Alex and took the kids," she whispered through her tight throat. "He was probably the one who took the shot at Alex down by the creek as well."

"Damn it!" He closed his eyes slowly and bowed his head for a moment before spearing her with a hard look. "You're goin' after him." Roger didn't ask, but Molly nodded anyway. "I'm comin' with ya. Sergeants gotta stick together."

Molly allowed herself one chin-quivering gasp of relief, then swallowed her fear and pain back down. "Come in."

It didn't take long to give Roger a brief situation report and share her plan, such as it was. While she got her weapons and ammunition together, Roger ran back home to get his own. He'd promised not to tell his son, Christopher, what they were doing, but he insisted sharing that Alex and Larry were going to the hospital in San Antonio so they could follow.

Molly knew Charlotte was a registered nurse and might be able to help translate what the doctors would tell them. She was surprised to learn Christopher had become a clinical social worker after leaving the service. Roger assured her he could help the kids with any trauma they may go through when they got them back. His confidence that they would get the kids back made her breath catch.

Molly had bought the same type of M24 sniper rifle she'd used in the service. The scope wasn't military grade, but she'd shot with it enough to be confident at ranges less than 400 meters. Its match-grade ammunition went in the backpack along with extra magazines for her pistols. Her tiny Glock G42 fit in an ankle holster under her jeans then she stuck the bulkier Model 19 in her shoulder holster. She had a carry permit, so she wasn't worried if someone saw them.

By the time she had loaded up Alex's SUV that she'd parked in front of her house, Roger returned dressed in old-school green camo and carrying a combat shotgun with a hip-holstered Glock 19 like her own. He raised a pair of large binoculars. "My eyes ain't what they used to be, but I can still spot for you."

Molly shivered as her emotions fought her control. "I can't thank you enough, Roger."

"We're neighbors," he said simply, as if this was a normal neighborly thing to do, and then he climbed into the passenger seat of the SUV. After Molly climbed in behind the wheel he asked, "Any word on Alex?"

"Not yet." He'd been alive when they left, but his lung collapsed again when they put him on the chopper. Larry said he'd call if there was any change, but she worried about his concussion.

"I'm so sorry, Molly," Roger said with a low, gravelly ache in his voice.

"Yeah," Molly whispered. She was sorry, too, but nothing was going to stop her from getting their kids back safe. She owed Alex for letting Troy get too close and she owed Troy a hot bullet.

Molly started the SUV and glanced at the tracker Larry had given her. All morning Troy's car had been heading south down I-37 and she had an idea where he was going. His family owned some hunting land near the Rio Grande Valley State Park, about four hours south of San Antonio. It was right next to the Mexico border. If he was going to hand off Alex's kids to his brother-in-law without anyone seeing them, Molly had no doubt it would be there. Troy had enough of a head start, so she floored it and spun out of her driveway.

Roger kept an eye on the tracker while Molly drove. Alex's SUV wasn't just armored, it had extra features like a top-of-the-line radar detector, GPS, and a satellite phone that would work even if there was no cell coverage. She had been flying down I-37, only slowing when the radar detector beeped, when the satellite phone rang. Roger picked it up.

"Yeah? Hey Larry, it's Roger." He mumbled a few times and sighed once, then said, "I'll tell her. Hang in there."

Molly steeled herself for bad news and bit her lip. "What happened?"

"They made it to the University Hospital trauma center. Alex crashed once, but they got him going again and then took him straight into surgery."

She let out a shuddering breath and eased off the gas for a moment to collect herself. "Oh, thank God."

The relief flowed like electricity all over her skin. He was still fighting. She wanted to tell herself that he would pull through, but she had too many friends die to lie to herself about it. He might die. If he did, she vowed to love his kids like her own for the rest of her life.

"Looks like Troy's pulling off just where you said," Roger said and looked over at the screen on the GPS mounted on the dash. "We're about forty minutes behind him at this point."

"Hopefully that's close enough," she said, then pressed her foot back down to send the SUV surging.

Molly loved to hunt, and the first few years she and Troy were married she'd gone on hunting trips his family held on their land. The terrain was dense with trees and supported a broad diversity of birds and other wildlife. One feature she remembered well was the hill to the north of the main camping area. There was an old farm road that she could use to get close enough without being seen.

She slowed down as she got closer, watching the side of the road for the old ruts she remembered. After missing them once, she caught them the second time she passed and headed the SUV slowly into the thick overgrowth. The solid rubber tires were good for more than stopping bullets as she bounced over sharp rocks and tree limbs. Eventually she found the rising hillside she was looking for and stopped the car.

"Let's go," she said to Roger and grabbed her rifle and duffle bag.

"I'm not afraid to admit being a little nervous about this," Roger said. "You doin' okay?"

"I'll be okay when I can hug Will again," she sighed. "Follow me up and I'll signal if I see him."

The hill wasn't tall, but a little elevation was better than nothing. With the sun beating down overhead, Molly crept her way through the tall grass and trees until she got near the crest. Then she got down on her hands and knees to approach the top, finally crawling the last few feet on her belly until she could see.

The old campsite was still standing, with its open sided pavilion and large brick grill. The ground was clear where they always set up campers and tents. That was where she saw Troy's yellow Camaro backed in to face the entrance. She held her hand up and signaled Roger.

Molly eased the rifle up to her shoulder to get a closer look through the scope. Troy was in bad shape. He was sitting in the driver's seat, his skin white. He had covered his left shoulder with his right hand. The front of his shirt and arm was black with dried blood.

"He's wounded," Molly whispered as Roger eased in next to her. "Larry was right about that blood in the hallway. Alex got off at least one good shot."

She felt a flush of pride that Alex had returned fire. She knew that there was no way to predict how a person would react in their first combat situation. Some people froze, others took crazy risks, but a few remembered their training and kept their heads. Alex was a soldier now.

Roger used his higher powered binoculars to study the car. "I don't think he's breathing."

"Do you see the kids anywhere?"

"Maybe in the back seat, but it's too dark to tell."

"I need to go check," Molly whispered.

"I can't cover you with a shotgun from up here. You stay and let me circle around behind his car first."

Molly nodded and Roger slipped back down the crest of the hill to work his way through the trees. She'd already lost track of where the stealthy drill sergeant was when the sound of a car pulled her attention to the road leading into the campsite.

"Damn it," she muttered and shifted her position to widen her field of fire to include the road. There was no way to warn Roger, so she just hoped he was paying attention.

A sleek black luxury car drove in and stopped across the clearing from Troy's Camaro. Two men with swarthy complexions got out to stand behind the open doors.

"Troy! Come out where we can see you," the driver called with a soft Spanish accent. When Troy didn't respond, the driver nodded to the man behind the passenger door and waved him forward.

The passenger bent to get a pistol from inside the car, then stepped around the door with his gun trained on Troy. When he got to the Camaro and opened the door, Troy spilled out on the ground at his feet.

"Dead," the man called back to the driver.

A cold numbness gripped Molly's chest. Her ex-husband, her son's father, was dead. Alex had killed the bastard for her.

"Where are the kids?" the driver asked.

"Tied up in the back seat. There's three of them, though. Looks like those knockout drops you gave him worked."

"We only need my sister's kids. Kill the other one."

Molly felt her heart race as the armed man leaned inside the car. Before she could do anything she heard the roar of a shotgun and the guy flew back against the open car door. *Roger!*

Swiveling in an instant, she zeroed in on the driver who had thrown himself back in the driver's seat. She fired a snapshot through the front windshield, creating a spiderweb of cracks, then she sighted and fired again where the driver should be. The car lurched forward as she sighted once more, but it slowed to a stop before she could fire a third time.

Roger ran out of the woods, pausing next to Troy and the man he'd shot to use the car door as a shield against the guy in the black car. Molly couldn't see through the broken window, but nothing appeared to be moving. She grabbed her rifle, jumped up, and slid down the steep face of the hill, keeping her weapon trained on the black car.

The driver had his hands over a hole in his chest. He was gasping for breath, his teeth stained a bright red from the blood he was aspirating. Molly watched his eyebrows draw up in confusion as he looked at her. Then the light left his eyes and he slumped forward.

"Molly, over here!" Roger cried from Troy's car.

Chapter 36: Molly

The solid rubber tires transmitted every bump and dip on I-37 to the SUV. Molly could only pay partial attention to the road because her eyes were constantly drawn to the rearview mirror showing the unconscious forms of three children belted in their booster seats.

None of them seemed injured, but they hadn't woken up when she and Roger loaded them into the SUV. At first she was glad because the messy deaths of Troy and the other two men would have been traumatic to the kids. But hours later, as she made the mad dash to University Hospital in San Antonio, her worry mounted about what had been in those knockout drops Troy had given them.

Roger had taken over when she crawled into the back of Troy's Camaro to cradle her son and the twins she'd come to think of as her own. While she had checked the children over and removed the duct tape holding their hands and feet together, Roger ran back over the hill and drove the SUV around to load up the kids for the trip back to San Antonio.

By the time she was leaving the campsite, Roger was on the phone with Larry who reported that Alex was still in surgery. Larry had a plan to help them avoid problems with the authorities and was giving instructions to Roger when she left. She hated leaving Roger there alone, but they were right to insist she get the kids back to safety.

"Mom?" A whispered voice called for her and Molly sobbed once in relief.

"Yeah, baby?" she whispered back, trying to keep her voice calm. In the rearview mirror, Will was rubbing his face and eyes.

"I'm thirsty," he mumbled.

"We'll stop soon and I'll buy you some water. Are you feeling okay?"

"Kinda funny in my head," he said as he looked around. "Why are we in Mister Alex's SUV?"

"Mister Alex was hurt early this morning and we're going to the hospital right now to see him."

The twisting fear in her guts kept her from saying too much. She wasn't sure she could keep herself under control if she spoke the truth out loud. His father was dead, and Alex had killed him, saving her from doing it herself.

Manny mumbled without waking fully. "Mister Troy said the bad men were coming for Daddy and he had to take us somewhere safe."

"Yes." The lie leapt to her lips before she had time to think about it. "Troy saved you all."

Hannah cried softly as she woke next. "Daddy?"

"He's gonna be fine, sugar," Molly said, praying that it was true. "We're gonna be at the hospital real soon."

Molly stopped at a gas station to check on the kids, fill up the SUV, and get them all some food and water. That was when she noticed Troy's dried blood on their shirts, but didn't mention it to the kids. When they went in the store, she picked out three of the smallest t-shirts they had on sale and hustled the kids into the bathroom before anyone noticed.

"I want the pink one," Hannah said as she picked the shirt out of the pile Molly put near the sink. "What's it say?"

Molly glanced over and shook her head at the curvy script over a compound bow. "I don't wear bows, I shoot them." That made all three kids giggle and the sound of their happy voices made Molly's throat tight.

Everyone went to the potty on their own. Then using paper towels and hand soap, Molly gave the kids a quick clean up and dressed them in the new shirts. The boys both had shirts that said *Vegetables Are What Food Eats*, and when Will read it to them, they all laughed again. Molly even gave a weak smiled as she tossed the bloody shirts in the bathroom trash.

"Let's get some snacks for the road," Molly said.

She let the kids pick out pretzels, pork skins, corn chips, and got bottles of water for them all, then paid in cash at the register. Whatever Troy had used to knock them out appeared to be wearing off without any issues. When they got back in the SUV again, it felt almost normal as the kids shared their snacks and argued about which radio station to listen to.

Molly called Larry on the satellite phone when they passed the San Antonio city limits to figure out where to go first. He had arranged for them to stay at a hotel near the hospital and coordinated extra security coverage. Since Alex was still in surgery, there was no point in taking the kids to the hospital yet. Larry also said that Alex's phone had been ringing off the hook with neighbors and friends who had heard about the shooting, offering their help and well wishes.

That made Molly remember she'd silenced her phone and found a dozen messages and texts, mostly from Jenna, who had apparently heard about what happened. She called her friend back immediately.

"Are you okay?" Jenna answered the call without a greeting. "Are the kids okay?"

"We're all fine," Molly said, keeping an eye on the kids listening in the back seat. "We just arrived in San Antonio."

"Oh, thank God!" Jenna sighed deeply and blew out a long breath. "What can I do to help?"

"We're heading to a hotel until Alex gets out of surgery. Would you mind coming and sitting with me?" Molly whispered through her closing throat. "Please?"

"Of course I will! And Roger's son, Christopher, is already there with his kids to keep yours busy. Do the police know who did it?"

"I don't know," Molly said. "I was only concerned about the kids. I haven't talked to anyone yet except Larry."

"I've been chatting with him here at the hospital. For a guy in bed with a minor gunshot wound and concussion, he's sure keeping busy."

"He's Alex's best friend," Molly said. "And he feels like he failed Alex."

The words echoed in her own heart. She'd failed Alex as well. She should have known Troy was involved somehow. The fact he worked private security in South America should have tipped her off to the possibility, and the timing of his sudden interest in Will was too coincidental.

"That's ridiculous! Alex survived and his kids are safe. I'm gonna go give Larry a piece of my mind," Jenna said with a burr of anger in her tone. "Then I'll meet you at the hotel."

When Molly ended the call, her phone rang again almost immediately. Alice Mayberry's name appeared on the screen.

"Alice," Molly breathed. "I've got the kids and we're safe."

"I know," Alice said in her usual even tone. "That lovely friend of Alex's, Larry Hanover, has kept me up-to-date. I understand you and the kids are staying at a hotel in San Antonio."

Molly blinked, confused. "Uh…"

"Terry will be driving me into San Antonio to stay with you at the hotel if you don't mind. I imagine it will be a while until Alex is fit to come home. The kids will need someone to sit with them while you are with Alex, and I would love to do that for you."

A sob broke out before she could stop it. "Thank you so much. For everything."

"Well, friends should come through in a pinch, and we're already good friends. I'll see you soon!"

Chapter 37: Alex

The noise was driving Alex insane.

Beep. Beep. Beep.

The kids must have left a toy under his bed. He didn't have the energy to find it and turn it off. *Why am I so tired?*

Opening his eyes took a supreme act of willpower. He wasn't in his bedroom. The beeping was coming from a screen next to his bed. Alice Mayberry was sitting in a recliner on the other side.

"Alice?" he whispered in confusion. His mouth was so dry that there wasn't enough spit to lick his lips. She heard him and looked up with her eyebrows drawn together.

"Have you come back to us?" Alice asked as she levered herself out of the chair, then gripped the bed rail to lean closer. "Praise God!"

"Water," he croaked.

Alice got a styrofoam cup with a bendy straw from the table next to the bed. "Here you go," she said and directed the straw between his cracked lips.

The cold water tasted wonderful as he sucked the cup dry. That little effort sapped his strength, leaving bright sparks shooting around behind his closed eyelids. His chest ached, but the distant pain wasn't enough to keep him awake.

Alex lost track of time, but his next coherent thought came when someone strapped a cuff around his upper arm and squeezed it tight. He opened his eyes to see a nurse reviewing the beeping screen as the cuff slowly released its tight grip. Alice was gone and he wondered if he'd dreamed her visit.

"Mister Thompson, do you know where you are?" the nurse asked with a loud, brusk tone.

"No," he whispered. His throat felt tight and his lips were dry again.

"You are in the trauma center of University Hospital. Do you remember how you got here?"

Visions flashed through his mind of a loud thumping and Larry's face covered in blood. Something was there, just out of reach, so he forced his mind to focus. His heart pounded as he remembered. "My kids. Where are my kids?"

"Anxiously waiting to see you," the nurse said. "We don't allow children that young in the trauma ward, but your friends and family have been here 'round the clock."

Hearing that made him doubt the memory of firing at the shadowy figure down the hallway at home. He needed answers. "Is Molly here?"

"Your wife? Yes, she's been here the most."

Wife? She'd refused his proposal. He remembered that too clearly. Everything was so confusing. "Can I see her?"

"Yes," she said. "I'll call her in for a little while, but you still need to rest. You're not out of the woods yet."

Alex forced himself to stay awake and became more aware of his body. He ached everywhere, despite the mental fog he knew was caused by narcotics. Even his hair hurt as he lay helpless in bed, too weak to do more than draw painful breaths.

When Molly came through the doorway, he was able to relax. She was lovely in khaki shorts and a soft blue top. Her face was lined with worry when she bent to give him a soft kiss.

"I'm so glad to see you awake," she whispered as her eyes searched his face.

"The kids?" Alex gasped.

"They're safe. Context Security got us a suite nearby with 'round-the-clock protection. Christopher has been helping them cope with... everything." She touched his hair and kissed him again, smelling of sunshine and summer, then took his hand in both of hers.

"How?" Alex whispered. Nothing made sense, but he couldn't think to ask the right questions.

"Don't worry about that right now. You just focus on getting well enough to see them. I got your back for now."

"Thank you." Tears filled his eyes but it even hurt to cry.

"Suck it up, soldier," Molly chided, but her eyes shone as well. "Your parents and sister are outside and want to see you."

"How did Mom take missing the wedding," he whispered with a faint smile.

Molly grinned and cocked an eyebrow. "She hasn't yet. We may be common law for now, but don't worry, we'll be setting the official date just as soon as you get out of ICU."

"But you turned me down," he sighed, but couldn't take his eyes off of her glowing face.

"I changed my mind." Her face flushed as she bit her lip to hold back tears. "I was an idiot not to see how special you are. I should have trusted my instincts instead of running scared."

"I love you so much," Alex whispered as he squeezed her hand.

"I know," she whispered back as she smoothed his hair. "I do, too."

"So you met Mom and Dad…" Alex closed his eyes and shook his head a little. "And you still want to marry me."

"They aren't that bad," Molly said. "Your Mom and I had a tense moment when she arrived and the nurse pointed me out as your wife. Once I got them updated on your condition and let them see the kids, everything's been fine. Oh, and your sister Pat is so great. I think Will is in love with her."

"Yeah," Alex smiled. He was having a hard time staying awake. "Maybe they can come visit a little later."

He faded away for a bit, but he woke again with his mother holding his hand. She was sitting next to the bed with her head bowed and eyes closed.

"Hey, Mom."

When she looked up, Alex was shocked by the change in her appearance in the year since he'd seen her last. She'd let her hair go white instead of fighting it, but the smooth skin on her face had softened into creases and wrinkles. He had always teased her that she had a painting somewhere that aged for her, but now she looked every one of her seventy years.

"Oh, Alex." She bent to kiss his forehead. "I wish you would've called us in Paris. I had no idea about any of this until we saw the news report that you'd been shot."

"I didn't want you to worry when there was nothing you could do about it." He felt stronger as he spoke. The fuzzy feeling he'd suffered so far was less, but soreness when he breathed had become worse. It was a good kind of pain, though. The kind of pain that felt like healing.

"It's a mother's job to worry," she said with a grim smile. "And I haven't done a very good job of it lately."

"You did fine. I know I pushed everyone away after Maria died." He shut his eyes for a moment as the memories swept through him. This time the memories didn't hurt as much. He loved her and she was gone, but it wasn't the kind of torment it had always been to remember. He opened his eyes and realized he was smiling.

"It's probably a horrible thing to say to a man who's been shot, but you look better." His mother eyed him and asked, "It's Molly, isn't it?"

"Yeah," Alex admitted with a smile. "She's great, and so is Will."

"I was a little shocked to hear she was your wife, but I understand why she did it. She's a real pistol. You do intend to invite us to the wedding, don't you?"

"Of course," he said. "Just as soon as I get up and around we'll start planning it out."

"Good," she said and sighed as she studied his face. "Let me go so I can send in your father and Pat. I know they want to see you, too."

"Thanks, Mom."

Alex watched her go as he considered his situation. His life had been completely upended. Moving had been stressful enough on its own, but the last few months had nearly killed him. Literally. But he'd also grown so much in the process.

The gut churning fear he'd lived with for the last five years had evaporated at some point, despite actually being shot. Maria would always be in his heart, but instead of constricting tight around her memory he felt himself opening up like a flower under the sun. His kids were finally safe and Molly loved him, which made him feel more alive than he had in years.

And suddenly the most exciting part prickled the skin all over as he realized what was going to happen now. "Holy shit, I'm getting married!"

Chapter 38: Molly

"Molly McDill?"

"Yes?" Molly looked up from her book in the waiting room of the ICU while Alex visited with his family. The two older guys standing in front of her were clearly feds. Dark, wrinkled suits, scuffed shoes, short haircuts. *This is it.*

"My name is Special Agent Harris, with the FBI. This is Special Agent Garcia," he said, handing her a folding leather wallet with his photo ID and badge. "We need you to come with us, please. We have some questions to ask you."

Her personal Context Security guard, Anthony, muttered into his throat mic to put Larry's plan into motion. She had written her description of events with Context Security defense attorney, Alicia O'Donnell, in advance of the inevitable FBI investigation into Alex's shooting and aftermath. She and Roger knew they would be questioned about their actions, so it was prudent to be ready with a statement and representation. It was all part of the plan to keep them out of jail.

"Are we going to the field office on University Heights? I'd like my attorney to be present." Molly stood as she spoke and watched the agent's faces harden. *Deal with it.*

"Yes," Harris muttered with a dry tone.

"Fine, I'll meet you there."

"We'd prefer you come with us." He tried to intimidate her by stepping closer.

"Sorry, but unless I'm being detained, I'll stick with my own security detail." Molly nodded at Anthony, who crossed his arms and stared at the agents. "You're welcome to follow us over."

"We'll do that," Agent Garcia interrupted as Agent Harris opened his mouth.

"CS central, Sarge is on the move. Bring our transport around to the main hospital entrance," Anthony muttered into his throat mic. "We'll be down in five." If there was a response, it only went into his earpiece.

Molly felt her stomach churn as they kept pace ahead of the FBI agents who were holding a whispered conversation behind them. This was the one part of the plan where things could go really wrong for her and Roger.

Alex was protected by Texas' castle doctrine that allowed property owners to answer attacks with deadly force in their own home. She and Roger, on the other hand, had loaded up assault weapons and followed Troy with the clear intent to kill him if necessary to recover the kids. While many people would agree with her decision, the law was clear about the premeditated use of deadly force.

After they all got on the elevator, Anthony pushed the button to take them to the ground floor. The FBI agents rode with them, but did not appear to agree with each other about allowing Molly to drive herself to their office. Agent Harris looked to be biting his tongue while Agent Garcia shot him hard looks.

Anthony kept his hand on his sidearm as he walked Molly out of the hospital and into the waiting black SUV. It was similar to Alex's model, with all the same advanced protection and tracking equipment built in. Molly climbed into the back seat and let out a slow breath to calm her heart as Anthony shut the door. Anthony got into the passenger seat and nodded to the female driver.

"CS central, Sarge is en route to the FBI field office," the driver said.

The male voice that responded over the SUV's sound system made Molly jump. "Roger that. Let her know that Ms. O'Donnell will meet her there. Under no circumstances is she to make any statements or respond to any questions until Ms. O'Donnell arrives."

The driver glanced over her shoulder to see Molly's nod. "Roger that."

It was only a ten minute trip, but it felt like an hour. Molly chewed her nails the whole way, unable to sit still in the comfortable seat. When they arrived, the driver pulled up to the front entrance where a slim, red-haired woman stood in a smart skirt suit with a laptop bag over her shoulder.

"Molly," Alicia called as she approached. "Don't look so worried. You've got this."

"I hope *you've* got this, because I'm not even sure I have bladder control at this point."

Alicia laughed and put her arm around Molly's shoulder to usher her into the entrance of the field office. After going through security, Agents Harris and Garcia stood waiting with matching sour expressions on their faces.

"Gentlemen," Alicia crooned. "Let's get this business over with. Do you have somewhere we can speak privately? And perhaps you should invite someone capable of…" She paused while looking between the two men. "…making decisions."

"We have full authority to investigate this matter," Harris growled.

"I'm sure you do," Alicia said with a condescending lilt and lifted her hand to indicate they should lead the way. "So let's begin."

Molly and Alicia followed behind them into a small meeting room with six chairs around a rectangular table. Agent Garcia shut the door while Agent Harris sat at the head of the table and leaned back in the chair.

"Let's start at the beginning," Agent Harris said.

"No, let's not." Alicia sat at the opposite end of the table and nodded for Molly to sit next to her.

Molly eased down in the indicated chair and watched as her attorney pulled out an array of printed documents from her laptop bag.

"I want it noted that my client is here voluntarily but will not be answering any questions. I represent both Molly and Roger Dunlop, who have prepared complete statements of the events surrounding the attempted murder of Alex Thompson and Larry Hanover, and their heroic efforts to recover the children after they were kidnapped by Troy Moore…" She paused dramatically for a moment. "… at the direction of Mexican national, and infamous drug lord, Vizcarra de Cervantes."

She slid the printed papers across the table. Agent Garcia grabbed a copy and sat next to Agent Harris to review the statement. Molly watched their expressions shift as they skimmed through the pages. It was obvious when they got to certain parts, because they each looked up at her with raised eyebrows. Garcia looked impressed, but Harris frowned deeper.

"This is basically a confession to premeditated murder for both Ms. McDill and Mr. Dunlop, aided by your company's employee, Larry Hanover," Harris said, pushing the documents away from him.

"I admit that might be one way to interpret the situation," Alicia pondered with an amused smile.

"What other way is there?" Harris asked her while Garcia pulled the documents back to take another look.

"The way that Jenna Banks will on her network the moment you indict my clients. She will tell the whole story, including deep background on the de Cervantes family connections to organized crime, scene photos, diagrams, timelines… I've only seen the rough cut and it's *already* Pulitzer Prize winning material."

"Is that a threat?" Harris growled.

"No." Alicia gave a small shake of her head. "The threat is you indicting my client for the murder of Vizcarra de Cervantes, the leader of the San Fernando drug cartel, which obviously has the resources to execute and kidnap US citizens at will. The FBI was aware of the threat to Alex Thompson, and even issued a public statement last week, but failed to do *anything* to prevent this tragedy. If my clients hadn't acted as quickly as they did, the outcome would have resulted in the death of Molly's son and possibly Alex's twins. And that is exactly what Jenna's story will conclude as well."

"We need to call the Deputy Director," Garcia whispered to Harris. "This is way beyond our pay grade."

"You call whoever you want, but understand this—I will be defending my clients with *vigor*," Alicia pronounced the word with a fierce smile. "Come on, Molly. We're all done here."

CHAPTER 39: ALEX

Alex's eyes snapped open when the reporter on the twenty-four hour news channel mentioned that the bullet-riddled bodies of Troy Moore, Vizzy de Cervantes, and Raul Martinez had been discovered near the Mexican border. Alex had been dozing in his hospital bed most of the day, but this news story woke him up. A statement from the FBI claimed it was a drug deal gone wrong. Alex wasn't surprised to learn that Vizzy had ties to organized crime and drug trafficking, but he didn't buy the official explanation for a second.

Molly still hadn't explained what had happened while he was in surgery. His last clear memory of the night he was shot was Troy taking the twins. Alex's obvious assumption—in hindsight—was that Troy worked for Vizzy and had been the shadowy figure in the hallway who'd shot him. But Molly wouldn't tell him what had happened and it was driving him nuts.

Since Alex had finally been moved out of ICU and into a private room, Jenna had been by earlier that morning to record an interview for a follow-up piece. He was waiting for Molly to bring the kids over from the hotel to visit him for the first time when his phone rang. His attorney's name, Peter Jameson, showed on his phone below a picture of his old friend.

Alex answered the call, happy for the distraction, "Peter!"

"You're sounding better. I expected Molly to answer your phone again."

"Nope, I'm out of ICU now. I'm still sore as hell, but the pain is manageable. And with less pain meds, my brain must be starting to work again because I'm going stir crazy."

"Good, because I need to share some news with you," Peter said with a giddy excitement in his tone. "I figured out what Vizzy was up to. It took a while because the trust document was written in Spanish and I had to hire some help to go through it. It turns out the kids, or you as their guardian, should be able to petition the court in Mexico City to give you access to the safe deposit box right now."

"I thought they had to be thirty, married for ten years, and have kids, just like Maria's requirements?" Alex felt his heart rate increasing at the idea of finally getting to the bottom of everything.

"That may have been the intent, but the lawyer that drew up the trust used an 'or' when he should have used an 'and'. Maria technically satisfied the trust conditions when she turned thirty, married you, had kids, but then died before your tenth anniversary. So the kids didn't just inherit the trust from her, they got it with all the conditions already met."

"So what do I need to do?"

"I've got an attorney in Mexico ready to assist us, but basically I just need your signature as their guardian on a court document. Then we can get them to courier the box from Banamex in Mexico City to their branch near you in San Antonio."

"Don't we need that key Maria kept all these years?"

"I don't know anything about a key. It's not mentioned in the trust document. Maybe the box itself contains something that's locked? I've sent the document to the local Context Security office, so someone should be by for your signature today."

"Thanks, Peter," Alex sighed.

"I'll let you know when to expect it to arrive. I may have to fly out to see what the big secret is myself."

"You may have to fly over for more than that," Alex said as a grin spread across his face. "I'm engaged."

"What?" Peter exclaimed. "When the heck did this happen? Why didn't Molly tell me?"

"I know it's quick, but when it's right, it's right." Alex felt the truth of the words in his heart. "I proposed the night before I got shot. When I woke up here in the hospital, she gave me her answer. You up for being a groomsman again?"

"Be happy to," he said and Alex heard the humor in his voice. "And lemme guess, you're gonna get Larry to be your best man this time around?"

"The guy took a bullet for me and saved my life. Be kinda hard not to ask him after that," Alex teased.

"You set a date yet?" Peter asked.

"Nope, but I'm thinkin' about Thanksgiving since Mom, Dad, and Pat will be coming back to spend time with the kids."

"You *are* in a hurry!" Peter chuckled and sighed. "But it's good to see you happy again, and it'll be... good to see your family."

Alex recalled the sparks the last time Peter and Pat had been around each other. Those two were oil and water, so it hadn't been the good kind of sparks.

There was a noisy commotion in the hallway that Alex recognized as the sound of excited kids. "Speaking of happy, I think I hear the kids coming. I'll talk to you later."

"Hug 'em for me!"

Alex had just put the phone down when the twins burst through the door. "Daddy! Daddy!"

Manny and Hannah climbed the bed in an instant and were in his arms. Ignoring the pain of his wound, Alex took a deep breath of their familiar scents as he hugged them tight. "Oh, I missed you so much."

Looking up, he saw Molly holding Will's hand. Will wouldn't look up at Alex. Molly's mouth was pressed in a thin line of worry. When she caught Alex's eye and mouthed, *He saw Troy on the news.*

"Hey, Will, you wanna come up and give me a hug?" Alex asked through his kids' excited babel. "I missed you, too, ya know."

Nodding, Will wiped his nose as Molly helped him climb up on the bed. Hannah made room to let him get closer to Alex.

"His daddy got shot, too," Hannah whispered loud enough for everyone to hear.

"I know," Alex said as he pulled Will closer with his good arm to hold him tight. "I'm so sorry that happened."

Manny rubbed Will's back. "But remember he saved us from the bad guys that were coming to get Daddy."

Alex shot a questioning look at Molly. She nodded and raised her eyebrows, letting Alex know this was something he needed to back her up on for Will's sake. "He sure did," Alex said. "But I bet that doesn't make losing him any easier."

"Mom says he might have done some bad things, but that didn't make him a bad Dad." Will had obviously heard the news about the shootout at the border.

"She's right," Alex said, torn between his own anger at what Troy had done to his family and Will's loss. He pushed himself to be there for the boy he'd grown so close to. "And you can always remember the good things he did."

Saying kind words about Troy tore him up, but Alex suspected Troy *had* loved his son. When Alex looked up at Molly, she was wiping her eyes with an overly bright smile.

"He did, baby. In his own way, I know he loved you more than anyone else in the world."

"I wish we could share our Daddy with you," Hannah whispered, and shot a wounded look at Molly. Clearly her abrupt refusal to his marriage proposal hadn't been forgotten and Molly hadn't told the kids about her change of heart.

"It wouldn't be the same, though," Will whispered into Alex's chest.

"I know," Alex said as he pressed his cheek into Will's hair. "Guess what, though?"

"What?" Will asked as he wiped his nose again and looked up.

"The greatest thing about love is that it never stops growing. I love both Manny and Hannah the same, even though they're totally different. Even though I loved their mother, Maria, with all my heart, that doesn't mean I never get to love again." Alex looked up at Molly with his throat squeezing tight. "And even if it's not exactly the same, it doesn't have to be. Love will grow anywhere you let it."

All three kids looked up at him with thoughtful expressions, but Alex only had eyes for Molly at that moment.

"That's why I changed my mind," Molly whispered without taking her eyes off Alex's face.

Hannah was the first to figure out what she meant and sucked in a sudden gasp of air. When Will and Manny looked at her, she cried, "She wants to be our Mom!"

"Miss Molly?" Manny looked up in wonder, then back at his dad. "Does that mean Will can be my brother?"

Molly nodded. "If we all decide to be a family, then yes."

"Will, Molly, would you like to make a family with us?" Alex asked as his heart hammered in his chest. He didn't want to say the next bit, but felt like he had to. "We don't have to if you don't want to. We'll still be friends and neighbors no matter what."

"Would Mom and I have to live in your house with you?" Will asked, his face showing hope warring with the pain he obviously felt.

"If you like," Alex said. "Or we could fix up your house and all live there if you wanted. Or maybe we could even live in both houses." He shrugged to show Will he was fine with any decision. "We don't even have to decide today, but I think you and your Mom are really special."

"Maybe we could try," Will murmured as he watched Manny and Hannah grin at him. He looked up at his Mom. "Could we try?"

"Yes," she sighed out in relief and joined the family on Alex's hospital bed. She reached around to hug all three kids. "Yes, we can try."

Chapter 40: Molly

The hospital's healing garden had raised beds of fragrant flowers. The yellow blooms waved as bees bumbled along from one to the next. Colorful kinetic sculptures made soft tinkling sounds in the light breeze. After the madness of the previous two weeks, Molly relaxed in the peaceful atmosphere on the wooden bench next to her husband-to-be.

"Penny for your thoughts?" Alex asked.

She looked over to take in his warm smile. Alex looked like his old self, albeit a little slimmer after his ordeal. He was wearing a loose white cotton t-shirt that hid the bandages over his healing chest and back wounds.

They had made a habit of getting out of the hospital room for a little private time each afternoon. The staff had encouraged Alex to get the exercise and, because the private garden had only one entrance into the atrium courtyard, their security detail didn't object.

"Just enjoying the quiet with you," Molly smiled.

Alex squeezed his arm tight around her shoulders, pulling her close enough to place a soft kiss on the top of her head. "So are you ever gonna tell me what happened?"

Molly shivered. After tucking her feet under herself on the bench, she leaned in to place her open hand over his heart and listened to Alex breathe for a moment. "What do you want to know?"

"The last thing I remember clearly was Troy taking the kids. I also remember seeing Larry leaning over me in the helicopter, but it's really sketchy. Then I woke up here after surgery. What happened in between?"

"After the helicopter took you and Larry off, I got cleaned up and went after Troy. Larry had placed a GPS tracker on his car when he came into town just in case. Roger came with me. We found him on his family hunting lease down near the border." The memories rushed through her, tearing her heart open again in the process. She wiped the silent tears from her cheeks and pinched her lips tight.

"So, no drug deal gone wrong?" Alex prompted as she gathered herself. "I'm sorry you had to do that to Troy. Even if you hated him for taking Will, I know you loved him once."

"I didn't do anything to Troy, though," Molly whispered as she looked Alex in the eye, hoping her news wouldn't change what they had started. "You did."

Molly watched his face carefully as he absorbed that information. Alex blinked and a frown slowly formed on his lips.

Molly had killed men in combat, but she remembered every single time she'd used deadly force with a heartbreaking clarity. The first time had been during an insurgent action and her training forced her hand to fire before she had time to think. The threat had been immediate, and her reaction saved her life and those around her. But afterwards she wondered about the man that attacked them. He had been a living person one moment and a second later, he was gone. Maybe his mother would cry for him. Maybe a child had been left as fatherless as she had been.

While she didn't regret anything, killing someone had undeniably changed her. Watching Alex process her revelation was hard because she knew it would change him, too. The confusion lifted and he looked away at nothing. His eyebrows dropped and his mouth hardened into that stubborn line she had grown to love. It was the same expression he'd had when he announced he was going out to work on the fence after that first attempt on his life.

"Well, shit."

"Troy was dead when we got there. Agent Garcia thinks he had a brain aneurysm at some point after he parked there to wait for Vizzy. Being shot can cause a spike in blood pressure that can burst weak blood vessels. Anyway, when you returned fire in the hallway, you hit him in the upper chest." Molly stopped abruptly to keep herself from babbling and allow Alex the chance to think.

Alex looked up with a thoughtful look on his face. "Poor Will."

Molly felt a fresh wave of tears rising. Alex's immediate reaction to worry about her son captured exactly why she loved him so much.

"The kids assumed Troy was saving them from *bad guys*, and I didn't have the heart to tell them the truth."

Alex nodded. "It would only hurt Will more for no good reason. What happened to Vizzy and that other guy?"

"We didn't know Troy was dead at first, so Roger was circling around to get a closer look. Vizzy drove up while I watched and sent his guy over to check on Troy. When they discovered he was dead, Vizzy told him to get your twins and kill my son."

"What a piece of shit," Alex growled. "I still can't believe it was him all this time."

"Roger fired before the guy could do anything, and I shot Vizzy before he could drive away."

The pair sat in silence for a few minutes. Molly wondered what else Alex was thinking, but didn't want to disrupt his thoughts quite yet. She waited until he was ready to keep talking.

"Why did the FBI say it was a drug deal gone wrong?" Alex finally asked.

"That was all Larry and Jenna." Molly took a deep breath before letting it out slowly. "Larry started an investigation into Vizzy right after he showed up at your housewarming party. Between Context Security and Jenna's network resources, they were able to put all the pieces together before the FBI came to talk to us about what happened."

"Good ol' Larry," Alex chuckled. "I owe him and Jenna so much after all this. I take it the leverage helped?"

"Yeah, definitely. The attorney from Context Security gave the FBI full statements from Larry, Roger, and me. If the FBI had brought an indictment against me for killing Vizzy, it would have brought the San Fernando cartel down on all of us. Then the attorney mentioned Jenna had a big exposé ready to air the day they filed charges against any of us that made the FBI look like a bunch of idiots. They had issued a press release that said they were investigating after Jenna's first report, remember? And they never did anything. Luckily, they backed down and agreed not to prosecute."

"Damn," Alex whispered and shook his head. "So, what happens now?"

"We get you out of the hospital tomorrow, go home, and get married." Her stomach churned as she looked into Alex's face. "I hope."

He stared in her eyes for a moment, then lowered his lips to hers. The kiss warmed her all the way through as he opened his mouth to taste her. He had shaved that morning, but the afternoon stubble was already rough against her skin. She reached up to run her fingers into his messy hair just as his phone rang and interrupted the moment.

"Sorry," he muttered, pulling himself away from her as he dug out his phone. "Hey, Peter."

Molly listened to Alex's half of the conversation without much interest. He was mostly humming and giving one word replies until he hung up.

"Good news?" Molly asked.

"Yes," Alex said as he put his phone away and pulled her into his arms. "Peter figured out why Vizzy wanted the twins. Maria's grandfather wrote Vizzy out of his will and left a mysterious trust to her alone. The kids inherited it, but their guardian remains the executor until they grow up. Vizzy wanted to be their guardian to steal their inheritance."

Molly nodded and looked away. She knew Alex was wealthy enough that he didn't seem to worry about money, but they'd never talked about it. The idea his kids had a trust fund wasn't that surprising either given what she'd read about the de Cervantes family.

"What's in the trust?" she asked at last.

"Beats me," Alex sighed. "We never had access before, but the circumstances of Maria's death satisfied the restrictions that were on it. The trust document refers to a safe deposit box, but doesn't disclose what's in it. When Peter figured out there were no more restrictions, he got a judge down in Mexico to order it released to us. Banamex is shipping it to the branch here in San Antonio. Wanna go with me tomorrow to see what's in it after I get out of here?"

Molly blinked, surprised at being asked to be a part of something so big. "Sure."

The thought of money brought back her own financial concerns. She hadn't worked since before he'd been shot, so she was obviously out of a job at this point. The bills were overdue at home, but she couldn't bring herself to leave. Living in the hotel and spending all her time with the kids and Alex kept her from thinking about her situation, but now it was impossible to ignore how broke she was.

Her worry must have shown through her face because Alex looked at her with concern. "You okay?" He asked as he moved a few stray hairs out of her face.

"I just realized I need to figure out what I'm gonna do when we get home."

"I thought we'd settled it," Alex chuckled. "You, me, the kids… happily ever after and all that."

"Are you really sure?" Molly asked with a tremor in her voice. She was embarrassed to admit how broke she really was, but he needed to know before they got married. "I lost my job. I'm behind on every bill. The house is a freakin' money pit. My son is heartbroken." Tears finally spilled over as she admitted it, "My life is a mess, Alex."

"But you're *my* mess," he whispered to her with a small smile on his lips. "Besides, we're getting married. Whatever I have is yours. We can fix up your house if you want. You can find another job if you want to, but I have more than enough to keep us going for the foreseeable future."

"What does that mean?" Molly didn't want to come off like a gold digger, but she was too curious to contain herself.

"Well, not to pat myself on the back or anything, but I was a pretty successful investment manager. You know I sold my business to move out here. I invested the proceeds but I haven't checked my portfolio since last month. Assuming the market didn't crash while I wasn't paying attention, we should have around ten million."

Molly felt her heart pounding at his casual mention of more money than she could ever imagine. "Dollars?"

Alex grinned at her. "Yes."

"Ten million dollars." Repeating it didn't make it feel any more real.

"Yeah," Alex shrugged, then pulled out his wallet and phone. "I'll get you a card in your name so you can take care of the immediate bills, then I'll add you on my accounts later."

Did this mean she was rich now, too? She sat up while Alex dug a card out of his wallet and called the number on the back. The hairs were standing up all over her body. She had always dreamed of having money, but had never imagined what it would actually feel like to not have debt weighing down her life.

Despite the disparity between them, Alex had always treated her as an equal. In fact, he treated everyone they'd been around like an equal. He accepted his neighbors' offer of help when he could have just paid to put the fence up from the beginning. His kids still had chores even though Molly was helping out around the house. In fact, he'd even folded the kids clothes with her. The idea of a millionaire sitting around folding his kids underwear made her head spin, but it was just like Alex to jump in and help.

She watched him speaking to the credit card company as her love for him spilled over. He had always helped her without making her feel inferior or pitied. He was generous with all their friends, but not in a showy way. Now he was going to marry her, a poor single mom, without any obvious worry or concern she would take advantage of him.

"Okay," Alex said as he put his phone and wallet away again. "There will be a card at the front desk of the hotel tomorrow morning. Spend what you need to get caught up, but start to think about what you might want to do next."

"What do you mean?"

"Well, I'm done with investing, but I still want to *do* something. Maybe raise horses. Grow heirloom tomatoes. I don't know. What have you always wanted to do?"

Molly sat back to think for a minute. "I always wanted to fix up Nanny's house for Will. but I still want to do as much of the work myself as I can. Repairs, painting, decorating, the works."

"If we're gonna live in my house for now, we could turn yours into a bed and breakfast if you wanted." Alex said nonchalantly. "That reminds me, I need to get that arbor gate put in the fence between our houses. Oh, and I also promised to help Terry dig out a bigger pond for his cattle when he came to help with the fence. And Roger wanted to fix up that picnic area by the creek."

Molly smiled as Alex continued to list his tasks after their return home as if he had been on a trip instead of in the hospital with a gunshot wound through his chest. Maybe a bed and breakfast would be a good idea. She could imagine the big house returned to its former glory, full of happy families and guests. They could even turn it into a family business and get the kids working there as they grew up.

"What would we call it?" Molly asked as her imagination took off. She hadn't realized Alex was still rambling about chores until she cut him off mid-sentence, but he didn't seem to mind.

"Call what?"

"The bed and breakfast." Molly stated, her eyes shining with enthusiasm.

Alex smiled at Molly, gazing into her eyes. "You're cute when you get excited about something."

"Like you and your fence?" Molly grinned. It was ironic that something meant to separate their properties was the very thing that had brought them together. It may have started as his summer project, but his determination to finish it in the face of the threats had made it so much more. And now he was offering to open a gate in that fence just for her and Will so they could join his family. The beautiful symbolism brought a possible name to mind.

"Hey, how about the Arbor Gate Bed and Breakfast?"

"I think that sounds perfect." Alex gave her a sweet kiss to bless her idea. "I love it."

"And I love you," Molly said as she ran her palm along his cheek. "How the hell did I get so lucky?"

"We both are."

Chapter 41: Alex

Alex watched Molly stuff the last of his clothes into the duffle bag on his hospital bed. "You ready to get out of here?" she asked him.

He nodded as she swung the bag's strap over her shoulder. Relief that he was being released from the hospital warred with the excitement of beginning the next phase of his life—of their lives together.

"Where are the kids this afternoon?" he asked.

"Uncle Larry and Aunt Jenna took them to the water park with Christopher and Noah. Hannah complained all morning that it wasn't fair that Jen and Lisa couldn't come, but apparently they've had some kind of stomach bug running through their family." Molly rolled her eyes and headed for the door. Two Context Security guards waited in the hallway just outside and one took Alex's bag from her.

"I think Uncle Larry's been avoiding me," Alex said as he followed Molly into the hallway. It had been two weeks since he'd been shot. While he'd seen evidence of Larry's presence everywhere, his friend hadn't come by once to visit.

Troy's first bullet had left Larry with a concussion, but he'd been released from the hospital after one day. He was supposed to have been on bed rest for two weeks, but he wasn't resting much from what Alex saw. He'd handled the research into Vizzy's drug cartel, arranged for Molly's legal defense, and now was at a water park with their kids, no doubt acting as a part of their security detail.

Molly glanced at the guards trailing them to the elevator before leaning in closer to whisper, "I think Larry blames himself for what happened. Honestly, I blame myself, too. If I had trusted my gut about Troy, none of this would have happened."

"No, you can't know that. We might have figured out Vizzy was behind everything sooner, but it wouldn't have stopped him. This played out as well as it could've, given what we were up against."

"That's what I keep telling myself. And what Jenna and I have both been telling Larry. But this has really shaken him up. He just needs some time to work through things before he can face you, I think."

It still stung Alex that his best friend would cut him off. Alex hadn't even been able to ask if he'd be the best man at their wedding yet. As if sensing his mood shift, Molly took his hand and interlaced her fingers with his. He gave her a grudging smile, then stopped to press the button to call the elevator. She hugged his arm while they waited.

"I bet you'll see Larry later today when he drops the kids off at the hotel." Molly commented as the security guards led them into the empty elevator when it arrived. "Is Peter meeting us here or at the bank?"

"At the bank. He called earlier to let me know he'd arrived and was getting his rental car." Alex caught a worried look on Molly's face. "You okay?"

"A little nervous," she admitted. "I mean, he's an old friend of yours. Do I look okay? Are you sure you want me there?"

Alex admired her slim jeans and bright green top. Her golden brown hair wasn't pulled back into a tail today. Instead it flowed down around her shoulders, framing her face. She had on a bit more makeup than she usually wore and the touch of green eyeshadow matched her top. His attention prompted Molly to display a self-conscious smile.

"You're lovely," he whispered as the elevator stopped to let them off on the ground floor.

Their guards moved ahead of them out of the elevator, sweeping the lobby as they made their way to the SUV parked at the hospital entrance. Alex felt like a weight was being lifted off of him as he passed through the glass sliding doors. The sunlight was hot, but Alex lifted his face to the sky as they paused for the guard to open the rear door of the vehicle.

I survived.

Once they were together in the back seat of the SUV, Alex pulled Molly close and took a deep breath as he nuzzled his face into her hair. She turned her face towards him, inviting the soft kiss he soon placed on her lips. They hadn't been intimate yet and it was driving Alex a little crazy. When he was recovering it hadn't bothered him so much. But as he healed, her loving attention and the lack of privacy in the hospital had kept him in a constant state of arousal.

"If you keep that up, you're gonna be in trouble when I finally get you alone," Molly purred into his cheek.

"I'm already in trouble," he whispered back. "You smell too good to stop."

"Be careful or I'll make you wait until our wedding night," Molly teased.

"Maybe I'll make *you* wait until our wedding night." Alex pulled back enough to give her a steady look. "I've already waited five years. What's another couple of months?"

"I was only kidding." She laughed before cocking an eyebrow as she studied him for a moment. "You're not actually serious, are you?"

He held in his laugh as long as he could, but his silent chuckle gave him away at last.

"Thank God," she whispered as she leaned into him. Alex squirmed as she traced her tongue along the curve of his ear. When his whole ear was wet, she uttered a breathy whisper, "We need to pick up condoms."

"Why?" Alex was still shivering when she leaned back to study him again. He didn't know if it was the thoughtless question or her warm tongue that made his heart race. "I mean, if you want to, sure. We'll get some."

"Do you want more kids?" she asked, and Alex couldn't tell her preference from her tone or expression. The bald question shocked him, but he should have expected it since they hadn't discussed their future in much detail yet.

"Before I met you I never even wanted to get married again," he said as he studied her reaction, but she still didn't give anything away.

"I didn't think you'd be willing to risk it again." Molly spoke gently, her expression softening.

Alex took her hands as he prepared to tell her the whole truth. "I'm not willing to live my life afraid anymore. Maria's family had a history of difficult pregnancies. Does yours?"

"No." Molly blinked back the tears beginning to pool in her eyes.

"We're getting married. For me that means we're together all the way. If you don't want any more kids, then I'll love the ones we've got with no regrets. But I have to admit the idea of you with our baby inside…" He smiled slowly as her lips curved up to match his. "Yeah, I'd love to have more kids with you."

"Okay. Good. No condoms then." She leaned in to give him a hungry, wanton kiss that took away his breath.

"Just remember I'm a little out of practice," Alex whispered, holding his performance anxiety at bay as she moved to his neck. "And I still get out of breath pretty easy."

"We've got plenty of time for practice," she whispered. "We may even have enough time at the hotel before the kids come back this afternoon. And I'll take care of the hard work if you take care of the other hard thing…"

"Oh, that sounds good," he murmured as all his blood rushed from one head to the other. "We definitely need to hurry back."

The rest of the drive to the Banamex branch took half an hour, but Alex was content to spend the time with Molly in his arms. His parents and sister had already left San Antonio when it became obvious he would recover, but they had promised to return at Thanksgiving for the wedding. He was getting married, and the thought constantly brought an irrepressible grin to his lips.

It had been amazing to watch the change in the kids since they announced their intentions. Manny and Hannah had dropped their polite *Miss Molly* in favor of *Molly Mom*. Will still called him *Mister Alex*, but he no longer held himself back like he had immediately after finding out about Troy's death. When they all came to the hospital for their daily visit, Will expected his hugs and attention right along with the twins.

His thoughts turned back to Larry as they sped along I-10. Alex owed his friend so much for his support and protection over the years, and especially for his help recovering the kids and keeping Molly out of jail. They had all underestimated the threat, not just Larry.

Maybe it was easier to be philosophical about the situation now that Vizzy was dead, but Alex knew Larry had done all he could do. If a couple of weeks in the hospital and two scars were what it cost for his new life, Alex was happy to pay it. Larry didn't need to feel responsible, but it wasn't hard to understand why he did.

They had exited off the interstate and were driving through a shopping center when Alex spotted the Banamex sign. The branch was a small freestanding building set apart from a large retail shopping center. When the guard parked the SUV, Molly leaned away to allow Alex to open the rear door and step out.

"Peter," Alex sang as he embraced the stout, muscular man who had walked up at their arrival. "Good to see you, man."

"You're looking better than I thought you would for just being shot," Peter said as he pulled back to look his friend over, then looked over his shoulder at Molly climbing out of the SUV. "And you must be the reason."

"Molly McDill," she said as she extended her hand to him.

"Screw that, I'm a hugger," Peter laughed and pulled her into a warm embrace.

Alex winked at Molly over Peter's shoulder. "I told you he'd like you."

"What's not to like! She saved one of my oldest and dearest friends, not to mention my godson and goddaughter." Peter was a bit shorter than Molly and smiled directly into her face. "Thank you, my dear. You've brought my old friend back from the brink in more ways than one."

"It's mutual," Molly said, Alex noticing her eyes flickering to him briefly. "He's the best."

Peter turned and put his hands on their backs. "I agree, but your security guys are looking twitchy with you two standing out here in the parking lot. Let's go see what all this has been about, eh?"

A finely dressed man was waiting for them as they entered the small bank building. "I am Jorge Mantegna, the manager of this branch," he greeted them with a nod of his head. "Alex Thompson?"

"That's me," Alex nodded as he extended his hand. "Nice to meet you, Jorge."

"We're ready for you near the vault. Just let me get your photo identification and we'll begin."

It only took a few moments for Alex to prove his identity, then they were led to a small room near the open vault door. Jorge led them to an old metal deposit box, that appeared to be sealed with lead, sitting in the middle of a table. Next to it were a metal chisel and hammer.

"I've been instructed to allow you to inspect the seal before I open it." Jorge extended his hand towards the box and stepped back.

Alex examined the box and saw an imprint of a key in the lead that covered the seal. "I bet that matches the key Maria kept," Alex said to Peter.

"I bet you're right," Peter agreed as he snapped a few photos of the box with his camera. "Let me get a shot of the imprint and we'll compare it later."

When Peter stepped back, Alex nodded to Jorge to open the seal. Jorge took the chisel and hammer and began to remove the lead in pieces. When he had cleared the seam, the top of the metal box opened to reveal two formal looking documents embossed with the de Cervantes family crest.

Alex took the documents from the box and saw the words *La Escritura del Isla de Cervantes*. "Peter, what's *Escritura*?"

Taking the document, Peter scanned the first page with his eyebrows raising slowly. "Uh… this appears to be the deed…" He looked up at Alex with a growing grin. "…to Isla de Cervantes."

That was the island Maria's family had lived on for generations and served as the flagship of their resort empire. Alex felt lightheaded as he realized what it meant for his kids. They were going to be wealthy beyond belief someday.

Glancing back down at the remaining document in his hand he saw *Certificado de Acciones de Lujo Jugar* and a very large number—250,000. Alex wasn't fluent, but his years working with the de Cervantes stock portfolio told him this was a stock certificate for a quarter million shares of common stock in their resort empire, Lujo Jugar.

"What's the other one?" Molly asked as she looked over their shoulders at the two documents.

"Probably about a quarter of a billion dollars all totalled," Alex whispered as he took the deed back from Peter. His hands shook as he realized what this would mean for the twins in the future. And that was without counting Connie and Rubin's part of the family estate.

"God, no wonder Vizzy wanted your kids," Molly whispered, her face slack with shock.

"I think Maria's Papi had the right idea," Alex said as his brain spun. His biggest fear was what would happen if his kids got all the assets at once when they turned eighteen. "Peter, can we wrap these assets up in another trust? Same conditions as Maria's, but with the error in that one clause fixed and some protections for the kids."

"As the trustee, you can petition the courts and argue the new trust matches the spirit of the original trust. What about the protections?" Peter asked.

"If someone murders me or the twins, everything gets liquidated and all the proceeds are donated to charity." Alex raged at the idea someone would try to murder his family again over this.

Peter shrugged and said, "We can only ask the court in Mexico. I'll draft it, but you need to do something about these assets now. The stock needs to be in a separate trust-owned account, but you also need to formally register the deed to the trust as well. If something happens to this piece of paper before you do, you'll be up to your ears in paperwork and legal invoices."

"We can stop by my bank on the way back to the hotel," Alex said. "The kids will be back soon and I have some things I need to discuss with Molly." When Alex looked over at Molly, she was suppressing a smile that Peter caught as well.

"I'll email you a draft of the updated trust. Take a look and let me know what you think." Peter patted Alex on the back, then hugged Molly one more time. Whatever he said in her ear made her laugh and push him away. "I'll see you at Thanksgiving if we don't get together before then."

After Peter left the small room, Alex raised an eyebrow at Molly but she just took his hand and led him out with a laugh.

Chapter 42: Molly

Molly's mind was still reeling when she walked through the door to the suite she and the kids had been sharing. Alex had stopped at his bank to put the deed and stock certificate in his safe deposit box. Then he'd surprised her by adding her name to his checking and saving accounts. Since her biggest credit card was through the same bank, he paid that off just before they left with a swipe and signature. Now they had a joint credit card and debit card, and their new checks, in both of their names, would be arriving in less than a week at the house.

Alex followed Molly into the room, and he paused for a moment to shut and lock the suite door while the Context Security guards remained in the hallway. Molly stood rooted in the middle of the room, anxiety spread across her face and she wasn't quite sure why. When Alex turned around, his broad smile faded a little at the expression on her face.

"You okay?" Alex asked with a touch of worry in his tone.

"A little overwhelmed, maybe," she whispered. He was generous, handsome, and wonderful with their kids, so why was she suddenly feeling so afraid?

"Wanna talk about it?" He took her hands and pulled her closer, running his hands up her arms.

"Are you sure about all this?" she asked, wincing at the pain in his eyes at her question. "I mean, when we were home, just us and the kids, everything made sense to me. The last couple of weeks have felt like some kind of crazy roller coaster ride. After today… I mean, you just… I never really knew you were so… *rich*."

"You make it sound like a disease." Alex's grip on her arms relaxed.

"I know it's not," she said in a panic. "It's just a shock to see it spelled out with so many zeros. All of a sudden, I'm terrified and I don't know why."

Molly looked into his eyes, and Alex searched her face for a moment, then pulled her into a tight embrace. "What can I do?"

"I don't know," Molly whimpered, tears brimming in her eyes from being so suddenly overwhelmed. "It just feels like I'm losing control of my life and I'm not sure how to hold on. I love you and the kids, but everything is changing so fast. The plans I made for my life a month ago are gone. I had finally figured out how to pay down my debt and was getting ahead for the first time in years. Then everything happened and you got shot… and I lost my job. And now, in one day, the debt is gone. It makes me feel like a failure because it was so easy for you to fix everything that I couldn't fix after trying for years."

She broke down into tears, crying hard against Alex's shoulder. He rubbed her back and kissed her hair. The outpouring of emotion was like a dam burst. Molly had never felt weak or helpless as she struggled through daily life before. In a perverse way, being a hard-working single mom had defined who she was. Now that Alex had blown into her life and changed all the rules, Molly felt unanchored and lost. Despite loving this man, she was having trouble grasping what that meant.

"I've had a lot of time to think while I was lying in that hospital bed the last couple of weeks," Alex whispered. "You've been busy keeping our kids fed and entertained. Taking care of me. Worrying about going to jail. Hell, if it weren't for you I'd probably be dead and my kids would be with that psychopath in Mexico by now. If you need some more time, Molly, then we'll take it. I never meant to make you feel this way."

Molly was quiet for a few moments. She tried to steady her breathing as she calmed down. "Thank you," she whispered. "I really don't know why I'm so scared."

"When was the last time you had someone you could count on who didn't let you down?"

The question stopped her for a moment as she thought. "Pawpaw, probably."

"And now you help take care of your Nanny. You've kept up with that enormous house she left Will, on a shoestring budget. And you've been solely responsible for raising your son. Then I move in next door, stir up a hornet's nest of trouble, and nearly die on you." Alex pushed back a little to look in her eyes. "No wonder you're scared."

Seeing the understanding in his expression made Molly's chest feel tight and her chin quiver. "I don't want to be, though."

"I know, but you can't just change how you feel because you don't like it," Alex said with a weary sigh. "Hey, I don't know about you, but I'm wiped out. Why don't we take a little nap. I bet everything'll look better after a nap."

"I *knew* you were pushing too hard for your first day out of the hospital." Molly speared him with a worried look. "Come on, the kids won't be back for a couple of hours."

She led Alex into the bedroom she'd been sleeping in for the last two weeks and closed the door. After dragging the comforter off the king-sized bed, she pulled the sheets back and tugged Alex in after her. He grunted as he collapsed into the soft mattress, toeing his shoes off the side of the bed.

"Come here," Alex whispered to her as he rolled over and pulled her back against his chest.

With one if his arms under her pillow and his other over her shoulder, she snuggled back against him with her own contented sigh. His breath tickled the hairs along her neck and sent chills down her arm. He rubbed his hand over her stomach one last time, then tucked his fingers between her side and the mattress.

His breathing evened out as he settled, but Molly couldn't relax. Knowing he was right didn't banish the fear she felt. She couldn't trust her own heart, and the strongest evidence of that was Troy's betrayals. First he'd left her with a baby to go play mercenary, then he'd stolen her son when he came back to kill Alex.

What if Alex got tired of her? Or what if he began to resent her son as he grew? Could she take the risk that he'd never hurt them? And if he did break things off, she had nothing left to fall back on, just like when Troy left. Her heart wanted to believe in Alex. Her head argued to trust him as much as he obviously trusted her. But it was her body that finally put the torment to rest.

Without really thinking about it, she'd been nervously rocking her hips against Alex while she worried. In his sleep, he began to rub against her. Then his lower hand slid up to cup her breast. While their temperature rose, she felt her core melt until his body responded.

When Alex held his arousal against her, she stopped thinking clearly. His breath quickened, but she didn't realize he'd woken completely until his fingertips squeezed her nipple. She couldn't stop the moan when he gently bit her shoulder and splayed his other hand down across her stomach.

Using his hand for leverage, he pushed his erection into her. She turned her face back towards him as his lips travelled along her neck to nip at her earlobe. Sparks shot down her body to swirl around her stomach as his hand moved lower. She lifted her leg to rest it on top of him, allowing him access to her heat.

"You feel so good," Alex whispered against her cheek as he rubbed between her thighs.

"More," Molly purred.

She unbuttoned her jeans, unzipping them enough for his fingers to reach into her panties. Her fingers guided his down and pressed him into the wet heat that waited there. That brought a gasp from them both.

With an aching slowness, Alex pressed his fingertips in circles where she needed them most. His touch wasn't hurried, but her breathing sped up as they rocked together. She wanted to feel him inside, but didn't want to move from his warm embrace yet. They spiraled higher, both of them breathing faster as Alex's fingers brought her closer to a quick end.

"So good," she breathed as her muscles began to tense.

Molly found it impossible to worry with Alex touching her like that. His soft kisses along her jaw communicated the love he felt more than words. She arched her back and held her breath, the peak moment stretching beyond time as she saw stars behind her closed eyelids. Alex kept the steady motion throughout her orgasm, humming his pleasure in her ear while she cried out hers. When she collapsed back against him with sweat beaded on her face, Alex pulled his arms tight around her to hold her shivering body still.

"What an amazing way to wake up," Alex whispered.

"Feel free to do that again anytime you want." She panted quietly.

Molly moved away to loosen his grip, then turned in his arms. She kissed his open mouth and pressed him to roll on his back. While she kissed him with a hunger she hadn't felt in years, her hands were busy opening the button and zipper on his jeans.

She broke the kiss long enough to pull his jeans and underwear down, taking his socks along with them as they passed his feet. Alex sat up to pull his shirt off, exposing the pink, puckered scar on his chest. Other than that singular imperfection, he had tight muscles and an attractive scattering of hair across his chest and down his stomach. Seeing him fully aroused made her fingers tremble as she stroked his impressive girth.

Unable to wait any longer, Molly lifted her own shirt off, exposing old battle scars as well. She smiled when he couldn't take his eyes off her breasts long enough to notice any of her own imperfections. After pushing off her jeans and panties, she climbed on top of Alex to kiss him again. Holding his face between her hands, she forced his chin up to kiss down his neck, then back up to his panting mouth.

When she couldn't take it anymore, Molly sat up and moved back against his firm shaft with a sigh, filling herself with him as her flesh prickled from the pleasure. Alex groaned a warning and gripped her hips to keep her from moving for a moment. He began breathing again with his eyes half-open and lower lip pinched between his teeth. Alex released his hold, moving his hands up her stomach to cup both of her breasts and thumb her erect nipples.

Molly moved then, giving them both time to warm like butter, slowly melting in a pan. Eyes locked together, she read his expression as she moved, gauging how fast or slow to move by how hard he bit his lip. She was focused on his pleasure, but enjoyed her own as well. As she built back up to the dizzy heights she'd just left, he stared up at her with loving wonder.

When he squeezed both her nipples at the same time, she had to bite her own lip. The pace was easy, but the pleasure was all the more intense for it. Feeling every inch of him, she let herself go again, knowing he would follow quickly. Her orgasm was still clenching her core when he shut his eyes to cry out. She bent down to capture his mouth with hers, welcoming his release deep inside her body.

She collapsed on top of him at the end and her heart finally accepted that this wonderful man would never hurt her or Will. The evidence was in both his patience and his passion. However it had happened, he wanted her just the way she was. The fear that had been shadowing her was blown away, like fog in the bright morning sunlight.

Just as she started falling asleep on his chest, the front door exploded open with the sounds of happy children.

"Shit!" Molly slipped off the bed, snatching a quick kiss on the way to lock the bedroom door.

"Hey, at least they didn't come a half-hour ago," Alex chuckled as he rolled to the edge of the bed and pushed himself up.

She smiled at her husband-to-be as they tossed each other articles of clothing. Her heart was overflowing when she whispered, "I love you."

"Love you, too," Alex said as he stood to button his jeans, his face flushed with pleasure but his expression full of peace. "Now let's grab the kids and go get something to eat. I'm starved."

Chapter 43: Alex

After dressing quickly and unlocking the bedroom door, Alex and Molly walked out into the chaos in the suite's living area. The kids ran up, hugging them both and describing their adventure at the waterpark at once with excited voices. Manny, Hannah, and Noah all looked like they'd been dusted in cinnamon from the sun, but Will's pink tint betrayed his Scottish roots. Alex and Molly sat down on the couch to give them a chance to run through their day, asking clarifying questions when needed.

Alex loved the big smiles on all the kids faces; they had clearly had a blast. Looking over, Christopher was relaxing in a chair with an echoing grin on his face. Larry and Jenna were sitting together on the loveseat, smiling indulgently at the kids' enthusiasm. Jenna gave Alex a wink, but Larry didn't meet his eyes.

"So, have you guys eaten dinner yet?" Alex asked with real enthusiasm. He was starving, especially after the wonderful way Molly woke him from his nap.

"Not yet. We wanted to order a pizza. Can we watch a movie before we go to bed?" Manny asked in his typical, rapid fire way.

"I'll sit with them if you guys wanted to go out and grab a bite," Christopher offered.

"Are you sure you don't mind?" Jenna asked him. Her windswept hair and casual outfit weren't her usual style, but Alex thought Jenna looked more relaxed and happy than he'd ever seen her. The affectionate way her hand cupped Larry's knee made Alex suspect another reason why his best friend might have been too busy to visit.

"Yeah, you guys head out and have some grownup time," Christopher said as he pulled out his cell phone. "I'm sure Alex is sick of hospital food. Why don't you go to that steakhouse up on I-10. I took Charlotte there last weekend and it was amazing."

"Sold!" Alex said as he hugged an armful of giggling children. "You kids be good for Mister Christopher while we're gone, okay?"

"Yes, sir," the chorus replied and immediately began arguing about which movie to watch as Christopher pulled the television remote from their sticky fingers.

Molly bounced up, clearly feeling better than she had before their nap. Her fear might be understandable, but Alex needed her to know he was there for her the way she'd always been there for him. Their eyes met for a moment, her face blushing as she gave him a sweet smile.

Even before the threat on his life, Molly had stepped up to help him with everything. She cooked and cleaned and parented right along with him, making him feel like someone had his back for the first time since becoming a single parent. Then when things got tough, she did too. He may have been a little crazy when he'd asked her to marry him in front of everyone, but it didn't change how he felt. Maybe she just needed a little time to get used to the idea.

Molly took his hand and pulled him up after her, the worry and fear he'd seen earlier seemingly gone now. He lifted her hand to his lips and gave the back a quick kiss, then they bumped shoulders as they wandered over to Larry and Jenna.

"You two seem to have made up for lost time," Jenna said with a suppressed grin as she glanced between Alex and Molly. "A certain glow…"

"Stop it," Molly laughed, then glanced to see if the kids were paying attention. "It was a busy morning. We just took a little nap, that's all."

"Uh-huh," Jenna said as she led them out the suite door. "Come on, this is my last chance to get a good Texas steak."

"You going somewhere?" Alex asked Jenna.

Alex immediately noticed the carefree look on Larry's fade before he turned to speak to the guards. To his surprise, they both stayed at their post rather than following along to the elevator.

"New York," Jenna announced with a breathless sigh as Larry caught up. "I took the network job offer and start on Monday."

"You don't waste any time," Alex laughed.

"This coming from the man who proposed in front of a room full of people after knowing Molly for two whole months," Jenna teased.

"Hey, I said yes…eventually," Molly teased back and pushed Jenna's shoulder.

"Smart girl," Jenna said and pushed the elevator button. "Just so you know, I made sure the network knows I'm going to be at a wedding over Thanksgiving so they don't book me."

Molly kept smiling and nodding, which allowed Alex to relax a little. "Good," Molly said. "I don't want to have to find another maid-of-honor."

That reminded Alex that he still needed to find out if Larry would be his best man, but didn't want to put him on the spot by asking in front of Molly and Jenna. When they got on the elevator, the girls got busy chatting about Jenna's new job and move.

"You're lookin' better than the last time I saw you. Your head doing okay?" Alex asked Larry.

"Yeah," Larry said, finally looking Alex in the eye. There was guilt in his expression, along with a measure of sadness. "You, too."

"I never had a chance to thank you." Alex spoke directly to him, but Larry looked down to break eye contact.

"Just doin' my job," Larry sighed as he held the door open button for the women to exit the elevator.

"So have they released you to go back to work or are you still violating doctor's orders and working anyway?" Alex asked with a wry smile, staying behind the women as they walked through the luxurious lobby to the front entrance.

"I'm cleared. I'll be flying back to Houston on Monday after you get home safe. We aren't recommending full time coverage anymore, especially with Sarge staying there with you now." Larry gave a thin smile at Molly's back.

Alex knew Larry didn't give his trust lightly, and Molly had certainly done enough to earn it. "You're gonna come back for the wedding, right?"

"Sure," Larry said with a shrug.

"Then I got a favor to ask." Alex turned towards Larry and stopped walking, leaning in closer as the girls walked outside. "I want you to be my best man."

Larry's forehead creased at the question. He waited so long to answer that Alex worried he might say no. After visibly swallowing he gave Alex the same thin smile he'd given Molly. "Sure. Be honored to."

"Good," Alex said with a relieved sigh and clapped Larry on the back as the men started walking again. "Good."

The ride to the steakhouse only took a few minutes. Larry drove and called in their movements to Context Security like the security guards had done all day. Alex sat up next to him to allow Molly to catch up with Jenna in the middle seats.

After they arrived and were seated, Molly and Jenna disappeared into the bathroom together, chatting and laughing along the way. The waiter returned with their drinks, then left Alex and Larry alone. Alex kept trying to get a bead on his friend's mood, but Larry was a blank wall.

"You seem down," Alex said at last, trying to open his friend up.

"Yeah, just lots on my mind. And tying up the loose ends the last couple of weeks has kept me busy." Larry continued to focus on stirring his straw around his iced tea.

"You and Jenna seem to be hitting it off." Alex was surprised that the blank wall blushed.

"It's not like that."

"So what's it like, then?" Alex sat back in the booth and sipped his iced tea, curious how Larry would try to explain himself out of it.

Larry's only reply was an embarrassed smirk.

"I can't believe you didn't take your own advice," Alex said with a small laugh.

Larry cocked an eyebrow. "What?"

"Remember when you told me that she was ambitious and I should be careful?" Alex teased.

"Dude, nothing's going on." Larry rolled his eyes upwards and sighed, but he was struggling to hide the smirk.

"Fine, kill-joy."

"Just because *you're* jumping in with both feet for round two doesn't mean everyone else is." Larry leaned forward over the table to huddle around his glass. "She did a great job on that follow-up piece. I mean, I obviously know all the facts, but hearing the way she broke the story down… It got me pissed off all over again."

"You know there was nothing you could have done, right?" Alex asked. "Considering what we were up against, this was a win."

"When the paramedics lost you on the ride in," Larry whispered. "Seeing you like that, knowing it was my fault…"

"It wasn't your fault. I should have fired first instead of standing there in the bedroom doorway like a dumbass."

"I'm the professional, not you. He never should have gotten close enough to take that shot."

"I hear what you're saying, but you need to hear me too. I don't blame you. Hell, if you hadn't thought to put the GPS tracker on Troy's car, my kids would be gone and Will would be dead. We *both* owe you for that. Give yourself a break, man, I need my friend back."

Larry pinched his lips into a line, but after a long sigh he looked up with a grim smile. "I'm tryin'."

"Good." Alex smiled in return as he rubbed his palms together. "So plan on coming out for the weekend in a few weeks. We've got some wedding planning to do. I was thinking about dragging you, Peter, Roger, and Christopher to Vegas for a bachelor party."

Larry laughed and shook his head. "Seriously? The idea didn't work out so well in the movies."

"No tigers in the bathroom for us. Just cigars, scotch, and poker. Maybe a show or two."

Chapter 44: Molly

While the family had been living in a hotel waiting for Alex to recover, Larry had a work crew clean Alex's house and repair the damage the shootout in the hallway had left behind. Molly's house was another story. The bloody clothes she'd left in the trash before going to save the kids was right where she'd left them and the rancid scent that arose from them had left the house unlivable.

The day after they arrived to live in Alex's house, Molly left the kids with Alex to straighten out the mess. After triple bagging the clothes to stifle the stench, she opened all the windows to air out the house, and then started cleaning in earnest. Tossing the expired food made a good start, but she couldn't stop until she had sorted the laundry and swept the dust out the front door. Before she started packing up everything she wanted to take over to Alex's, she stopped with the broom in her hand to think about the layout of the house.

Alex was right, it would make a wonderful bed and breakfast. The downstairs was divided between a living room that stretched across the whole front of the house and the large dining room and kitchen behind it. The guest bathroom was under the wide staircase near the front door. The basement, with its laundry room and root cellar, was at the bottom of a narrow staircase behind the kitchen. The upstairs was made up of four large bedrooms arranged around a turn-of-the-century tile bathroom with an enormous claw-footed tub.

If she gutted the upstairs, she could add more bedrooms and give them each a smaller private bathroom with a shower. There was even a finished attic area that she might be able to use for additional bedrooms or storage. The downstairs living room was dominated by a crumbling stone fireplace that shared the central wall with the kitchen. It would add a rustic charm once the masonry and mantel had been repaired. The rough wood floors throughout the house had been worn smooth by generations of feet, but could do with some sanding to even them out before refinishing back to a shine.

Molly had always loved her spacious kitchen, but working in Alex's kitchen had spoiled her. His appliances, storage, and equipment had modern, commercial features. Reimagining her kitchen as the center of a bed and breakfast filled her heart with joy and her head with a million ideas. Maybe she could even open for dinner on the weekends to feed the locals as well as the guests. The project would give her a creative outlet of her own and help her bring something tangible to their marriage as well.

The feeling of being overwhelmed by her impending nuptials faded as she began to plan what it would take to pull off. She still didn't feel comfortable spending Alex's money, no matter what he said. But if she considered the money as a loan, she could track the income generated by the Arbor Gate Bed and Breakfast to pay back his investment and eventually add the income to their joint assets. Even if it amounted to the same thing in the end, thinking about it that way helped her adjust to the idea.

Grabbing the filled trash bags, she took them out the back door to the large bins she had to drag to the county road once a week. When she was going back to the house, she saw Alex and the kids standing at the fence between the properties. Will was holding one end of a measuring tape and Alex was dragging the other end along the top of the split rail fence. Molly waved as she walked towards them.

"Whatcha doin'?" she called as she got closer.

"Dad's gonna put a gate here so we don't have to walk out by the road," Manny yelled as Hannah counted off the numbers with her finger.

Molly shot Alex a knowing smile as he jotted down the measurements. "He is?"

"Yeah, we found a cool one online that we can put together ourselves," Will answered. He was clearly excited but fought to keep a serious expression as he held his end of the tape measure. "We could even plant flowers that will grow over it!"

"I was thinking passion vines might be nice," Alex said, echoing her own idea back with a playful glint in his eyes.

"Good idea," she smirked.

Molly warmed in his attention. Alex was as generous in bed as he was in life. His injuries might have slowed him down a little, but every night they'd spent together had been better than the last. She had to do most of the work so far because the muscles in his chest were still healing, but he more than made up for it with his relentless focus on her pleasure.

Troy had been her best match sexually before meeting Alex. He'd had a strength and charisma that demanded her response, but she had to bite and claw her way to her own satisfaction. Sex was a kind of battle between them. Because Alex had a different kind of strength than Troy, she had worried it wouldn't be as good as what she had been used to.

Luckily, it wasn't the same at all—it was better. Alex brought the same single-minded focus to sex that he displayed working on the fence or protecting his kids. He loved her with his whole body and it showed in a thousand little ways. Every touch, every look, every sound amplified their connection. It wasn't a battle between them, it was a dance and he matched her passion for passion. And when Alex finally let himself go, he gave her everything. Feeling his heat blooming inside her and watching his face as he whispered her name made her shiver at the memory.

Alex smiled at Molly, apparently understanding where her thoughts were. The kids were busy having fun measuring the fence posts and each other, so she leaned over towards Alex and invited a kiss. He leaned over from his side of the fence and gave her a quick peck.

"How's the house?"

"Smells awful. The trash went off while we were away, so I opened the windows to air it out." She sighed when the brush of his hand along her arm made the hairs stand up. "I was thinkin' more about the bed and breakfast idea."

"Yeah?"

"I'll need to gut the second floor to arrange the rooms, remodel the kitchen, and fix some minor structural problems, but I wanna do it." Saying it out loud made it feel more real and his approving smile thrilled her.

"Let's sit down tonight after the kids go to bed and make some plans. The general contractor that built my house mentioned how much he loved the look of your place. Maybe we could get him back up here to give us a quote."

Looking back over her shoulder, she went over the house with a critical eye. Sitting up on the slight hill made the imperfections hard to see. Over the last year she had painted it, repaired it, and learned it secrets inside and out. A remodel was going to be a big project, but she loved the old house too much to do any less.

"I wish Nanny could see it," Molly whispered.

"Why can't she?" Alex asked. "Her retirement home is just a couple of hours away, right?."

With a sigh, Molly said, "She's not doing well. She's gone from assisted living to nursing care in less than a year. The last time I was there she thought I was my mother."

"Oh. I'm sorry. I hadn't realized it was that bad." Alex took her hand and squeezed in his.

"She always said getting old isn't for sissies," Molly sighed again. "I know she would love the idea of bringing guests into her home."

"Maybe we could take pictures. She's bound to have some lucid days and the staff could tell her about it for us."

She smiled back at Alex. "We'll send her lots of pictures."

In the middle of her and Alex's quiet moment, Molly felt a gentle tug on her hand. "Molly Mom, we're hungry," Hannah said, speaking for the two boys who were wrestling over the tape measure on the ground.

The endearment always made Molly smile. It made her heart swell that the twins had accepted her so fully into their lives. Thinking about their new life together helped get her mind off her grandmother's failing health for the moment. Molly had so many new possibilities open to her now that Alex and his twins were apart of her and Will's life.

Alex walked over and plucked the tape measure away from the wiggling boys. "Let Molly go finish cleaning in the old house and we'll make her a grilled cheese sandwich for lunch."

"See y'all in a bit." Molly left them to walk up the hill with plans whirling bright through her mind.

CHAPTER 45: ALEX

It had taken two weeks recovering at home for Alex's weakness and pain to subside. He'd wake each morning next to Molly, with the kids bouncing on their bed demanding breakfast. The pleasant ache of love had replaced the pain of the wound in his chest. There were sweet moments each day when he was overcome by a tight feeling in his throat for the life he still had.

The kids had adapted to the new living arrangements with amazing speed. It seemed like one long sleepover to them. Despite a few bumps over territory and toys, they had embraced their new blended family without complaint. Alex had been careful with Will. It was a tough balancing act between setting limits on his behavior and encouraging him to express his grief, but other than a few angry outbursts that dissolved into tears, Will seemed to be healing.

Each day, Alex found some way to thank his friends and neighbors for their support. He went to Alice's Women's Circle and spoke openly about his life, accepting their prayers and well wishes along with the wonderful casseroles they brought to share for lunch. Talking about what had happened had been freeing. And sharing Molly's plans for the Arbor Gate Bed and Breakfast with the group generated more curiosity and interest than he'd expected.

Alex learned how to drive a backhoe when he helped Terry dig out the pond on his cattle ranch. He also rode out with Grant in his large air conditioned tractor to inspect the fields. Roger and Bubba stopped by regularly to invite Alex to join them at the ice house by the highway, which he usually did. And as each day passed, Alex felt the tension and worry he'd carried over the last five years bleed away.

Molly had run with the renovation of her family home with Alex's blessing. The meeting with the architect and general contractor had gone well, providing a nice punch list of items that needed to be done. After a work crew moved all the furniture into storage, Molly spent her free time working at the house and researching what was required to run a bed and breakfast. Her excitement was infectious and Alex joined in when there were jobs the kids could help with.

The day after the new arbor gate kit had been delivered by Bubba and his sons, Alex was working with the kids to sort, cut, and assemble the pieces on the flexible frame of the arbor. Molly gently reminded Alex that he might not be strong enough yet to do a lot of the heavier work, so Roger came over to removed the railing on that section of the fence and run the gas-powered auger to sink the gate posts.

Alex had just shown the boys how to use a hand saw to cut dozens of redwood strips that would criss-cross the arbor when his cell phone rang. Peter's smiling picture was on the screen when he swiped across it with his finger.

"Peter!" Alex sang. "Good news?"

"I just got word from my liaison in Mexico that the judge ruled to approve the new trust today. As expected, there were questions about the clause to sell everything and give the proceeds to charity. When we explained that someone had tried to kill you to steal the trust from the kids, the judge agreed with the justification and signed off on it."

The relief Alex felt was expressed with a slow exhalation. "Finally."

"As of this moment everything is locked up for thirty years or so."

"Give yourself a bonus when you send me the bill for all this. I know it's been a pain getting it done, but I can't thank you enough."

"Buy me a bottle of that 25-year-old Macallan and we'll call it even. How're Molly and the kids?"

"We're settling in just fine. Molly is hard at work getting the bed and breakfast ready in time for the wedding and I'm in the yard installing the arbor gate we're getting married under right now."

"Can't wait to see it! I gotta run, but I'll send the notarized copies of everything for you to keep. Talk to you later and give Molly my love."

"Will do."

Alex watched the kids work for a while until Manny suggested having a sword fight with the redwood strips instead. While they ran around yelling *en garde* at each other, Alex continued cutting the remaining redwood with the hand saw. It was dull and repetitive work, but just what he needed to relax and enjoy his afternoon with the kids.

When his phone rang again, Alex assumed Peter was calling back, but the screen displayed the logo for the Lujo Jugar Resorts, the luxury resort and spa Maria's family had grown into a multinational corporation. Pausing a moment to let the shock wear off, Alex answered the call.

"This is Alex."

"Alex, this is Rubin de Cervantes."

Hearing his former client and father-in-law for the first time in years made Alex's heart race and dried his mouth. He suddenly wanted to pour out the rage he'd felt for all the years living in fear. Alex remained silent until he could trust himself to be civil.

"I know I'm probably the last person you want to speak to…" Rubin started, but then the silence stretched out for a moment. "My… uh… my son, Vizzy… he tried to have Connie and me killed."

That unexpected revelation forced Alex to cough out an inappropriate laugh. "Yeah, me too."

"I know that now." He sighed heavily. Alex could imagine Rubin running a hand over his bald head, a common habit when he was stressed. "It's changed… everything."

"Well, it's changed nothing for me," Alex hissed, unable to keep his cool anymore. "You blamed me for Maria's death. You tried to take my *children* from me. I'll never forget that, Rubin, and I'll never believe that you didn't know Vizzy was capable of this."

"He was my son." Rubin growled in wordless frustration. "You have a son as well. Imagine how it would feel to find out he's a murderer. That he would try to kill you. And for what? Money?" Rubin's words were choked off by a whispered plea to God in Spanish. "Whatever I felt about you, Alex, I never wanted you dead."

Words lost their meaning. He felt like he was in a dream where odd things happened for no apparent reason. His mouth spilled a confession before his brain could intervene. "Vizzy never thought I was worthy of Maria. None of you did."

"I admit I didn't like the idea of you two getting married, but her happiness was more important to me than that. I thought you understood that."

They both stopped speaking, Alex looked over at his kids playing. Rubin's words about his son haunted him. Whatever else he was, Rubin was still a father who'd lost both of his children. Alex knew that fear too well. It was impossible for Alex to not empathize with his pain.

"Did you know that Vizzy was in Houston the day of Maria's stroke?" Rubin asked in their silence.

It took Alex a few seconds to process the information, and when he did, he could only sputter out, "What?" Alex felt his knees weaken, forcing him to lean against the fence before he fell. His head spun as his vision dimmed. Vizzy had been there? *No!*

"The policia found all kinds of things at his house in San Fernando. Vizzy kept meticulous records. Connie's gone through his personal diaries, trying to make sense of what he'd done. This morning she discovered Vizzy had picked up a dangerous concentration of a prescription drug just before he flew to Houston."

"What are you saying?" Alex whispered.

"It was a drug that had been banned in the US for causing hemorrhagic strokes in pregnant women," Rubin said, his voice squeezing tight at the end. "It would have been lethal to someone with preeclampsia and hard to detect unless the doctors knew to look for it immediately."

Alex felt hot tears rising as he swallowed down the anguish in his throat. "He killed Maria?"

"I don't know. Does it matter now?" Rubin wept into his phone. "I've lost them both."

He was staring away in horror when Hannah came up. "Daddy? Are you okay?"

Wiping his eyes, Alex tried to give her a smile. From her fearful reaction it didn't work. "Would you run go get Molly?" he asked her as he covered the cell phone with his hand.

The boys took notice when Hannah ran through the open fence. They glanced a question at Alex, who nodded at them, then they dropped their wooden swords and tore off after her.

"Connie is falling apart," Rubin continued, his tone strengthening. "It's worse than when Maria passed. It would help if she could see Manuel and Hannah, but I know how much that is asking at this point."

"I'm getting married in a few weeks," Alex said. *Vizzy killed Maria?* But then another thought struck him—*my wife-to-be killed your son.* "It's not a good time right now."

"You're…" Rubin cleared his throat. "I don't know why it surprises me. It's been five years after all."

"Don't worry, it surprised me, too." The new revelations had Alex feeling an odd kinship with Rubin, but he still debated with himself how much to share about his personal life. "The kids already love her."

Rubin let a slow breath out, hissing through the phone. Alex knew him well enough to imagine his broad hand sliding over his pate again. "Just think about it and let me know. I won't keep you. I just wanted to clear the air between us."

"I understand," Alex said. "I'll be in touch."

He dropped the call and turned to watch Molly and the kids make their way back. She must have seen something in his face as soon as he turned towards her.

"Kids, go run in the house and wash up. I'll be in to make us a snack in a minute." As soon as they were out of earshot, Molly stepped close and drew Alex in. "What happened?"

Alex buried his face in her neck. "Rubin de Cervantes just called me out of the blue. He thinks Vizzy killed Maria."

Saying the words tore open a scarred place deep inside, making him pull Molly tighter. The guilt he'd always carried around now scalded him as it burned its way out.

"It wasn't your fault," Molly whispered. "There's no way you could've known."

"Oh, God," Alex cried and allowed her to hold him up for a while.

"I got you," she whispered and kissed his cheek. "Let it go."

Even in the midst of his fresh sorrow, the irony of mourning his first wife while clinging to his second wasn't lost on Alex. Molly's unwavering support had gotten him through the hardest trial he'd ever faced. The thought of dying and leaving his kids vulnerable to Vizzy had been even harder than losing Maria. Molly loved him enough to risk herself to save his kids and now she was his rock as he realized how much Vizzy had taken from him.

Chapter 46: Molly

I'd bring Vizzy back just so I could kill him again. The acid rage at Alex's revelation woke Molly's inner mama bear. They'd just gotten into a routine; then there was Vizzy, reaching out from the grave and stealing what little peace of mind Alex had managed to recover.

"What kind of bastard kills his own sister?" Molly whispered.

"The same kind who tries to have his parents killed, apparently."

Molly pulled back to look at Alex's face to check if he was serious.

"That's why Rubin called. Vizzy hired someone to kill him and Connie, but they survived somehow. The police over there have been going through Vizzy's house and found some diaries. Connie's been going through them and discovered he took some kind of dangerous drug to Houston the day Maria had her stroke."

"So her parents weren't involved in any of it?"

Alex shrugged. "They still sued me for her wrongful death, but I see how Vizzy could have used their grief to coerce them. He must have been after the trust when he tried to kill her to begin with. When the twins lived, Vizzy went after them through me."

Watching Alex struggle with the news hurt Molly's heart. She pulled his hand to lead him towards the back porch. "Let me get the kids something to snack on and we'll sit outside and talk this out."

Molly left him sitting in the patio and got the kids settled in front of the television with fruit snacks. When she returned, Alex had gotten himself a beer and was staring out at the clouds scattered across the blue summer sky. She sat next to him and pulled him to lean against her chest.

"I feel stupid for getting so upset before. Maria's been dead for nearly six years. It's not like the cause changes anything."

"But it does," Molly said. "I lost friends in the service through accidents and insurgent action. It always feels different knowing someone made the decision to take their life."

"I guess I can see that." Alex took a long pull on his Shiner. "Rubin and Connie want to see the twins."

Molly already knew how Alex felt about that, but now his expression showed he was conflicted. "What do *you* want?"

"I'll never fully trust them," Alex said as he met her eyes. "But I also know how I'd feel if I lost the twins. Am I being stupid if I let them come for a visit?"

"I don't think so," Molly said. "Why don't you call Larry and see if we can get a team up here one weekend. Have them come for a little supervised time and see what happens."

"I don't want the kids getting hurt," Alex whispered.

"You can't stop that from happening. The best you can do is be there for them when it does."

Alex nodded and drained the beer. "I know, but getting to know their grandparents is a one-way ticket. It's gonna change everything."

"So is getting married," Molly said. "We're gonna have security out the wazoo at the wedding, so why not have them come then?"

Alex turned to see her face. "You wouldn't mind my old in-laws coming to our wedding?"

"Maria's going to be a part of our lives forever, Alex. I already love her kids. I'm gonna help her daughter pick out a wedding dress someday. Her son is going to dance with me at his wedding. She has given me such a gift." Molly pinched her lips to collect herself before confessing the rest to Alex. "She's given me the family I've always dreamed about, and I'll do my best to honor her memory."

Now Alex pulled her into his embrace and she let herself be comforted. "You're a special woman, Molly Thompson."

Hearing Alex join her name with his said more than the words alone. He really loved her, she could feel it to her core. Feeling his arms tighten around her broke her control and she cried into his shoulder.

"I love you so much," Alex whispered into her hair.

Molly kissed him then, tears and all. His hands moved up her back and into her hair while the kiss deepened. The warmth in her stomach moved lower and she craved his touch like an abiding hunger.

They had made love every night since he had been discharged from the hospital. Sleeping wrapped up with him had kept her fears at bay and strengthened the bond that had grown since he moved in next door. Sex with Alex could be gentle or wild, funny or passionate, and Molly had found herself responding like she never had before. Her thoughts were interrupted by a quiet trio of giggles.

"Look, they're doing it again," she heard her son whisper loudly.

"Molly Mom and Daddy, sittin' in a tree," Hannah sang loudly and the other two joined in for the rest. "K-I-S-S-I-N-G! First comes love, then comes marriage, then comes Daddy with a baby carriage!"

Molly choked back laughter at the unintended irony in the song. She wondered what the kids would say if they knew that baby carriage might be arriving by spring.

"I assume you're done with your snack?" Alex asked the kids. "Well, there's not gonna be a marriage if we don't get that arbor gate finished to have the wedding under. Come on and help me."

Molly followed her family back to the gate between the properties with her hand resting on her stomach. If she was pregnant already, their baby was just tiny now, but the possibility made her heart sing.

Working with Alex, she herded the kids through the rest of the cutting and began to assemble the crosshatched pattern that made up the arbor. The kit was easy enough for the kids to help. It only took an hour to finish weaving and tacking the thin wood strips to the frame.

"Help me get this end secured," Alex said as they stood the curving arbor over the wooden gate. Will grabbed the hammer and nails while Molly, Manny, and Hannah held the arbor in place. Alex and Will made quick work nailing it into the gate posts.

"I wanna do this side," Manny said. Without protest, Will handed over the hammer to Manny and then took Manny's spot holding the wood in place while Alex helped drive in the nails. When the arbor was secure, the family stood back to inspect their work. Alex slipped his arm around Molly's waist while he let out a satisfied sigh.

The arched arbor over the gate reached about nine feet at the crest. The double gate was done in a picket style, with spaces between the narrow pickets. Molly thought the redwood was beautiful and would age well.

"What are we gonna plant to grow over it?" Alex asked her.

"I was thinking about a passion vine," Molly said. "But Alice said that she had a clematis that would grow faster and makes beautiful purple blooms. That would go well with the pale lavender dress I was looking at."

Alex grinned down at her and nodded. "You wanna get the kids cleaned up and fed while I pick up out here?"

"Maybe they'll go to bed early," Molly suggested. "So we can go to bed early."

Alex picked up her hint and gave her a gentle squeeze. "Sounds like a plan."

"Come on kids!" Molly rounded them up and chased them inside. "Wash your hands first, then come set the table."

While she made the grilled cheese sandwiches, Molly smiled around at the kitchen that had once awed her. Alex may have had it built, but Molly had spent more time in it. She had always felt at home here, even when she was just helping Alex watch the twins.

After they all ate, Molly washed the dishes while Alex ran the kids through the showers and into their pajamas. They all listened as Alex read three of their favorite stories using his special comical voices, then she and Alex tucked them all into their beds.

Alex took her hand and led her toward the living room. They both knew the kids would be up at least twice before finally going to sleep. He left her at the couch where she picked up the tablet to lock the house and turn on the alarm. When he returned, he had two glasses of red wine and a sparkle in his eyes.

"I thought a little celebration was in order for finishing the arbor gate."

"None for me, thanks," Molly teased as she set her glass down on the side table.

"Why's that?" he asked, puzzled.

"I'm late," she whispered and raised an eyebrow.

Molly watched Alex's face shift from amused to confused to surprised. Then he looked down and pressed his open hand low on her stomach. He grinned back up at her face. "Late enough for a test to be sure?"

"Maybe next week," she said and gloried in his reaction. When she told Troy about Will, his first response was for her to *take care of it*.

"So we'll be around three months along at the wedding then."

Molly nodded with a pleased smile. "It should be right after the first trimester by then and safe to announce if you wanted to."

He pulled her into a tight hug. The shuddering breaths on her neck betrayed his overwhelming response to her news. Joy filled her until she chuckled.

"Are you sure you're ready for another one?" she asked.

Instead of words, he pulled back and kissed her deeply.

Chapter 47: Alex

Alex stood on the wide porch of the new Arbor Gate Bed and Breakfast with Manny and Hannah holding his hands. They had been so excited that they hadn't been able to sleep. Alex hadn't slept either, but his excuse was the anxiety of seeing Rubin and Connie again for the first time since the trial.

The plan to have his former in-laws come to their wedding made sense when he and Molly had discussed it in the middle of summer. Now that Rubin and Connie were pulling into the new riverstone parking lot Molly had put in a week ago, he wasn't as confident. For the safety of his former in-laws, as well as for the safety of Alex and his family, Larry had somebody from Context Security pick them up from the airport. A black SUV came to stop at the bottom of the porch Alex stood on. Alex held his breath while the driver raced around to open the door, feeling panic creep up his spine.

Connie had aged more than the years alone could explain. It was like her body had shrunk in on itself and her wrinkled skin hung loose on her neck and arms. She was still dressed impeccably, but if anything the contrast made her look worse. The desperate expression on her face lifted as soon as she saw the twins.

"*Mis nietos*," she cried as she covered her mouth with her hands.

"Is that really my *abuela*?" Hannah asked with a skeptical expression.

"Yes," Alex whispered, making sure to look her in the eye while keeping a calm expression on his face. He looked back to see Rubin exiting the SUV after Connie.

Rubin appeared unchanged, especially compared to his wife. He wore his customary dark suit and red tie like a suit of armor. The Texas sun reflected off his shiny bald head. He looked around at the house before settling his gaze on Alex and the twins. With a deep breath, he put his arm around his wife and ushered her towards the three steps that led to the wrap-around porch.

"Alex," Rubin said by way of greeting. Connie was still enraptured by the twins.

Alex made no move toward them. He wanted his kids to feel comfortable before taking them any closer. "Manny, Hannah? These are your *abuelos*, Papi Rubin and Mama Connie."

Both kids held tight to Alex's hands as they watched the old couple come up the stairs. The air buzzed with tension for a moment until Connie dropped to one knee and threw open her arms.

The kids eased forward, taking glances back at Alex who plastered a reassuring smile on his face and nodded. When they entered her embrace, Connie let out a long shuddering sob. Rubin slowly stepped around them and approached Alex.

"Thank you," he said as he extended his hand. Two simple words, but Alex could feel the emotion Rubin had put behind them.

Alex gave the firm grip a tight answer. The rising emotion at seeing his old client again surprised him. This man, the father of his first wife, had remained aloof and disapproving ever since he and Maria had begun dating. Nothing Alex did had ever been good enough for Rubin's little girl. Glancing at Hannah being doted on by her grandmother, he felt an uncomfortable empathy. Someday his daughter would bring a young man home and then Alex suspected he would truly understand.

"You're welcome," Alex said after a moment. He turned to wave Molly and Will forward. "Rubin, this is my fiancé, Molly McDill, and her son Will."

"Hi." Molly gave him a nervous smile.

Rubin's stoic expression softened as Molly walked up with her son clinging to her side. "I'm pleased to meet you both." He looked down at Will with a bit of humor peeking through his normally gruff countenance. "So, you're going to be my grandchildrens' brother on Saturday?"

"Yes, sir," Will whispered with wide-eyes.

"I suppose it wouldn't be fair if I brought them presents and didn't bring you one as well."

Alex saw Rubin's mouth twitch when Will grinned and glanced up at Molly to seek her reassurance.

Rubin continued with an amused twinkle in his eyes. "And if they both call me Papi Rubin it would be confusing if you had to call me something else, yes?" He looked up at Molly and asked, "Would you mind if he called me Papi Rubin as well?"

Molly shot Alex a questioning look, but he returned a bemused shrug. "That's fine with me," Molly said. "Will, what do you say?"

"Thanks, Papi Rubin!"

"Will," Hannah called as she and Manny pulled Connie over. "This is our Mama Connie!"

Alex and Molly stepped back to allow the grandparents their moment with the kids. The Context Security driver had finished unloading the luggage from the SUV and was carrying it inside when Connie snatched a colorful woven bag on his way by.

"Wow," Molly whispered to Alex. "Not what I expected at all."

Rubin and Connie had moved to sit on the rough hewn bench by the front door to distribute their gifts while the kids sat on the porch and tore open the paper wrapping.

"I've never seen this side of them before," Alex whispered back.

She slipped her arm around Alex's waist and gave him a one-armed hug. "Let me go make sure their luggage ends up in the right room."

Alex watched her go inside while pride warmed his heart. His bride-to-be had taken the broken down old house and made something precious. From the construction to the decorating, Molly had brought her vision of the bed and breakfast to life and she made it all look easy.

As a result, the wedding planning fell largely on Alex. Molly asked for lavender and cream colors to match her dress, but gave him free reign for all the other details. Classy invitations had gone out to their friends and family a few weeks earlier and they expected around fifty people to witness their nuptials on Saturday afternoon.

An event company would be bringing in a large canopy and folding chairs on Friday so they could have the ceremony in front of the arbor gate. The caterer would arrive Saturday morning with the cake and hors d'oeuvres, and then clean up everything afterwards.

Rubin and Connie were the last guests to arrive before Thanksgiving dinner. Alex's sister arrived with his parents earlier in the week to help prepare for the big family meal. Jenna Banks had managed to get off from her new job in New York for ten days to help Alex with the last minute wedding details. Alex noticed something going on between Jenna and Larry as they stalked around each other all week, but he wasn't quite sure what it was.

Connie stood up, leaning heavily on Rubin's shoulder as she did. "Do we have time to unpack and rest a bit before the Thanksgiving meal?"

"Of course," Alex said as he offered his arm. "We won't be eating until five, so you have a few hours."

"We have much to speak of later, but I want to begin by saying how sorry I am for everything that has happened. Words mean nothing, I know, but I hope in time you will be able to forgive us."

Alex felt his throat tighten at her heartfelt apology. Connie was a battleship that cut her way through high society and left weaker opponents sinking in her wake. Now she was the one battered and bruised and alone.

"For Maria, for the twins, we'll find a way."

Uncle Larry showed up to wrangle the kids while Alex led Connie and Rubin through the common room up to their room. His in-laws paused a moment to take in the downstairs room that defined comfort. Overstuffed couches and chairs, bookcases, and artwork all centered around the massive stone fireplace. He then led them up the wide staircase to the second floor bedrooms. McDill family pictures and photos of the area lined the stairway.

The rooms upstairs were all named for gemstones instead of numbers. Alex led Rubin and Connie to the Garnet room where Molly waited outside the door.

"Your room is ready. Please let me know if you need anything."

"Thank you," Rubin said as he assisted Connie through the door.

Alex took Molly's hand to return down the back stairs into the kitchen. His mom and sister were busy but looked like they had the meal under control.

Mom wiped her hands on a towel as she walked up. "How'd it go?"

"Better than I feared. Rubin asked if Will would call him *Papi* Rubin and Connie gave me a sincere apology. You'll see at dinner."

"I made your father promise to be civil, so don't worry about him getting out of line."

Alex laughed. "I'm more worried about you two!"

"I heard that," his sister Pat said. "Just for that you have to set the table."

Alex left Molly to watch the kids and he slaved away for his sister to place every plate, utensil, and decorative doodad to her exacting specification. The dining room table had enough room for the capacity of the bed and breakfast. This inaugural weekend would test the whole operation.

With Alex's parents, Pat, Larry, Jenna, the de Cervantes, and the attic bunkhouse reserved for the kids, every bed would be filled. They had planned it that way so Alex and Molly could have their wedding night alone in the house for the first time. And Alex couldn't wait to sleep with his wife without the kids bounding into the bedroom at first light.

Molly gathered the guests while Alex poured the wine in the glasses around the table. Introductions and reunions made the room noisy until everyone took their seats leaving Alex standing at the head of the table.

"Last Thanksgiving was just me and the kids. That was my fault. I hid us away because I was afraid and moving here was just another example of that fear. This year I have so much to be thankful for. My neighbors have helped me overcome my fears and showed me what being part of a community means. And to my great surprise, Molly and Will have taught me love will grow anywhere you let it.

"And now for the first time, I can celebrate this time of Thanksgiving with my whole family. Some of you are mine by blood." Alex raised his glass to his parents and sister. "Others are family because of love." He raised his glass to Rubin and Connie, then to Molly and Will. "And some are family by choice." He raised his glass to Larry, Jenna, and Roger. "I love you all and hope that as our family grows larger, you'll return occasionally to celebrate here again."

"Hear, hear," Alex's dad called for the toast and drank.

Alex looked at Molly, who held her wine glass to her lips, but didn't drink. He eyed her for a moment with a small, secret smile. He wasn't sure when she planned to make their big announcement, but wasn't surprised that this was it.

Molly made eye contact with him and he nodded.

She set her untouched wine glass back on the table and said, "And speaking of our family growing larger, you'll forgive me if I don't partake."

Chapter 48: Molly

"It's gonna be tight," Jenna said.

"I'll suck in as much as I can. Zip it!" Molly's baby bump had a growth spurt since she'd bought her wedding dress a few weeks earlier. She'd even had it altered to leave some room, but as Jenna worked the zipper up, Molly realized she should have let it out another half-inch.

"Can you breathe?" Jenna laughed.

"Yup. Sitting might be an issue, but as long as I can breathe and walk I can make it through the ceremony. The bouquet will hide my bump and I'll change before we eat anyway because the brisket Roger brought is going to be messy."

Her dress wasn't a traditional wedding dress, but Molly wasn't a traditional bride. Her life had led her into the Army out of high school, then into being a wife and mother with a man who wasn't ready for marriage. With that man entirely out of the picture, Molly was ready to grow her family with a better man; a man she could trust with her whole heart. Now the future was opening up like the gorgeous blooms on their arbor gate.

The clematis plant Alice had given them for the arbor was part of a seedling her grandmother had originally brought over from England and planted all around their family homestead. It was a rare twice-blooming variety that flowered in both spring and fall. Molly's lavender colored wedding dress had accents in the same blue-purple shade as its blooms.

"You look amazing," Jenna commented as she stepped back to allow Molly to turn in the full length mirror behind the bedroom door.

"I feel amazing," Molly sighed. "I swear sometimes I wake up in the morning and have to pinch myself to make sure I'm not dreaming."

"After all you've both been through, you deserve this. You both do." There was a bittersweet expression on Jenna's face in the mirror that made Molly turn to face her friend.

"What's wrong?" Molly whispered. Jenna instantly put her reporter mask back on.

"Nothing! I'm just happy for you."

"Don't lie to me." She gave Jenna a look that brooked no argument.

Jenna smiled blankly for a moment more before her face fell and her shoulders slumped. "It's Larry."

"I thought you two might have been up to something before you moved to New York."

"We were. It was amazing." Her emphasis on the last word she spoke contrasted with the anguished expression on her face.

"So what's the problem? You both make good money, so a long distance thing shouldn't be impossible to work out."

"I can't. Not right now. I've got to stay focused on my career."

Molly sighed and bit her tongue. She'd drop the subject for now. Molly and Jenna had gotten to know each other over the summer. Jenna had a blind spot where her career goals were concerned and nothing Molly said would change her mind at this point. Molly slipped on the comfortable flats she intended to wear down the aisle while Jenna checked her makeup again.

Jenna got their flowers from the dresser and handed Molly her bouquet. "Ready?"

"Oh, yeah," Molly said, standing up tall and waiting for Jenna to open the door.

The bedroom doorway was where Alex had kissed her the first time after they discovered the attempt on his life had been real. It was also the place he had been shot when Troy came to take the kids. She stepped through and past the spot where she stopped Alex from bleeding out. Nothing remained in the hallway to remind her, but the memories were enough to cause her to shiver anyways.

When she'd gone down the aisle the first time to meet Troy, she'd been pregnant with Will. Troy's family had welcomed her and she had convinced herself Troy would step up to be a real husband and father. The biggest difference in marrying Alex was that he had already stepped up and proven that he was willing to take on this new life with Molly. Alex wanted her to be his wife and even wanted Will to be his son. It made taking those steps through the living room and out the patio doors easy.

Alex's old friend and lawyer, Peter Jameson, had already drawn up the adoption paperwork. Part of their wedding vows would include officially taking on the role of mother and father for each other's children. The kids were ecstatic about being real brothers and sisters. And as soon as the service was complete, they would sign the marriage certificate and other documents that would legalize the family that already existed in their home.

Molly stepped into the side yard where Alex had arranged for the wedding to take place. A large pavilion was ready for the reception and rows of folding chairs created an aisle leading up to the arbor gate their family had made. Friends and family all turned to watch her approach as a string quartet started playing Pachelbel's Canon in D. In the crowd, Alice Mayberry wiped her eyes with a lace handkerchief. Her son Terry had a sour look on his face, but Molly knew it hid a heart of gold. Grant Singleton was stoic, but she was certain his chin quivered when she passed.

Roger stood between her and the crowd with his elbow extended to walk her down the aisle. He looked handsome in his dark suit and tie.

"You sure about this?" Roger asked with a twinkle in his eye. "I bet between the two of us sergeants we could bust you outta here easy."

"You know I don't want to be anywhere else," Molly replied and kissed his rough cheek as she slipped her hand behind his elbow.

Hannah was wearing a lovely lace dress and carried a basket of clematis petals to toss before them as they moved down the aisle between the rows of chairs. Molly smiled as she passed Bubba Caldwell's clan, Roger's family, Rubin and Connie de Cervantes, and so many other people who had supported Molly and Alex. Jenna was following close behind and Molly thought she heard a shuddering breath and sniff. So far she was holding it in, but it didn't sound like her maid of honor was doing as well.

Molly made the mistake of looking up at Alex. He was wearing a dark suit with a tie that matched the purple blooms of the clematis growing up the arbor. He looked like a man who had been struck by lightning. His wide eyes were focused on her to the exclusion of the world. The feeling of utter devotion he projected made her own eyes fill with tears.

Their boys, wearing matching suits and ties, were standing on each side of him with broad grins as Molly approached them. Roger gave her hand to Alex and they turned to face the pastor of Alice Mayberry's congregational church, Reverend Roy McCormick, standing before them in the black robes of his calling.

"We are all here to witness the union of two families," Reverend McCormick intoned. "It's not simply the marriage of Molly and Alex we bless today, but the union of their lives and the lives of their three children, Will, Hannah, and Manny. The events that led up to this moment are likely familiar to you all, but I'd like to call your attention to the one thing I've learned from talking to all of them about this service today."

Reverend McCormick paused to scan the eyes of all those around them. "They know that being a family isn't something that happens by accident. You have to want it, to work at it, and to be willing to sacrifice for it. After spending time with Alex, Molly, Will, Manny, and Hannah I can tell you that this ceremony is merely a recognition of what many of you already know: They already *are* a family.

"So in the presence of these witnesses, I ask you, Alex, do you take this woman, Molly to be your lawfully wedded wife; to love and honor her and her son Will as a husband and father."

Alex visibly swallowed his emotion to whisper, "I do."

"And do you Molly, take this man, Alex, to be your lawfully wedded husband; to love and honor him and his children Manuel and Hannah as a wife and mother."

Molly smiled so hard her cheeks hurt. She looked at their kids grinning up at her with adoration on their faces, then glanced back at her husband, the man she had saved and who had saved her. Squeezing Alex's hand she declared with her whole heart, "I do."

###

READ TWO BONUS CHAPTERS!

To read two bonus chapters featuring what happens between Larry and Jenna right after the wedding, visit my website at **http://awtrey.com/** and sign up for my newsletter, *Writing on the Edges*.

The two chapters provide a preview of the next book in the series, *Holding On*, coming in the spring of 2017.

As a bonus, you'll continue to be the first to learn about special offers, book giveaways, and insider information only available to subscribers.

About the Author

I've been writing novels for fun and practice since 2012. After completing eight novels and a few dozen short stories, I felt ready to publish my latest novel *Letting Go*. I'm a member of the Central Florida Chapter of the Romance Writers of America and Florida Writers Association. When I'm not writing, I'm the CTO for a technology consultancy and a professional singer.

To connect with Tony online visit **http://awtrey.com/** or email at **tony@awtrey.com**.